LIGHT RECLAIMED: BILLIE KNIGHT

The Spirit Reports

A series about Billie Knight and Randall Delphine, queer BFFs and artists who, reunited after decades apart, must heal their personal and shared trauma in order to move forward into a future together. Including the behind-the-scenes perspectives of Billie's and Randall's spirit armies—ancient goddesses, dead rock stars, animals, ETs, and ancestors among them—these novels explore addiction, queer love, and music, from opera to grunge.

Set primarily in the Pacific Northwest—Seattle, the Olympic Peninsula, and Humboldt County—the Spirit Reports also extend abroad, to Berlin.

Light Reclaimed: Billie Knight is the first book in the series. Book two, *Life Review: Randall Delphine,* is forthcoming.

LIGHT RECLAIMED: BILLIE KNIGHT

a novel by
Teja Rhae Watson

DAGMAR MIURA
LOS ANGELES

Published by Dagmar Miura
Los Angeles
www.dagmarmiura.com

Light Reclaimed: Billie Knight

This is a work of fiction. Names, characters, businesses, places, events, and incidents are either the products of the author's imagination or used in a fictitious manner. Any resemblance to actual persons, living or dead, or actual events is purely coincidental.

front cover image by Mateusz Wyszyński on Pixabay

First published 2022

ISBN: 978-1-956744-76-7

for all of the survivors of sexual assualt

I always wondered why survivors understood
other survivors so well.… Perhaps it is not the
particulars of the assault itself that we have in
common, but the moment after; the first time
you are left alone. Something slipping out of you.
Where did I go. What was taken.

—Chanel Miller, *Know My Name*

You're not coming for me
I'm coming for you.

—Karen O and Danger
Mouse, "Redeemer"

Table of Contents

Willa

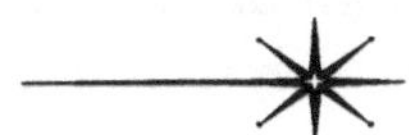

*T*he dream is a living kaleidoscope, a symphony of symmetry. Dozens of dervishes spin; some fast as a top, others leisurely, like a carousel. As their skirts lift and fall, the circles widen and contract, out and then in. Around and around, like they're screwing into the unknown.

The dervishes are children, their little faces lively as they turn. Coats of mint, saffron, rose become teal, tangerine, watermelon as they pass one another. *Whump!* like the wings of a dragon, as their weighted skirts lift, fall. *Whump, whump.* Out, and then in—a void, and a gathering.

And then, dizzy, one by one they all tumble down, in a tangle of limbs and laughter.

Willa stands, laughing and out of breath, her dark-blue eyes brilliant with intent. She pushes her bangs out of her eyes, leaving a streak of dirt on her cheek. And then she runs—in a second she's gone, into the trees. The night forest covers her, but for a tracer here and there to follow. As she runs, the darkness tunnels into her body, burrows deep in her bloodstream.

Up ahead, an old house emerges out of the woods. Willa runs in, leaving the front door flung open wide.

Inside, her muddy footprints bisect the broad stairs, the house's heart. Her laugh echoes through its bones, delight and mischief roaming the walls—like the house is laughing.

But now, it begins to wail. Willa is weeping. The cry of something being taken—the house quivers with it. Upstairs, the dark slashes mark a long, narrow hallway, leading to the last room on the left. Empty rooms line the hall on both sides, their windows open, moonlight on the bare wood floors.

And now, near the door of the last room on the left, the walls begin to shriek: the sharp, high scream of a child. The windows shatter; the doors slam shut.

The floor drops away.

Billie

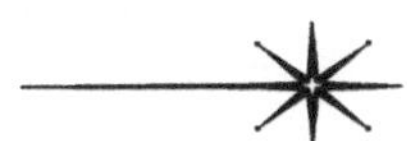

*B*illie Knight jolts to sitting, her nocturnal eyes turning on in the dark. Terror slithers through her blood.

Something woke me up. She grabs her water, drinks, then quiets, listening. Fresh air floats down through the boards that will be her roof—Billie breathes it in.

All is quiet. *Must have been the trees.* The first night Billie slept in the new cabin, during a rainstorm a couple weeks ago, the stand of surrounding spruce trees squealed their displeasure about being knocked around by wind and rain. Between them and the drumming on the tarp covering the roof, it was like an experimental noise rock concert.

Scenes from the dream play on the dark cabin walls as if projected there: the circling children, Willa tearing through the trees, the empty old house.

And that scream.

I know that scream. She's never really thought about it; it's always just been inside her. She'd subconsciously assumed it an imprint from her mom—the high shriek Petra makes when displeased. But this sound came from a child. *From me, little Willa.* Her own five-year-old body had raged out that ferocity, and almost-fifty-year-old Billie feels it rattling around inside her, wanting out. She shivers, and pulls on a hoodie.

The scream is an alarm. Everything lost in it, devoured by it. An animal in pain.

She wants me to save her. That's what woke her up: Willa calling to her—urgent, unmistakable.

Billie finds her headlamp and drags it on, squinting at the light. The ten-by-ten cabin is a mess of tools and clothes, all of it covered in sawdust. She pulls her hood up and the lamp shines out like a headlight in a tunnel.

As she pushes herself up from the floor, her six-foot frame feels extra heavy. Pocketing her phone and pulling on her boots, she opens the door and steps into the dawn.

At a bluff not far from here, there's cell service. She heads out on the narrow trail to the bluff that she blazed the week before. It had been painful work, clearing the dense brush—Scotch broom, with its bright yellow flowers, grows heartily on the Olympic Peninsula, and its stiff, sharp branches are notoriously hard to remove.

As she walks, the darkness fades, the air above her blooming like a robin's belly. She clicks off the headlamp, pulls it down around her neck. She wants to run but she can't, the brush too tight around her. She puts her arms up to protect her face and forges through, claustrophobia filling her limbs.

It's been a week and two days since George Floyd was murdered. *I can't breathe,* Billie hears him say in her head, as her own breath falters.

Since he died and the protests began, the first thing Billie does every morning is check on how the protesters across the country fared overnight, braced for more bad news. The revolution is needed, and a long time coming— but she worries about more harm to Black bodies. It's because of this new, urgent need for news that she made the path to the bluff—reducing her commute to the office from over an hour, to only fifteen minutes.

Finally she breaks out into the wide-open vista—a

few more feet and she would've gone over the edge. An epic valley ahead, and beyond that, water. The Salish Sea sails west to the Pacific Ocean; to the east, the Puget Sound and Seattle. On a clear day she can see Canada across the water.

Turning on her iPhone, Billie leaves herself a reminder: *New trail needs widening*. She sits down on soft pine needles and leans back against the log, catching her breath.

She bought these six hilly acres on the northern Olympic Peninsula ten years ago. The Land was too cheap to pass up, less than two hours to Seattle, where Billie teaches at the Seattle Art Institute. With the help of a few energetic students, a year later she had built herself a small cabin. Over the next four years, she and many others—including, notably, Billie's dad, Joe—had built a lodge, with kitchen, living room, and three bedrooms; as well as an outhouse, a treehouse, and a hen house. Billie and her three Landmates have a solar panel, to charge their devices and cook; they use headlamps and lanterns for light, propane for cooking, and fire for heat.

Billie sees a voicemail from Lisa, her stepmom for the last three decades, which came in just a few minutes ago. "Shit," she says, eyeing her phone warily. "This can't be good."

Billie's mom and dad split up when Billie was in high school, and her dad and Lisa got together a few years later. Lisa being with her dad in Humboldt County, far-northern California—especially these past few years, when his energy has started to fade a little—has meant that Billie could focus on her work and the Land.

Billie hits play and puts it on speaker. Lisa's deep voice starts and then stops, then forges forward.

I'm so sorry to have to tell you this, Billie, especially by voicemail, but I know your cell service is unreliable and who knows when we'll be able to talk....

Your dad has passed. He had a heart attack in his sleep. He was fine when we went to sleep, but when I woke up early he had no pulse, so I called Dr. Lathrop, who just left. Sudden cardiac arrest, he said.

Billie freezes, stares at the phone on her palm. *He can't die, I'm coming to see him next week.*

Lisa is crying, but continues:

I want to talk with you about a memorial service. He wants—he wanted to be cremated. We talked about it not that long ago, he said he wants his ashes in the Mad River. We were like, if the coronavirus gets us....

It's quiet, then Billie hears Lisa blowing her nose.

Maybe it did, actually. Your dad was always so healthy, but then he was so afraid of getting sick, he lost a couple friends to the virus—he couldn't even go to the hospital to say goodbye. And then George Floyd's murder.... He was afraid, and then he was angry. All that emotion...maybe that's what killed him. He never had a bad heart before.

Billie knew he was winding down, at seventy-three, but she thought he still had a lot of years left. A decade at least. He'd always seemed invincible. She'd planned to see him in April, but when air travel was suspended because of Covid-19, she'd postponed it till June.

He died of a broken heart, Lisa says then, crying harder. The message cuts off.

Billie drops her phone, as if it's infected, and it lands in a nest of brown pine needles. She sits, staring at it. *No. This can't be real.*

She's afraid to call Lisa back. She knows she has to.

Billie wants to switch to manager mode. Call Lisa.

Get a plane ticket. But she can't move.

The Strait of Juan de Fuca sparkles obscenely under the sun's first light. She can even see Victoria Island waking up across the pond.

She wishes she could just get in the car and go, but after all the heavy labor—clearing the trail, building the cabin—she knows her body isn't up for thirteen hours of driving. She puts her head to her knees and rests it there, wrapping her arms around her legs.

She takes a breath and, as if coming up for air, grabs her phone and dials Lisa.

Air travel was just finally reinstated, but it's still a little risky to fly; a lot of people have the virus without knowing it, since testing is not easy to access. Billie has been out on the Land for the past eight weeks, barely even seeing her Landmates, so she's 100 percent sure she doesn't have it; anyway, she's healthy, and not high-risk, so she's not too worried about getting it. She needs to be in Humboldt, to help Lisa deal with her dad's affairs and plan the memorial, and driving there would take too long.

Billie gets off the phone and buys a ticket with the credit from her canceled flight. She leaves at seven tonight: Sea-Tac to SFO, SFO to ACV, Humboldt's tiny airport. She texts Lisa the info and Lisa says she'll be there to pick Billie up.

On the dense path back to the cabin, Billie puts up her arms like a boxer and punches at the Scotch broom, a fury of yellow flowers flying around her.

When she finally bursts out into the open air, she's gasping for breath. She finds a big rock to sit on and pulls the neck of her hoodie up over her nose, concentrating on deepening her breath. Eyes closed, she remembers the dervish dream. The children spin like multicolored crystals in her mind, catching the light and reflecting it.

Her breath calms. She pulls down her hood and shakes out her black hair, which settles around her scruff.

I woke up when he died. She suddenly knows: Willa's scream, Billie's nightlight eyes opening, and Joe leaving life—they were simultaneous, connected.

And now he's gone.

Why couldn't it have been Petra? Billie's sure that her mom, who was diagnosed with Alzheimer's five years ago, would want to die, given the choice. *I'll have to go to Petrolia, to tell her Dad is gone.*

Back at the cabin, she grabs her water bottle. There's no room to stand inside, so she sits on the door frame, thinking, *I need to bring over more water.* Pulling out her phone to make a note, she shakes her head and throws the phone to the ground, yanking at her hair.

Stop, she tells herself. *It's over, he's gone. So you might as well chill.*

The new cabin is meant to be a place for her to charge herself back up, a mile from the lodge, which is the center of the Land. She is taking the summer off for the build. But when her classes were canceled due to the coronavirus in mid-March, Billie had started on the cabin right away. The uglier things got in the rest of the country, the harder she worked, like she was building herself an escape boat—which she sort of was.

She sets out for the lodge now, tucking some toilet paper in her pocket to pee on the way. Everyone pees outside, on the Land; it makes the bathrooms less smelly and the job of emptying the buckets easier.

Her dad being gone feels abstract, out here on the Land, since he'd only been here three times. The first time, he came to help build the lodge. He'd camped in a tent for weeks, in his late sixties, and by the end he was a legend among Billie's friends. She couldn't have done it without his massive expertise.

Billie stops in her tracks as she realizes, *Now I can't ask him. About what happened when I was little.*

For a moment, she can't breathe. A suspicion has been growing in her, that she was harmed in some intimate way, a long time ago. Her mind doesn't remember, but her body is starting to.

I'll ask Petra about it, when I'm there. The thought turns on in her head, and lights her up for a moment.

She shakes her head, dimming the bulb. *One thing at a time.*

The wooden compass rose appears ahead, arrows pointing to each of the four structures—lodge, outhouse, Billie's cabin, treehouse—and to four cities: Portland, to the south; Tokyo, to the west; NYC, to the east; Vancouver, to the north. Billie remembers her dad standing here with her on his second visit, a couple summers back, and pointing toward Tokyo, where he and Lisa were headed next, to see Billie's new mural there.

It was a big one, the biggest: forty stories high, taller even than the tallest redwood, solid and grounded in the neon mayhem of Shibuya. Its roots, she likes to imagine shooting through the concrete to the earth below. *My dad saw that one,* she thinks. He'd been so excited upon seeing the mural, he insisted on stopping at the Land again on their way back to Humboldt, to fawn over Billie, his only child.

That was the last time I saw him.

She walks into the lodge, lightheaded, and leans on the kitchen counter. *I have to eat something.* She pulls her headlamp from her neck and puts it on its base to charge, gets the water boiling. As the coffee steeps, she eats a banana and takes her herbs.

She remembers her dad up on a ladder above where she's standing now, for a week, as they built the stairs to the second-floor bedrooms. How happy he was, leading the job, thrilled to get to help her. He was sixty-seven and it was his last major project. The past few years, he had done smaller jobs, making custom furniture, consulting and designing—less heavy labor.

She remembers with shame that she'd been embarrassed when he called her "my girl," when he was here building. Ruining her butch image in front of her friends.

He never would have hurt me. How could I have thought it might have been him?

In the middle of Billie's last sexual encounter—almost two years ago now, in her old cabin up the hill—when the person inserted their hand in her without asking for consent, Billie had a kind of flashback and a siren went off in her body, filling her with noise and fear. She pushed the person off of her and ran to the outhouse, where she hid until they finally got in their car and left the Land.

It had been especially humiliating because Billie had always considered herself sex-positive and a good communicator in bed. The trauma response, occurring in such an intimate space, shook her to the core. It told her what she didn't want to hear: something had been inside of her that shouldn't have been there.

She had considered asking her dad if he knew anything about it, but hesitated, because what if he was the one who had hurt her? He was the only man who'd been around when she was little. If there was even a slight chance it was him, she told herself, it would be awful if she brought it up.

But it wasn't her dad who hurt her, she's certain now. *No. I was just afraid of what I might discover. And now it's too late.*

A sick feeling settles in her stomach as she heads out to start her chores.

Jane

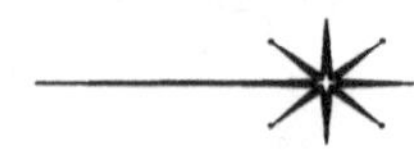

*E*arly summer, the bulk of Billie's work is in the garden. The two large veggie boxes she built after she finished her original cabin are still serving them well, along with eight smaller ones they've added over the years. Since she was a kid, she's had a knack for bringing things up and out of the ground—an ongoing conversation with the earth.

The tomatoes are plump and she picks a few just-soft ones, and a few others to ripen off the vine, removes dead leaves. Breaks off several stalks of kale that are starting to yellow, pulls up a dozen carrots, gathers several handfuls of chamomile. She waters everything. In the summer it can get into the nineties out here; miss a day and lettuce dies.

Billie had lost her first chicken, Lennie, to a mountain lion. In the early days she would talk to Lennie—"Just me and you," Billie would say when she fed and watered Lennie or looked for eggs. Then she found what remained of Lennie's mangled face and it was just her again. Until Jane came, bringing with her two chickens; teaching Billie that it's inhumane to keep just one chicken, since they're such social creatures.

They have twelve chickens now, and most days a dozen eggs. More than enough for four vegetarians to eat, gift, or trade. Billie lets them out of the coop for the day and places their eggs (lilac, gray, and light-green) in the carrier.

On her way to the coolers outside the lodge, she runs into Jane. Both women are early risers, having grown up where there was always lots of work. That they are both accustomed to working hard is one reason their partnership has been so successful. Jane was the first to join Billie on the Land, and she helped build every structure except the original cabin. She and Joe had gotten along famously during the lodge build. He called her Janes, after the road Billie's childhood home was on.

It's Lisa's house now, Billie realizes.

Jane was integral in setting up their early systems, getting things running smoothly. She and Billie always have their eyes on the next project and clearly communicate action items so that anyone visiting the Land can easily offer help.

"My dad died this morning," Billie says. As she says it out loud, the fact drops into her body like a heavy rock in a riverbed. She settles her heavy frame on an overturned bucket.

Jane is shocked. She sinks to her knees on the dirt next to Billie and puts a hand on Billie's knee. Jane is naturally quiet, and right now she doesn't know what to say. Her eyes are huge as they search her friend's face. She seems to take a cue from Billie's stoicism and sinks back onto her heels. The chickens squawk, in some sort of squabble.

"Heart attack," Billie says. She takes a deep breath. "I'm headed down there tonight. I'll need to stay at least a few days." She takes a sip of coffee and hands the cup to Jane.

Jane drinks the rest and sets down the mug. "I'll cover your chores. Unless you want me to come?"

"Up to you. He adored you, you know that. But he's

not going to know the difference."

Billie and Jane met in 1990 at a poetry reading at a punk bookstore down by Pike's Place. They had similar mohawk-mullets—Jane's was blond, Billie's black. Game recognized game, and they struck up a friendship.

Jane's short hair is mostly gray now. Billie's hangs down just past her shoulders, bone-straight and heavy as a horse's tail, her bangs still perpetually in her eyes. She's big and broad like her dad was; Jane is slight, spare. Billie admires Jane's seemingly effortless grace—Billie feels like a Sasquatch in most settings.

Billie and Jane aren't really each other's type, so in their eight years out here together they've only kissed once: at a party, someone dared Billie to kiss Jane on the lips. Billie was drunk, and in her bravado she had even slipped in some tongue. Jane had kept her eyes open through the whole thing, and when Billie opened hers with a sheepish smile, Jane was staring back at her and shaking her head.

Jane says she'll stay on the Land but offers to drive Billie to the airport. Billie decides to leave her truck at the airport instead, so she won't have to worry about a ride home. After they get their business sorted, Billie trudges the mile back to the new cabin, undresses, and gets back into bed. Under the covers, she closes in on herself. She hugs her knees and begins to shake. The tears burst out of her as if from an unclogged drain.

I'm all alone. Petra's lost in her mind maze, and now Dad's gone, too.

The lonesomeness she felt as an only child—until she met her best friend, Randall, in middle school, and then again after Randall left—resumes with full force. Her heart hurts; she presses her knee against it, holding herself tight. She pulls the heavy black comforter over her head.

It's dark under there and, far from any human who might hear, she lets herself wail. She clenches her fists, squeezes herself tight so she doesn't fall apart. She cries and cries, shaking her head, fighting against the pain.

The only way through it is through it. The grief advice floats in from somewhere and Billie clings to it in the darkness.

In the airport, Billie enjoys the anonymity of her soft black mask: not just protecting her from Covid, it's also a barrier between her tender self and the outside world. After another dizzy spell, she forces herself to eat some trail mix. Fighting back tears, she refuses to give in to grief. It's only five hours of actual travel, but if she accepts that Joe won't be there to meet her, really takes that in, she's afraid she won't make it.

Lisa picks her up instead. Under her beautiful big chestnut eyes are circles so dark they look like bruises. After climbing into Lisa's Jeep, they embrace for a long time, and though she can feel Lisa's chest heave under her own, Billie still doesn't let herself cry.

As they drive to Billie's childhood home on Janes Road, a country road outside the sweet little city of Arcata, Billie realizes she's never spent time with Lisa alone before, but their mutual shock and the work to be done keeps things from feeling awkward. Since Lisa met Joe after Billie went away to school, they've never lived together. Lisa is sixty-three, ten years younger than Joe had been and only thirteen years older than Billie.

For the first few days, they sort Joe's things like

zombies, Billie keeping her distance, monitoring herself for symptoms after flying. The quiet suits them. People bring food, but mostly they're alone in their own halves of the house. When they do meet for distanced meals, Lisa is easy to be around, open and grounded despite everything.

In addition to planning Joe's memorial, they discuss the business of what Joe left behind. Billie is relieved to hear that there's more than enough retirement savings for Lisa to retire from her Fish and Wildlife job as soon as she likes. And Lisa has her wonderful family on the nearby Hoopa reservation. If Lisa dies, the house will go to Billie.

A week later, after testing negative for the virus, Billie climbs into her dad's old Chevy truck on a Sunday morning and pulls the heavy door closed.

She rests her head on the steering wheel, breathing him in. The truck smells sweet, like the peachy weed that Joe's friends grow. Billie starts the engine and heads south, for Petrolia and her mom—to the least-developed coastal road in California.

Mattole Road, death drop to the Pacific. Leap of faith, say your prayers, hold your breath, here we go. Not just steep, or narrow, or potholed, or curvy—but all four, all the way down. Sometimes it turns into just one lane; elsewhere it's a dirt road for a while. But if you make it to the end, black-sand beaches beckon. This part of the world is called the Lost Coast, and its epic wildness feels like home.

With the ocean on her right, Billie winds up and down over the broken roads, then through the tough and tiny town of Petrolia, with its *go back where you came from then* attitude toward complaints about road maintenance.

The danger deters the less hardy, even makes some turn back, and they like it that way. She likes them that way.

Billie is tempted to stop at the store, to say hi and get a sandwich for later, but she has no clue what she'll find when she arrives at her mom's place and decides to wait.

It's just like Petra to move somewhere that sounds like her name, as if she's a legendary or mythic goddess—as if maybe she herself is the town's namesake. Where she lives is one of the only things Petra seems to remember about herself. She recites it under her breath like a mantra sometimes.

Petra from Petrolia. Petra from Petrolia. Petra from Petrolia.

An answer to the question—"Who am I?"—that, Billie imagines, consumes her mind.

When the road mellows out, Billie calls Ann, her mom's childhood friend and caregiver, to say she's about an hour away. Ann asks if she can take the opportunity to do an overnight with her grandkids, and Billie agrees to look after her mom tonight and tomorrow morning. Petra needs more hands-on care these days than she used to, and Ann fills Billie in on what to do, says she'll give Petra an early dinner before she leaves.

Ann is her mom's conservator—the person Petra chose to manage her affairs, before she became mentally incapacitated. It makes sense, since Ann lives here with her, and Billie is far away in Washington. Ann is Petra's childhood friend, they grew up together, and Petra and Ann are much closer than her mom has ever been with anyone—so the arrangement seems to suit them all. Billie certainly doesn't have the bandwidth to care for her mom right now.

Thinking about all of this, she yanks her hand

through her hair, then shakes the hairs that come away out the window.

The Alzheimer's makes Petra easier for Billie in some ways. Her mom's impulses and intentions are more clear. She's a simpler creature, incapable of manipulation. She knows that the way her mom treats her is not about her—her mom doesn't even know who Billie is anymore, so it couldn't be. It's like Petra is becoming a child again. In fact, Petra's remaining memories are mostly of her own childhood. "First in, last out," the doctor had explained.

For years, Petra had refused to see a doctor about her increasing mental impairment. Finally, on a visit home five summers ago, Petra and Ann had made her go—it had to be done. That was when they learned it was definitely Alzheimer's.

Billie has wondered if it could have been her mom who abused her, but her sense memory is one of being penetrated. A feeling of being filled, stretched. Although it could, of course, have been a hand or some other object....

She's been afraid to be intimate with anyone since the embarrassing flashback. The scariest part of all is that she has no desire to, after having always had a very healthy sex drive. *What if that part of me is gone forever?*

Though she can't remember any details, she senses that whatever it was, it happened multiple times. She thinks it happened around age five, because she has a clear sense of herself before and after that age. But that's old enough to remember—if it had happened only once, she thinks she would remember. The shape of this thing is more complex.

And now Billie's headed to Petrolia to ask her mom if she remembers anything—literally the last thing in the world that she wants to do. As she pulls onto the gnarly dirt driveway to her mom's place, after two hours on the road from hell, the truck bumps up and down so hard, she hits the brakes. Her skull snaps forward and smacks the wheel.

"Arrrrgh!" She pulls over and shuts off the ignition, putting her hand to her head, where a headache has bloomed. *Fuck! I didn't bring any painkillers.* The closest drugstore is up on the other side of the road from hell.

Maybe I should just skip the whole thing. It's not like Petra would care. Billie's visits are always stressful and disruptive for her mom.

Shit! I told Ann I'd take care of her. I have to go.

Without the option of turning back, Billie starts to panic. The headache is scaring her—how will she deal with it, out here without her meds? She digs around in the glovebox to see if her dad has any ibuprofen or aspirin; he doesn't, though she does find some pot and a pipe. *Smoking will just make it worse.*

Billie gets out of the car and paces up and down the driveway. *Fuck.* The headache is coming on strong. She worries about the headache, which makes it worse, and then suddenly she can't catch her breath. She gasps like a fish out of water.

What if this is a heart attack? There are no neighbors for at least a mile in both directions, and Ann will have left by now.

Should I go back to town? At least there'd be people who could help. She feels weak, dizzy.

What if I'm dying?

The last thing she wants to do is get back in the truck. *Maybe I'll try and walk up,* she thinks. It's about a half-mile, but at least Ann has a land line she can use to call

911 if she's having a heart attack. Ann probably has pain-killers, too.

Then Billie remembers that she brought some THC gummies for Petra the last time she was here; Ann had thought they might help her mom to relax. Billie doesn't know about that—she's never seen Petra relaxed in her whole life—but she knows that the gummies do very much help with her own headaches. They're the best thing for them, actually—they help the pain, and the stress that comes with it. *Maybe there's still some left.*

Sun beating down, Billie goes back to the truck and gathers her stuff. Digging around under the seat, she finds a Sharks ball cap of her dad's, puts it to her nose, and breathes him in.

Pulling on the cap, she shoulders her backpack, taking care with the flowers she picked, and locks the truck. As she walks, she tries to breathe. "In, out"—*yeah, right.*

Trudging up to her house, Billie realizes that she's never trusted Ann, though she's not sure why. Maybe it's the strange confidence that Ann and Petra seem to have in common, a superiority complex. Petra has always been very contained in herself, like an island, and Ann is the only person Petra ever invited onto it. Usually when she's here they're busy with the logistics of Petra, but here without Ann, head and heart pounding, Billie feels unsafe, unwelcome.

Billie's chest aches, which scares her. Before the bend, pressing down on her heart, she looks back. It's weird seeing her dad's truck out here. Her mom and dad reside on separate sides of Billie's mind. Joe would never have had reason to visit Petra here; they broke up when Billie started high school, and once she graduated they didn't stay in touch.

Feeling dizzy, she plops down in the dirt.

Wait. She remembers a friend saying that when he gets panic attacks, he always feels lightheaded, like he's about to pass out.

Is this a fucking panic attack?

"It's a panic attack," Billie says, laughing. "Just a panic attack!" she yells out to the empty field ahead. "I'm not dying."

Nothing like a Petra visit to yank up Billie's anxiety. There's the standard stress of dealing with her mom, of course, but also a darker fear: that dementia is waiting around the corner for Billie as well. She has to remind herself, every time, that her mind is sharp and her memory is strong—with the notable exception of those first five years.

She fishes trail mix out of her backpack and eats a few handfuls, drinks most of her water. Her fear fizzles out, loses its charge. Anticipating Ann's house, dark and cool, she gets up and starts walking again. She's never been in Ann's place alone. Usually Ann is there, and Billie's always felt awkward around her, so she never wanted to stay long. It will be sweet to have some alone time.

Later. I need to go up and give Petra her meds.

Breathe. In, out. It sort of works now.

Ann's house comes into view, an old, dark thing with moss crawling around the perimeter—much higher up the walls than it was the last time she was here.

"Okay," she says out loud, psyching herself up.

And then, further up, she sees her mom's place, the renovated barn—and the fear returns like a punch, taking her breath away.

Ann left the big front door unlocked, and Billie enters. It's dark and cold inside, up here in the trees. Her mom's place has a heater, but this old house does not.

The wood stove is the house's heart. Billie goes to it, finding it still warm, and starts a small fire. Then she goes to the kitchen and finds the gummies and a bottle of Advil; she takes three Advil and eats one five-milligram gummy, pockets another. She pulls the dahlias she brought out of her backpack, runs them under the kitchen faucet.

I really don't want to go up there. She looks at the note Ann left about her mom's meds and slips the pillbox in her pocket.

Back at the fire, she fights off memories of her dad teaching her how to make a fire, at the beach—blocking the wind with his powerful frame. His absence gets heavier every day, as if his energy has moved from the external world, into her bones. The hopelessness of him being gone forever is unbearable. She has to come back out into the light periodically, take a breath.

I need hope right now, to stay sane. If I can just get some clue from her, something to go on...

But the hope makes her vulnerable. Because Petra never once told the truth if it painted her in a bad light.

I should make some coffee.

Just get up there and get it over with.

A quick cup of instant.

While the water's boiling, Billie uses the bathroom, washing her face with a cool cloth. She looks longingly at the beautiful clawfoot.

Later. You have to go check on Petra. You promised.

She stirs up her coffee and adds some milk. In the living room, she moves an armchair closer to the fire and spreads the coals, watching them breathe, burning bright.

Separate from one another, they must fight harder to stay alive.

Petra

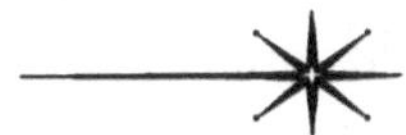

$\mathscr{B}$illie steps out of Ann's cabin with her coffee. The headache has ebbed a little. She assesses her mom's old silver Prius as she passes it—tries to look inside, but it's locked. *I should talk to Ann about selling it.* As far as she knows, it hasn't been driven in years.

As she rounds the corner to her mom's stairs, she takes the last sip of her coffee and sets the flowered teacup down on the first step, to grab on the way back to Ann's place. An anchor outside her mom's space, a beacon to bring her back.

No more avoiding. Let's do this.

As she heads up the stairs, she knocks on the wooden railing, so she doesn't surprise Petra. Once her mom thought Billie was a man there to rape her and yelled at her to get away. Since then, Billie tones her appearance down, when she can—today, her dad's royal blue cap softens her punk rock style a little.

It's been two years since her mom recognized Billie. In the interim, Billie has learned that trying to explain that she's Petra's daughter, especially when she presents as masculine to Petra, ends up just degrading everyone involved.

The only other part of her mom's adult identity that's still partially intact is that of art teacher, so a couple times Billie has pretended to be a former student of her mom's—it makes sense to Petra and is generally greeted with interest. Petra taught individual students, in the detached studio her dad built to her precise specifications, soon after he finished their ranch house. Billie always hated going in there; even now, she feels nauseous at the thought of it. It smelled stale, like secrets. And her mom was hugely protective of the space. She never let Billie in when she was teaching, rarely when she was painting.

Billie decides to start as herself this time. "Petra?" she calls cheerily as she crests the top step, her heart doing a little spin. The first thing she sees is the ocean. In front of it, her mother sits on the deck, looking out at the sea.

Then Petra turns to look at Billie, as if in slow motion.

Oh, my god, she looks so much older. It's been a year since Billie's seen her, and her mom has shrunken.

She doesn't have any idea who you are. Billy reminds herself that it's not personal.

"Hi Petra! I'm Billie," she tells her mom quietly. "Your daughter."

She holds out the bright peachy-orange dahlias to Petra. They were always her favorite, but now she takes them from Billie as if seeing flowers for the first time.

"Can I put those in some water?" Billie asks her mom, who holds the flowers to her chest and shakes her head with a quiet but forceful "no." She turns back around to the sunset that's starting.

Billie and Petra have in common a love of the sea. Billie can remember being in the studio and watching her mom paint the ocean, full of awe. Once she told Petra, "It's even more beautiful than the ocean itself," and she distinctly remembers Petra receiving the compliment with a nod. Those paintings had destroyed any dream little Willa might have had of painting the ocean herself. There was no point in even trying.

But Petra had, for some reason, been determined to teach her how to paint eyes, and for this Billie will always be grateful. A lot of the redwoods in Billie's murals have eyes in their trunks, usually vertically, up and down along the bark. Once, to fill a particular space, she painted a tree horizontally, the eyes running the length of the wood, like fish in a shallow sea.

"The white of the eye," she remembers Petra saying as Billie sketched, "is not actually white—it's gray." Petra taught her to use many different colors in the pupil, which created brightness, realism, and depth. She'd learned so much just watching Petra mix paints. "The lines around the iris must be jagged, not straight, because the eyeball is spherical, not flat."

Billie enters her mom's space. It's cold in here, too, so she turns on the heat, noticing that Petra has covered the bathroom mirror with a scarf.

Why should I even bother telling her about Dad? She'll just have forgotten again in a few minutes. But it has to be done—Billie can't say why. Something about ritual. She wants to do it right.

She breathes in. *Get back out there. Be strong.*

Out on the deck, she pulls up a camp chair, testing it before letting her large frame fall in. From behind her mom she sees only Petra's wispy gray ponytail, the tips of the dahlias over one shoulder, and behind that the sun disappearing, only a sliver now, an eye on the horizon. And then it's gone.

Right away, the fog starts rolling in. Realizing she will soon need to start ushering her mom inside for the night, Billie takes a deep breath, then starts. "Petra, I'm sorry but I have some bad news."

Her mom goes rigid.

"So, I am your daughter, Billie. My dad, your ex-husband, Joe, had a heart attack and died a few nights ago." *If anything, she remembers the studio.* "Remember your studio? Where you taught art?"

Her mom's shoulders relax. She stays still and silent. They both look out at the ocean, so dark it's like it was never blue. For the millionth time—in an ongoing obsession from childhood—she wonders what her mom is thinking. What it's like in there. The question is further complicated now by the disease, of course, running rampant like a looter with a baseball bat. But her mom has always been an enigma to Billie.

"That's where the dahlias come from. You planted them there. Right outside your studio." The studio is more a storage space for all her mom's stuff now, but Petra's dahlias have flourished ever since she planted them there several decades ago. They are, mysteriously, more amazing every year.

"Thank you," Petra says, her voice cracking. She clears it. "Thank you."

Billie doesn't know if she means thanks for the dahlias, or for telling her about Joe, but it doesn't matter. *I'll take it.*

It's almost dark. *Just say it.*

"I'm your daughter, Billie, like I said." Sitting behind her, she doesn't have to see the skepticism in her mom's eyes, the proof that she thinks Billie is lying about who she is. "And I have to ask you something. Do you remember anything from when I was little?"

Her mom is still, then shakes her head. "That's hard."

"I know it's hard. But it's important. Something bad happened to me when I was little, and I want to know what it was. I *need* to know. I need your help."

"*My* help?" Petra laughs. "My help! Why don't you hire someone for that?"

"Well, I would if I could," Billie mumbles confusedly. *Fuck.* Continuing will risk further activating her. She closes her eyes, waiting.

"Why didn't you put these in water?" Petra asks, throwing the dahlias on the deck. "Now they're going to die."

Billie picks up the flowers and walks inside, where she lets out a deep sigh. *It's so hard to breathe around her.*

The one-room cabin has a bed, a desk, and a small bathroom and kitchen. Billie looks for a vase. Ann recently told Billie that she's going to have to disable the stove, after Petra burnt food on it more than once. If this place caught fire, the whole hillside would be close behind. After the willful wildfires of the last few years, they have to be careful, even here where it's so green.

Finding a large Mason jar, she fills it with water and places the dahlias in it, stem by stem. She puts them on the kitchen table and looks out the window, into the redwoods. She considers what to say to Petra next, what new tack to try. She's always envied her friends who have moms you can just talk to, without having to perform complicated calculations.

What was I thinking? Of course I won't get anything useful from her.

Billie decides to conserve her energy and come up with a new plan for trying again with Petra tomorrow. Coming out on the deck again, she settles on a bright "You ready to come inside?"

She leans on the deck's railing. Her mom is still, in the dark. She is mumbling another of her mantras: "It comes again tomorrow." The mantras have worn a deep enough groove in her mind that they've survived the rogue waves that wash everything else away.

The fog has the place surrounded now. *Hopefully tomorrow it will be clear.*

"Let's get you inside," Billie tries again. If Petra stays out too long in the damp she'll have trouble warming up, thin as she is. It's nearing nine, which is when Ann usually gets her settled in for the night.

Walking over to Petra, Billie pulls gently on her arm, but the older woman just grunts and pulls away. She has joint pain, Billie knows, and decides to leave it, goes inside to get Petra's meds ready. She's taking more pills now, too—four in all.

Petra walks slowly in, then. Upright, she's as imposing and intimidating as ever. Billie watches from the kitchen as her mom walks in and sits on the foot of her bed, which is tucked into an eave. Billie closes the door and brings her mom her meds and her glass of sparkling water with a squeeze of lime.

At her feet, she carefully pulls off Petra's Crocs. The socks underneath are thick and warm, but the feet feel frail.

The cabin is warm and cozy from the heater, so Billie crosses the room to turn it down.

When she turns around, Petra is right behind her.

"Shit!" Billie says, startled.

Her mom's eyes hit Billie at chest level, and she stares through her, as if through to the wall. She *still* makes Billie feel like she's invading her, colonizing her—and, at the same time, like Billie isn't worth the bother.

Her mother is the queen still and she needs Billie to know it—that much, Petra remembers. *Seventy-seven and still playing power games.* Billie can't help admiring the effortlessness of her authority, inborn in her.

Petra goes in the bathroom and closes the door. After a minute the toilet flushes and Petra walks back out, giving Billie a dirty look. She's still wearing her day clothes, though they're not much different from her sleep clothes. *Screw it. I'm not touching her again right now.*

Her mom goes to her bed and scoots under the covers, like an animal into a cave.

You don't want me here—noted. Feeling's mutual.

"Music?" Billie asks.

Her mom shakes her head. "Mountain stream."

Billie goes to where her mom's phone is charging and opens her meditation app, which basically amplifies the sound that can be heard just downhill at the Mattole River. She adjusts the volume and turns on the nightlight across the room, switches off a lamp.

Her mom looks out at her from under the eave, one eye narrowed.

Billie says, "Sleep well. I'm going to lock the door, but I'll be sleeping in Ann's cabin tonight. If you need me you can press the alarm by your bed." Billie doubts Petra would even remember the alarm, if she did need something. She scans the room for anything dangerous. *It's a leap of faith, leaving her in here. Who knows what kind of shit she gets up to in the night.*

Backing away, Billie says, "I'll be back in the morning." She turns off the last light, closes the front door, and locks it, which makes her feel super creepy. Ann says it's the only way to keep her safe, after Petra wandered into the trees once or twice and got lost in the dark.

Billie walks quickly down the steps, picks up her teacup from the bottom stair and holds it to her heart. She takes a big gulp of air.

Walking toward Ann's place in the dark, she turns around and looks up.

Her mother is highlighted in the window above, looking down on her daughter, a stranger in the dark.

Ann

Billie reaches the cabin, locks the door, and leans back against it.

First, fire. Then food.

Ann had mentioned that her cousin just brewed some cider. Billie helps herself to a bottle, sipping it as she builds the fire.

Her eyes wander the living room, where Ann's photos cover the walls. *Hmm, reminds me of someone else I know.* Though Billie enjoys getting recognition for her work, she doesn't want to look at her own work in her living space. She would rather be inspired by the art of others.

These small differentiations reassure her. *I'm not a narcissist. Thank you, universe.*

Whether I'm going to get the Alzheimer's, too—that's a story for another day. Billie knows her chances of getting it are much higher than most. But as with the loss of her dad, she can only spend so much time with those dark thoughts before she needs to escape, to breathe again. In fact, after telling her mom that Joe had died, Billie had forgotten about it until now, absorbed in Petra's night-time routine. Grief, like Alzheimer's, seemed to be a terrible process of forgetting and then remembering, again and again; presumably at some point his loss would sink in and become part of her.

She gets up to look at Ann's photos, sipping her cider, stomach growling. Some of them are actually pretty good. She used an old Seagull, a square-format camera that now has pride of place on the mantle. It takes little square photos, smaller than a Polaroid and without the border. Several large, old silver frames are filled with the small black-and-whites, stacked up and down and side to side like bricks. Trees, horizons, lots of faces and body parts. The patterns they make are interesting, their grays and blacks a through-line, connecting one to the next.

Billie's body feels heavier than it used to. She would never admit it to anyone, but she knows that, now almost fifty, she's starting to slow down. She tires more easily, and keeps experiencing strange new aches and pains. The headache is mostly gone though.

She wanders into the kitchen. Ann had said to help herself to whatever. She gets another cider and looks into the fridge, the freezer. She sees a frozen mac 'n' cheese and throws it in the microwave, then wanders the house with it, eating as she inspects Ann's pictures. She sees a few of Petra as a young adult, a couple of herself as a toddler; one, centered in one of the arrangements, features a young Petra and Ann. A couple other kids besides Billie—Ann's grandkids maybe—but no other women besides Ann and Petra.

Wait. Suddenly she feels uncomfortable. The further away from the living space and into the house's innards she gets, the more intimate they seem—lots of sun-kissed lolling, Petra posing with pursed lips and her dazzling smile.

Did Ann and Petra have a thing?

She tosses her food in the kitchen trash and goes back to the couch, grabs her cider. As she drinks, her eyes scan the photos. The fire releases a loud *pop*.

Billie takes another sip. *Maybe there are clues here.* A picture, perhaps, of the man who hurt her.

She goes back to the frames, searching for men, dark eyes moving quickly over the images, not seeing but seeking.

But there aren't any men here. Not one human adult male in any of the oversize framed pieces. There are lots of bare feet, elbows, shoulder blades, and some of them must be men's, but there are no men's faces anywhere to be seen, which seems strange, perhaps even intentional.

Suddenly it seems obvious that Ann is a lesbian. Billie tries to recall what she knows of Ann's history, her parents or siblings. She knows Ann and Petra grew up on the same street in Modesto, and they both got out of there as soon as they could, cutting ties with their families back in the sixties. But why?

And then she realizes, *Because they had each other.*

It's suddenly so obvious. Of course they were more than just friends. They were lovers, but they had hidden it. They had lied about everything, even after Petra was married. Billie remembers now Ann visiting them from Petrolia, and sleeping out in her mom's studio, the two of them staying up late into the night out there—talking, she had thought.

She looks at the images and it's obvious: They were in love. Her mom looks happy like Billie has never seen her before. Young and bathed in light, drenched in love, blond and bright. Turning her eyes on the camera, bewitching, ingesting the adoration coming from behind the lens and digesting it into power.

Jesus fucking Christ. These two. How could I not have seen it?

She's already going to have to talk to Ann tomorrow,

about her mom—and now this, too? It feels impossible.

Wait—Ann could also have answers about what happened to me.

Oh, god. What if...

She runs to the bathroom and throws up in the toilet, then sits down on the cold tile floor, resting her torso on the edge of the tub, hair falling in her face, sweat beading on her neck.

After a moment, she leans over and turns on the faucet, plugs the drain, resting her head on her arm as she watches the water rise.

Don't think about it. She fights off images of young Petra and Ann with her five-year-old self. *But what if it was them?*

The rest of her mac 'n' cheese comes up and out, into the toilet, and a little gets on Billie's T-shirt. She strips it off, cups a small handful of water, and rinses her mouth, then pulls off the rest of her clothes, turns off the light, and gets into the hot water.

She tries to focus on recalling what Ann and Petra were like together. What did they do? Had Petra ever left Willa alone with Ann? Ann must have been living here, in this house, then, though Billie doesn't remember ever coming here as a kid. She thinks she can remember Ann showing her how to shoot with the Seagull, in an open meadow somewhere.

Most of the photos of Petra are from before she'd had Billie—probably before Petra met Joe. *Did Petra and Ann live here together, then?* She can't remember the details about how or when Ann bought the house; inheriting it from her family seems unlikely, since she burned that bridge when she left town with Petra.

It's possible the two girls had only been in an innocent

young love, and that one or both of them had simply grown out of it. Or maybe Ann just stopped taking pictures of Petra. Or maybe the later photos aren't up, for anyone to see. Maybe they're elsewhere in this house.

Billie, Jesus. You need to relax and rest. Just lie down, watch some TV, and fall asleep.

Billie washes her hair and body, and gets out feeling better. She wraps her wet hair in the towel and walks nude to the guest room, where she puts on briefs and a black T-shirt, breasts unbound. She falls back onto the twin-size bed, feet dangling over the edge. Grabs the remote and turns on the TV, scans the channels.

After a hot bath, this is perhaps her most soothing activity, and something she gets to do even less often. She leaves the volume muted as she looks for something to watch, browsing the moving images like a walk through a strange village. Pure, mindless distraction. The control of it, too, the power; Billie still feels it now. She had needed this small control after Petra lorded her power, again and again. The remote, as a kid, was a way to regain autonomy. However small and pathetic it seems now, then it had been essential.

She remembers the coffee she drank when she arrived and realizes it might keep her up. *I need to sleep.* Taking the towel off her head and tossing it to a chair, she slides under the covers, then remembers the gummy she stashed earlier, fishes it out from her jeans on the floor, and eats it.

Next thing she knows, it's three-thirty and a robotic "Alert" is repeating at a deafening volume. *She remembered the alarm alright.* It won't stop now until Billie goes up there and turns it off. The likelihood of Petra really needing help is slim, but Billie doesn't have a choice. She pulls on a hoodie and jeans, grabs the keys, and rushes out of the cabin barefoot. The closest neighbors are more than a mile away, but for her own sanity the sound must be stopped now.

She unlocks the front door. Every light in the place is on. Petra is in the bathroom, on the toilet, when Billie walks in. She shrieks on seeing Billie and slams the bathroom door.

Billie turns off the alarm and all but a couple lamps. "Petra?" she calls into the bathroom, with no response. "You okay?"

Her mom exits the bathroom like a cat, stealthy and on guard.

Billie rolls her eyes. "It's okay. I'm here because you pulled the alarm, remember?" *No, she doesn't remember, stupid.*

Petra sits down on the bed.

"Are you okay?" Billie kneels at her mom's bedside. Petra climbs back into bed and Billie pulls her heavy quilts around her. She knows her mom is often up in the night; the Alzheimer's interferes with circadian rhythm.

As she looks at Petra, strangely, an image of herself as a kid enters her mind, hovering over her mom's face. *One of the photos in Ann's collages?*

No, I would have remembered it. Willa is fierce, defiant—she looks angry. Billie can't imagine what happened to piss her off like that. She wasn't allowed to show anger to her mom.

Billie shakes her head, shaking away the image, her mom coming back into focus. Petra seems more peaceful now, somehow, maybe because Billie is there. She was probably scared, up here alone in the dark.

I wonder if she ever sleeps with Ann?

Billie shakes her head again. *One thing at a time. Jesus.*

In the nether nighttime space, they're both a little softer. Billie still feels a little high from the gummy, which had knocked her out. *I'm here, and she's wide awake, and seems peaceful for once. Maybe I should try again, while I have her attention.*

Billie sits back on her heels, places her hands on her thighs, and decides to go for it. *Try the name Willa, instead of Billie. First in, last out.*

It had never occurred to her to use her old name before. "So, Petra, I am your daughter…Willa." She looks for recognition in her mom's eyes. Petra looks curious. "I need to talk to you, about when I was a kid. You're the only person I can ask. If you can think of anything at all that might help me….I need all the help I can get."

She's never spoken to her mom about this stuff. Petra looks out at her, in the low lamp light. Her hair is messy where she slept on it, and she seems open and innocent, like a kid.

Billie takes a breath, continues. "I know that something happened to me…was done to me. At around five years old…. I don't know what happened, but I am starting to remember little things."

She goes to brush Petra's bangs out of her eyes, then stops, pushing her own hair away from her face instead. "I know it wasn't Dad." *God, that feels good to say.*

Her mom looks up at her, a wildness in her eyes like a flash of memory.

"Dad is dead," Billie says. "Do you remember me telling you that yesterday?"

Watching her mom for recognition that never comes, Billie's heart breaks. *It must be such a mess in there. Like an obstacle course.* Billie watches Petra's face go back to being blank, wary.

Or maybe it's just like a fog that covers everything. Some people search their whole life for that kind of peace. Numbness sounds pretty good right now, to Billie. Opening a jar of trauma is something one should only do if one absolutely must. She wants to put the lid back on and close it tight, bury it where no one will ever find it.

Maybe I'm not ready for the truth.

"Special," Petra says. "That's what he said."

"Who?" Billie asks breathlessly.

Her mom's light-blue eyes lock on Billie's dark-blue ones. When she was small, she thought her own eyes had been made from her mom's sky-blue mixed with her dad's dark-brown.

Petra blinks several times. Billie can see the story retreating, blurring inside her. Petra blinks to get it back, but it's gone. Her eyes close.

"Mom? Special how? What do you mean?" Her mom has never used this word with her before, but hearing it, saying it, Billie has a sensation of almost-memory, a feather floating beyond her reach, carried away by the wind.

Petra turns her back on Billie, withdrawing into her warren.

Billie wakes again, in the tiny guest bed, at eight. She tries to retrieve her dream, but it evades her.

That image of Willa, though—the wild eyes still burn bright in her brain. A face she would never have made at

Petra, who would have knocked it right off of her. She'd only hit Billie a handful of times, but she would never have tolerated such insolence.

It comes back to her, from the middle of the night: Petra saying "he" had said she was "special." *What the hell does that mean? Special-education? Could it have been a teacher?*

She goes to get the coffee brewing—good coffee that she brought from Seattle on her visit last year. While it brews, she wanders the house. In Ann's office she finds three photo albums, full of all kinds of photos, not just the little square ones.

You can look later, she tells herself. *After you go see Petra.* A reward for good behavior.

She makes her bed and packs her stuff, so she can hit the road as soon as Ann returns. As Billie zips the zipper, and sets the backpack out in the hallway, she feels herself continue down the hall, to the last door on the left. She's almost in a trance, her body guiding her down the hall, past Ann's bedroom to a small room at the back of the house that she's never noticed before.

She enters, sees it's a kind of studio. More cameras, and a few rolled-up backdrops.

She turns around, and in front of her on the wall, there it is.

An enormous photo of her—of Willa, looking angry, wild-eyed. It's black-and-white, and square, so must have been taken with the Seagull, and enlarged to four feet around.

This is where she saw the image. But she doesn't remember having ever been in this room before. She looks around but nothing else is familiar.

Did I sleepwalk in here last night? Holy shit. She's never sleepwalked in her life that she knows of. *Maybe because of the gummy...*

She looks at herself on the wall, looking seriously pissed. *What in the actual...?*

What the fuck. Is this doing in here. Why so big?!

She can't be in this house anymore. She rushes down the hall to the front door, slips on her shoes and runs outside, up the trail behind Ann's cabin. She runs hard, up and up and up until she can't run any more, then sits down on the dirt path, chest heaving. The image of her five-year-old self fills her mind and she tries to shake it out.

Do not fall apart right now, she tells herself.

Everything is fresh, up in the trees. Being in the redwoods is like coming home. She feels it, breathes it in. She's protected.

Her eyes, when she opens them, fall on something shiny, in the grass at the side of the path. It catches the light and reflects it to Billie.

She reaches down and picks it up. It's a little piece of igneous rock, glittering in the sunlight, shaped like a tiny heart. Her middle finger falls in the valley and her pointer and ring fingers press down hard on the peaks, her thumb pushing up on the point. She pushes so hard, it leaves marks on her fingers.

Petra is locked in. I need to let her out.

Standing up, she puts the rock in her pocket, takes another deep breath in, and heads back downhill.

Billie leaves the same flowered teacup at the bottom of the stairs, to remind herself that she's coming back soon, to the land of the living.

I need to hold on to my sanity. It's what I have that she doesn't.

She knocks, then unlocks the front door and walks in slowly. *Just be a student. It's easiest. You don't have to be yourself right now.*

"Hi Petra," Billie says quietly in an upper register as she enters, scanning for her mom. "It's me, one of your art students…just coming to check on you."

Petra isn't in bed or in the bathroom. Billie looks around, panicked. *Could she have gotten out?*

Petra cranes her neck around the refrigerator, from where she sits at the kitchen table.

"Oh, hi, you scared me," Billie says in a girly voice. "Are you hungry? Do you want some tea? Ann is going to be home soon." At the thought of seeing Ann, Billie feels sick.

She opens the fridge. "I could make you scrambled eggs?" She peeks over the fridge door at her mom. "Petra? Eggs?"

No response. Her mom's eyes have nothing in them, no life to be seen.

Billie takes out the eggs, puts some bread in the toaster, gets the kettle and skillet going. She sits at the table next to her mom, cracks some eggs into a bowl and whips them up, then melts some butter in the pan, pours in the eggs, then some cheddar. Soon the eggs are scrambled, the toast is buttered, the tea is steeping, and Billie sits to eat with Petra.

I know this woman. I know what she likes. Even if I don't know what she's thinking, some things never change. Billie had been trained by Petra, in how to take care of Petra. How she liked the house cleaned, her eggs cooked, every preference of the queen in her kingdom. *I can do this.*

Billie drinks her tea and eats, watches Petra from behind her bangs.

That's better. I needed something solid in my belly.

She suddenly desperately wants to be home, on the Land. She has a flash of worry, wondering if she reminded Jane to water the flowers up by her old cabin. *She'll remember,* she assures herself.

You just have to get through this last little bit.

She clears their plates, sits back down. Considers taking Petra's hand and decides against it. It would be too painful if she pulled away. Billie doesn't want to scare her off.

There are so many things she wants to ask. About Ann and Petra's relationship. Her mom may be gay—that's new. And the picture of Billie in Ann's room—why is it there? Does Petra know it's there? Does she ever sleep in the cabin? She knows she's going to have to talk to Ann about moving Petra in there for good; it's no longer safe for her to stay alone. But maybe this is all a ruse. Does her mom normally sleep in the cabin, when Billie isn't here?

Billie has way more questions now than when she got here. *Pretty sure that's not how detective work is supposed to go.* She suppresses a physical urge to go back to the cabin and look at the photo albums.

She flashes again on the big, angry black-and-white of her. *What the fuck did she do to get me to make that face?*

Pulling Petra's pills from her pocket, she gives them to her with a glass of water—not sparkling in the a.m., but still with a twist of lemon.

Petra looks like she could use a nap. Who knows if she even went back to sleep after the alarm debacle.

See if she remembers the "special" comment.

"Petra?" Billie says softly.

Her mom isn't able to keep her lids open. They're falling down.

"Let's get you back in bed."

Back in Ann's place, Billie rushes through the photo albums at the kitchen table, seeking anything that could help, taking pictures with her phone of anything interesting: more images of her mom as a young woman, of Petra and Ann together, of small hands and feet that Billie thinks might be her own. And the original of the huge Willa in the studio.

She moves quickly, one eye on the time. Ann had said she would be back by noon, and Billie wants to be gone by the time she returns. She can't deal with Ann right now, doesn't want to get stuck here talking to her. But she also can't leave Petra alone for more than twenty minutes.

It's 10:45 now. An hour to clean up in here and feed Petra lunch. Shit, the walk to the truck will take fifteen. So, leave here by 11:30.

The priority is trying once more with Petra, to see if she knows anything. Once Billie leaves, there will be no way to contact her. *This is it.*

What if I just ask her directly: Was it you? Was it Ann? Her heart falters at the thought. After the panic attack yesterday, she knows she can't push herself too hard. She still has to make it up that diabolical road and back to Arcata.

She returns the photo albums to the office and paces the hallway—every time she's about to enter Ann's studio again she hesitates, imagining Ann arriving home and finding her in there. Being trapped in that room with her, with that image.

Get a hold of yourself. You were a damn cute kid—it's an interesting photo, that's all. She loves you, she would never do anything to hurt you.

Does she, though? If she loves me so much, why am I scared to see her?

Billie desperately wishes she could just leave now, but she has to give Petra her midday meal and meds first. She forces herself to breathe, searches the fridge for something to feed Petra. Ann had said she made some soup; Billie finds it and heats it up, then puts a lid on the ancient enamel pot and carries it over to Petra's.

At the foot of the stairs, she stops, realizing she doesn't have anything to leave behind, to ground her back in sanity land. *It's okay. You're just going to go in, get her fed and medicated, make sure she's safe, and then you can get the hell out of here.*

She walks up and unlocks the door, then knocks loudly, her mind spinning for another identity to try on as she enters Petra's space. *You don't have to say who you are at all. It only confuses her.*

"Hello?" she calls out. The bathroom door is closed, Petra must be inside. Billie takes the soup to the kitchen and pulls two bowls out of the cupboard. She puts her mom's pills on the table, next to a tall glass of water with a squeeze of lime.

With her mom out of the room, Billie takes the opportunity to do a brief inspection, making sure all the outlets look safe, nothing is too close to the heater. She looks in the cabinets. *What am I looking for?*

Petra comes out and catches Billie looking through her desk drawers. Billie's cheeks turn red; she turns away and inserts some authority into her voice. "Come on over, I've got your pills laid out and some soup heated up. Ann made the soup, she told me you liked it."

She looks for a sign of recognition in her mom's face at the name, to no avail. Petra walks into the kitchen and sits in her chair like a hungry kid. Billie ladles soup into the bowls and brings them over, sits to eat with her.

"Does Ann take pretty good care of you here?" Billie asks.

Her mom's eyes are on her soup, picking out the veggies she likes, pushing aside the ones she doesn't.

"Is Ann your good friend from childhood?" Billie tries.

Nothing. Billie's not sure if Petra even heard her.

"Do you sleep in her cabin with her?" she suddenly finds herself asking.

This gets her mom's attention. She looks at Billie curiously, like she has a newfound respect for her. *Does that mean I'm right?*

Billie looks at the clock. It's 11:20. *Fuck. Gotta wrap it up.*

"Ann will be back at noon." Does Petra still know about time? About math? "I'll be leaving soon. Unless there's anything you want to tell me, about when Willa was little?"

Billie looks deep into her mom's eyes, desperate to find something there, anything. She thinks she sees fear. Or it could be resignation, or regret. Does Petra remember enough to feel guilty, even if she doesn't know what for, even if she doesn't remember what happened?

"Petra?" Billie says. "You okay? What are you thinking about?"

When Petra drops her head, Billie does, too, tries to capture her mom's eyes again. *Maybe if I can keep her thinking about this, not let her look away... Maybe the looking away makes her lose the connection.*

Just then Billie hears a car pull up. She looks out the kitchen window. Ann's Subaru wagon.

Of course she's fucking early. God damn it. Ann gets out, wearing a red shirt and jeans, then looks up at the window, catches Billie there, waves. Like Petra, she's tall and fair.

She's coming up. Billie starts to panic. *Fuck. Focus on getting out of here.*

"Heyyyyy!" Ann says to Billie as she enters the small space. "Long time no see!" She comes over and gives Billie a perfunctory hug.

It's all Billie can do to allow the physical contact, as she stands. She feels like her heart is going to come up out of her mouth. *Please let me not vomit, or have another panic attack.* She takes a breath, then realizes she's holding it in.

Both women are looking at her. She exhales. "I'm so sorry about Joe," Ann says.

Normal small talk. She knows nothing of your mind-state. Just stay cool.

It's so obvious now that Ann is a lesbian, Billie can't believe she didn't see it sooner. Other than the intervention, when Billie and Ann got Petra to see the doctor, Billie hasn't really spent time with Ann as an adult; in her few short visits since her mom moved here, they'd been busy with logistics. Now, next to Petra, though they're both in their mid-seventies, Ann looks decades younger than Petra. She wears her health proudly, shoulders back. Billie wonders if she enjoys finally having some power over Petra.

Her mind goes to her mom and Ann in the studio together, under the Willa photo....

Ann speaks to Petra, her voice calm and steady. "I see you had some soup." She nods at Billie. "And your meds?"

Petra stares blankly up at her.

Billie nods, clears her throat. "Yep, just now."

"Pretty flowers," Ann says.

"Aren't they? From the Janes house. Petra planted them herself, way back when."

They are all silent, looking into the flowers' ball florets and contemplating their strange provenance. Petra appears entranced, lost in their miniature caves.

That would be the place to take her, if she's going to remember anything significant. Her studio. Where she went to escape.

Billie clears her throat. "I should get on the road."

"Saw your truck down there," Ann says. "You didn't break down, I hope?" Billie shakes her head. "Can I give you a ride down there?"

"Nah," Billie says quickly. "I just felt like a walk. I do now, too." *This was my last chance and Ann fucked it up.* Her frustration makes it hard to meet Ann's eyes. She catches Petra's eyes again instead. "It was nice to see you, Petra. Hope to see you again soon."

Her mom's eyes register some pain or surprise. *She doesn't want me to go. Is she scared to be left here with Ann?* She looks down at Petra, who casts her eyes down.

In ten minutes she'll forget she ever met you. Don't be so paranoid.

Her mom looks up at her. "Good luck with that drive."

Billie and Ann laugh and Petra looks pleased. Another of her invincible lines.

"Thanks, I'll need it," Billie says, laughing as she moves for the door. When Ann follows, she says, "No need to walk me out. You just got back, you probably want to settle in."

"Don't be silly," Ann said. "I need to get something from my car anyway." She locks Petra in.

Billie is suddenly sure that Ann is going to walk with her, all the way to the truck. "Maybe I will take that ride after all. Save my strength for the drive."

Ann nods. "Hop in."

Billie grabs her backpack from the house and gets in the front seat. "The fam is okay?" she asks. "Two grand-kids, right?"

"Three now," Ann says.

"Oh, wow, congrats. Everyone's healthy, virus-free?"

Ann says, "Yeah, thank goodness."

As Ann politely returns the inquiry, Billie speaks over her. "We should talk soon about my mom. We had talked about moving her into the cabin—"

"Already in the works," Ann says. "I'm getting her set up in the guest room."

Will she fit in that little bed? Billie wonders but does not ask. After all, Petra does seem to have shrunk.

"Okay, well, let me know if you need anything," Billie responds vaguely. Her view of Ann has changed completely. She doesn't feel guilty, like she used to, about Ann doing all the work of caring for her mom; about not offering to do it herself. *She likes it this way,* Billie sees now.

Billie changes the subject. "I saw a lot of photos of my mom that I had never seen before. Beautiful. She looks good in black-and-white."

Ann nods, and Billie sees her wondering where Billie is going with this. *Does she know I know about her and Petra?* That seems obvious now, just based on the photos of them together. Can they just talk openly about this, now that Joe is gone? She wants to ask Ann about it, but she can't make the words come out.

She can't bring herself to ask about the photo in Ann's studio either. *Because what if it was her who hurt me?*

They're almost to her dad's truck. *Get me out of this fucking car.*

"Thanks for taking such good care of my mom," Billie says. "We're both very lucky to have you. I'm sorry I haven't been around much. After the summer…"

"After summer," Ann agrees.

She realizes they've been saying Billie will help more with Petra "after summer" for several years now. Hearing Ann say it back, she feels what an empty promise it's been all along.

Ann also seems very ready for Billie to get out of her car now. Billie sees half-moons under the armpits of her red polo shirt as Ann leans in for another uncomfortable half-hug.

Billie gets out, starts up the truck, waves bye to Ann, and they both turn their cars around.

What the fuck was that.

Billie pulls over in Petrolia for a sandwich to go, kombucha, coffee, and a brownie. Knowing the road out is even more harrowing than the drive in, after ordering her sandwich she climbs back in the truck, pops the glovebox, and smokes the last of the pot in his pipe.

His mouth was on this less than a week ago. The thought is sweet, not weird or gross. Her intuition has cleared Joe entirely. *The only thing he did wrong was have a heart attack and leave me with these lunatics.* She desperately wishes her dad were here right now, to drive them up out of here. He had a way of making everything easier. Slipping the glass pipe—a dark blue, like her eyes—into her hoodie pocket, she rubs her thumb along its grooves.

Can I say the same about Petra—that I'm sure it wasn't

her? Does that feel true? And what about Ann? She feels less sure about those two.

After picking up her sandwich, she heads out over the undulating roads along the black beaches. The sky is a cloud-free cornflower blue. She rolls down the window and breathes the sea breeze in like medicine, pulling her hood up to keep her hair out of her face.

Would she really hang a giant photo of you looking super pissed off if she'd had a sexual relationship with you? That would make her a full-on psychopath pedophile.

Billie is pretty sure Ann isn't a psycho pedo. But there was also the fact that seeing Ann in the same space as her mom had the strange emotional effect of making her want to stay with her mom—which had to be something to do with Ann and Petra, their relationship. Not anything to do with Billie, probably.

Fuck.

Ann clearly loves Petra, Billie tells herself. *That's only a good thing. There's no evidence that Petra isn't being well cared for. I certainly couldn't do any better.*

The idea of Ann and Petra as a couple is blowing Billie's mind. It certainly wasn't what she had come here hoping to discover. *But it is good intel,* she realizes, *even if it doesn't end up tracing directly back to whatever happened to me. It rounds out my picture of my world back then.* The new images, in her mind and in her phone, can populate her memory void.

She pulls over to eat half of her veggie sandwich before the road heads away from the ocean, powers on her phone since service usually starts back up around here.

She's always felt weird about Ann, she understands now, because subconsciously she just didn't trust someone who would be good friends with Petra. *'Cause Petra seems like she would be the actual worst friend. But lovers… that's something else entirely.* In this new light, their relationship makes a lot more sense.

The thought of Petra being queer makes Billie feel uncomfortable, though—after thinking she was the only one all this time. When she had come out to Joe and Petra, neither had seem surprised, and Billie wonders now if that's why. Was Petra not surprised because she herself was queer? Was Joe not surprised because he knew about Petra and Ann? *Now I can't ask him about that either.…*

She lets out a big sigh, looks down at her phone.

The first thing she sees is a text from her mentor, Gloria: a news story about the city of Minneapolis, where George Floyd was murdered. Their city council has announced that they will disband their police department, and replace it with a community-based public-safety system.

Billie's mouth drops open. She reads the story again, then breaks into a huge grin and texts Gloria back, so excited her hands are shaking: *I have the chills. Thank you for telling me. I love you.*

After belting down some coffee, she pulls the truck back onto Mattole Road: up, up, up, like the first leg of a roller coaster.

Lisa

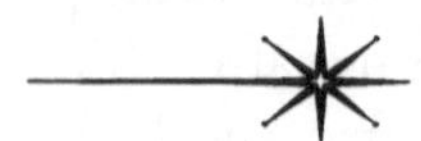

*B*illie makes it home alive, after on the way out almost being run into the canyon by a fast-driving local. Driving through Eureka, there seemed to be half as many people on the streets as there used to be. Last she heard, Humboldt County had 200-some Covid cases. Even though they stopped having to shelter in place a couple weeks ago, people seem to be scared to be outside.

She parks Joe's truck where he always parked it, under the cherry tree, and heads inside the old ranch house, which Joe built in the late 1960s.

It's quiet without her dad, who would always greet her with "My girl!" when she came in the door. Billie never wanted to be anyone's girl but she also never wanted to correct her dad. *My existence brought him great joy. Why couldn't I have just been grateful for that?*

The couch, when she falls into it, still smells of freshly cut wood. She can practically feel him sitting next to her. It's a torture, to feel his presence, so tangible yet so elusive; in a couple months she'll be desperate for it, and his scent will be gone. *How is Lisa going to manage, as his energy shifts and fades away?*

Lisa. I should have brought her some food or something. Lisa has never really seemed like someone who has needs—unlike Petra, who always had *all* the needs—and so Billie has never worried about her. But as she lies on the couch feeling like she should at least go collect some wildflowers, she can't make a single muscle move. She falls into a deep sleep before another thought enters her head.

She's outside, under the trees. Sunlight wavers in and out, echoing the waking-life sun moving through gaps in the curtains. Billie's head is warmed by the sun in both places, an energy brewing there.

Something moves up ahead, in the dream, flickers in the corner of her eye. She moves toward it. Then another flash—an animal, maybe. Leaves rustle in the trees. Billie is light on her feet, the soundless steps she perfected in childhood, on the trail of some small animal she really wanted to meet.

Heading toward the sound, she sees something duck behind a tree, but as she moves toward it she trips over a root, and falls, falls, falls….

Just before hitting the ground, she startles awake. Her eyes open but she's still seeing the dream images. She tries to remember. The corduroy of the couch has striped one cheek. It seems like every dream she's had lately ends with a fall.

I need to get a notebook and carry it with me, she thinks. *Write them down. There could be clues.*

Hearing Lisa in the kitchen, she calls, "Hey Lisa? Do you happen to have a little notebook you're not using?"

"I think so," Lisa says, and Billie hears a drawer opening. Lisa walks over with a small black notebook, flipping through to make sure it hasn't been used, then hands it to Billie. "Your dad always had an extra around for the next project."

Billie takes the notebook and thanks her. "Guess I'm the next project now." She remembers her dad dictating measurements and notes when they worked together, her writing them down in a little notebook just like this one.

Except—he had liked all the colors but she'd never seen him choose black. He never wore black either, now that she thinks of it. *It's like he bought it for me—like somehow he knew I'd need it.*

"You writing something?" Lisa asks, sitting on the couch at Billie's feet.

Billie smiles. "A detective story, kind of. How are you doing?"

"Oh…you know. I still can't believe he's not coming back. But he would want us to keep going. That's what I keep telling myself. I don't have to move on yet, but I do have to keep moving."

"Yes," Billie responds. His death has created momentum for her as well. Sitting still would hurt too much.

"How's your mom?" Lisa asks.

"Still Petra." Lisa and Petra have never met, but Joe had told Lisa stories about Petra.

When she was a kid, Joe never spoke badly about Petra to Billie, but after they split up he had explained to teenage Billie about her mom's narcissism, what he understood of it. But Joe was also generous in praising her gifts, too, even with Lisa, as if answering Billie's unspoken question, "If she was such a nightmare, why did you choose her?"

Her mind; how much it had held. Petra was an autodidact who knew a lot about a lot of things. She would have made a good academic, had she been born a little later, or into a family of intellectuals. Joe liked to say that he was glad that Billie had his heart and Petra's brain—until her Alzheimer's diagnosis, anyway.

He also was entranced by Petra's artistic abilities. And her beauty, her confidence. Her fashion sense—even out here in the sticks, there was an elegance to her outfits; he enjoyed seeing what she would put together next.

As the story goes—although Billie is now wondering if any of the family lore is actually true—Joe had met Petra at a wedding. They would have both been in their early twenties. Petra had been wearing a long, ethereal cream-colored dress, so Joe had assumed she was the bride. Seeing her off on her own in the garden, smoking a cigarette, Joe had been worried something was wrong, and went to talk to her—soon realizing that she was just a friend of the bride. Within a year he had made Petra his own bride—she wore the same dress to their City Hall ceremony.

Billie wonders if she should tell Lisa what she discovered in Petrolia. Lisa and Joe had been close—if he had known about Petra's potential affair with Ann, she's sure he would have told Lisa about it.

Across the couch from her, Lisa looks tired. Billie thinks she sees more gray in her long hair, which is pulled back at the nape of her neck. But her eyes are clear, not red from crying. Keeping gentle eye contact, Billie decides to go for it.

"Actually, I have an odd question for you. Did my dad ever say anything about my mom and Ann having an affair? Or about Petra possibly being bisexual?"

Lisa's big brown eyes darken, as if a cloud has covered her. She's quiet as she looks out the window, toward Petra's studio. Lisa has been living with the remnants of Petra's heavy memory ever since Petra moved to Petrolia and Joe moved back in, bringing Lisa with him. Lisa is the one who has been caring for the dahlias—the reason the flowers have flourished, all these years.

Billie is uncomfortable in the silence, regrets bringing it up. "I'm sorry, I know this is really awkward, and you just lost my dad, and here I come with my conspiracy th—"

"No, you're right," Lisa interrupts. "About your mom and Ann. They were together. Joe told me they were together before he and Petra met, and that he suspected they stayed in a physical relationship even after he married her. I guess Ann would come and visit periodically, and Petra always was happier after, so Joe just let it be. He said he had no idea how to make her happy. For most of the marriage, there was nothing physical between them. He seemed to think it was because Petra was gay."

Lisa looks at Billie thoughtfully, her eyes soft. "Then you started high school, and it made sense for them to split up. He got his place in Eureka, and you and your mom stayed here…. Your mom probably figured you didn't need to know, on top of the divorce and everything." Lisa raises an eyebrow hopefully.

Billie cocks her head at Lisa, like *Yeah, right.* Petra was 100 percent not factoring Billie into her equation. "This would have been a good thing for me to know." Her voice breaks; she fights back tears. It seems so obvious now, and Billie feels stupid for being the last to know. *Ann was just waiting for me to say something, today in her car, to let her know I know so she could talk about it.*

"I'm sorry, Billie. Your dad and I did discuss whether he should tell you, once she got sick and moved out to Ann's place. I think he felt it wasn't his news to share. I guess he figured Ann would tell you one day. So did she, finally?"

He was protecting Petra, she realizes. Here in his house, Billie's regret about the time she lost with her dad consumes her. Her body feels like it's filled with sand.

Billie explains that no, Ann didn't tell her—that she'd

pieced it together from looking at her photos. She doesn't mention the giant photo of her in Ann's studio; she can't even wrap her brain around what it means, in light of this news.

Later, in her room, she processes the info. *Petra is gay. She's been gay all this time.*

Why didn't I see it? Those photos have been up this whole time I've been going to visit Petra at Ann's. Why did I never look at them? Did I not want to know?

She sits on the queen-size bed Joe and Lisa had replaced her full-size bed with. Out her old childhood window is the view she always had: her mom's studio in the near distance. *I should go look in there for clues.* But Billie knows there's no way she's going out to the studio. Her body feels practically leaden at the thought.

Joe

Joe's favorite thing to do had been to shoot the shit over a beer—but it was the talking, not the booze, that he really loved. The activity of drinking just provided a framework for the long, meandering conversations on his porch, his sock feet propped up on the railing. He might nurse the same beer for hours, but he could sit and talk all day long.

So, to memorialize him, his loved ones meet at the Logger Bar. But most of them aren't really in the mood to chat. Joe had been in good physical health, so his death was unexpected, and some people are in shock; a few of his friends only found out about it today. People are also upset about George Floyd's death—and the virus has people shaken, too. Joe's death is just the latest terrible news of 2020.

All these people loved my dad. Almost everyone is wearing a mask, and those who aren't wave and blow kisses from afar. The masks make small talk unnecessary, and the mood is somber. Hugs are mimed. Hand sanitizer bottles around the bar are pumped. In Humboldt County, people are mostly staying safe.

Billie sits down on a couch by the fire and breathes through her tears, a dry, heaving breath. She's been afraid to let it all the way in, that he's really gone. Now she realizes that's what the memorial is for: a safe place to let it sink in.

The Logger Bar houses enormous chainsaws in its eaves, and the helmets and boots of the loggers who drank here in the early 1900s. The chainsaw blade above Billie's head is at least ten feet long. She imagines it cutting through a redwood, then closes her eyes at the thought.

When Billie opens her eyes, Lisa is standing at the bar—itself made of reclaimed old-growth redwood—and pulling down her mask. "Thank you all so much for coming. This is just what Joe would have wanted. To be here with all of you. All of us." She laughs nervously and looks around at everyone. Billie catches her eye, smiles in encouragement.

And then Billie smells pot, breathes it in—a peachy waft of sweet and skunky. *Dad?* Her eyes scan the space, as she rubs his pipe in her pocket.

"Me and Billie are grateful to the Logger, for having us." The bar's owner nods her head behind the reclaimed-redwood bar. She and Joe went to prom together in the sixties. Drinks are on her today.

Lisa continues, "Joe was so important to so many of us. It's a big hole he leaves behind."

On the other side of the bar, Billie sees Hank, her dad's best friend, and she desperately wants to go to him, hug him. But she doesn't want to interrupt Lisa in front of all these people, most of whom she doesn't know. Guilt eats away at her gut again, that she wasn't around the last few years. She'd thought she had time.

Though her dad had never mentioned it, Lisa had told Billie that the electric outages they'd gone through the year before had really affected Joe, too. He'd been angry that the electric company could and would just shut off power to so many Californians, rather than risk responsibility for starting another fire; they've recently been fined $4 million for causing the awful 2008 blaze that razed nearby Paradise. Without heat in the house for days on end, Joe's defenses had been weakened, and he caught a case of bronchitis that took six months to kick. Billie hadn't gone home for Thanksgiving because of the outages—without lights or heat, Joe had said it didn't make sense. He had downplayed it, though, so she wouldn't worry.

And then this fucking virus. She realizes this is the biggest gathering she's been to since it all started. *Thank god people came out.* It would have been awful if Joe had died a month or two sooner, during quarantine.

She thinks then of all the people who died from the virus, how lonely it must have been for them and their families. For the many who were alone as they were dying; and after, for the families who had to suffer alone, not able to share their grief and receive supportive touch from their communities.

She thinks of George Floyd. Of the video of his murder, which had broken Joe's spirit. *It's been ten days since he died. And he died ten days after George did.*

She breathes in deep, sniffing for the peachy scent again, wanting him here, wanting something to hold on to, whatever she can get. She cries quietly, letting her hair cover her face like a curtain. He had been so constant, so solid. It had never occurred to her that he wouldn't always be here.

Across the pool table, Billie sees her tenth-grade history teacher standing, his Afro mostly gray now, rolling the cue ball from one hand to another. She struggles to remember his name, wonders how her dad had known him. Joe was never really a teacher conference kind of dad—he was pretty hands-off, and he worked a lot, from morning to night on tight turnarounds. By high school, she was at his house only on weekends, so school stuff was less of a concern. He did make an effort to spend time with Billie, though, and she was often out working with him.

Lisa looks around at all of them, her beaded earrings swinging slightly. "Anyone who wants to can talk about him...talk *to* him. Knowing Joe, I'm sure he's here now, listening."

Billie looks around at the faces dispersed around the bar. *Maybe I'm not the only one who feels him here.*

Lisa sits down next to Billie on the couch, her big cheeks dotted with salt from her tears. Billie says, "I probably should say something." She puts her hands on her legs as if to push herself off the couch, but can't do it.

"No one expects you to," Lisa assures her.

She pushes herself up anyway. As she ambles over and settles onto a stool, her mind is blank. She wishes she had planned something, but nothing could ever be appropriate to the circumstances. The entire year has been absurd, like it was written by a first-year film student who just kept adding in more catastrophes, upping the tension.

She pulls her mask down, scanning the dozens of faces standing, leaning, hanging on each other; sitting on barstools that have been dragged all over. Lisa, on the couch, her brother now next to her.

To her left, she sees Hank, who was like an uncle to her—who still is. He nods at her comfortingly. *You got this.*

She nods back uncertainly, then smiles and looks around again, remembering that she's part of this community. She holds up her glass, and everyone in the bar does, too. "To Joe."

They all drink. Billie empties her gin and tonic, and sets it on the bar. The owner takes the glass and mixes her another.

As Billie clears her throat to speak, she sees a puff of smoke, in a corner across the room. She blinks and breathes in deep again. The weed smell is gone but she recognizes earth, dirt on someone's boots.

"My dad was always there for me," Billie says. "I assumed he always would be. And now, I can't accept that he's gone. It seems impossible that the Earth is still spinning, without him here."

She swallows. The owner slides her fresh drink over, and Billie smiles her thanks and takes a sip. "It's a beautiful thing, having his memorial in this place." She looks out at the people before her, feeling lost. As her teary eyes meet theirs, some of them pull down their masks, so she can see their sad smiles.

She takes a breath. "As most of you probably know, my dad grew up in Mobile, Alabama, where the majority of the population is Black. Most of his friends growing up were Black. And George Floyd's murder was…well, Lisa and I think it's what broke his heart. If you have a little extra, please consider donating to the Black Lives Matter movement in Joe's name. That would make him very happy.

"And also, he would want *you* to be happy. To smile, and laugh. To take care of each other. Thank you for being so good to him." Her voice falters, and she blurts, "I wish I had been better," before bursting into tears and walking back to the couch. She sits down, and Lisa switches places with her brother, puts her arm around Billie.

Across the room, atop a barstool, a young auburn-haired girl pulls aside her mask. "Your dad was such a good boss," she says shyly, looking over at Billie. The girl's name is Allie, Billie knows, and she worked for her dad, like Billie had in high school. She's about half Billie's size, and on her barstool she looks uncomfortable, like a kid in a room of grown-ups—which she is. She has the dark circles, too.

"Joe taught me so much," Allie continues. Billie knows the girl is in foster care, and that her dad been assigned as her advocate, a volunteer supporting role; taking Allie on as an employee came later. She was basically another child for her dad. Billie feels bad, realizing she had barely even considered Allie until now—other than Lisa telling her that Joe had left Allie his truck, along with a college fund.

Billie moves for her phone, to write a reminder to check on Allie in a few months, then tells herself, *No. Stop. Not now.*

Someone else starts to speak, an older woman whose house Joe had built. Billie tries to pay attention, but she hasn't been sleeping well and can barely focus. She sips her gin and tonic and breathes in through her nose, trying to catch his scent again.

Later, after a drink or two, the thirty-three mourners who are still around walk from the Logger Bar to the Mad River, each with a Chinese takeout carton of Joe's ashes. The darkening late-afternoon river beckons to Billie, and she heads straight down to the bank, pulling off her shoes, rolling up her skinny jeans as far as they'll go, wading into the cold, clean river. She loves the shock to her skin, how it wakes her up.

Others descend to the sandy beach behind her, staggered at the river's edge; some stay on the bridge above.

On the count of three they all empty their cartons into the Mad.

A huge cloud of ash covers the river—Joe is as big in death as he was in life. Everywhere, but then gone so quickly.

Billie suddenly feels scared to lose him, slips her shoes on and scrambles downriver, following him. Soon the ashes are absorbed by the rushing water, but she keeps pace with where they went, watching, as everyone else heads back to the bar.

She can remember walking this path with her dad, singing Bill Withers.

Ain't no sunshine when he's gone.

The dust of his body is being pulled to the sea, as he wanted. If she kept walking, in about ten miles she'd be at the Pacific.

Something on the other bank grabs her attention, but she can't see anything there. *Willa?* she wonders. *Is my inner child playing hide and seek with me?*

Something inside her creeps out of hiding. Now that he's gone, really gone, there's nothing to stop her from pursuing the truth of her own history—the mystery of what happened to little Willa.

Billie feels the tiny hope flicker inside her again. Maybe she can root out whatever infected her, like a rotten apple core. Get it *out.*

From here on out, she knows, there's no controlling how things will go. The current is pulling her, too, and the wild sea waits.

On the way to the airport, after buying face masks in Eureka, Lisa and Billie drive past the house of Billie's old best friend, Randall. Billie hasn't seen him in thirty years.

As they pass the big old country barn, she remembers the parties they'd had in it, Randall and Billie falling in love with *Ziggy Stardust* and *The Wall.* They fell in love with art and music and dance. With each other, and even with themselves—even if it didn't always stick.

They had discovered that if they strung a few extension cords together, they could watch out in Randall's barn. And so on weekends, in 1987, the summer before her senior year, that was what they did. The TV mounted on a few hay bales—often with the sound muted and new wave playing on the boombox—they danced below, feeling understood, inspired, transformed. They'd found the antidote to what ailed them.

In the film, David Bowie is Ziggy Stardust and the Spiders from Mars are his band—in black-and-white, a shot of light bursting through every now and then onto Ziggy. Billie and Randall danced to him, with him, because of him. He was worth worshipping. He changed people's lives, opened them up. Got them to see the world differently—like an alien. Billie remembers how she and Randall had loved to imitate the audience members, all gaga for Bowie.

She remembers, too, how she had always wanted to watch Pink Floyd's *The Wall,* but Randall had always said it was too heavy. That was before he was attacked. He seemed to want to exorcise his darkness, escape it.

Randall had helped Billie embody her inner rock 'n' roller—all black-and-blue, like a bruise. After shaping her brown hair into a messy shag, he dyed it black. Black eyeliner, to emphasize her brilliant midnight-blue eyes. Black jeans, black T-shirt, black boots. In all these years, her look hasn't really changed.

Randall had also been the one to rebrand her Billie—she'd been Willa all her life until they met.

Once she settled into the solidity and security of her uniform, Billie remembers, she had even let Randall paint her like a girl for a night here and there. She'd trusted Randall to make her up however his little gay heart desired. She can't imagine trusting anyone that much now.

In the mirror, he had found the real Randall, too—though unlike her, that was constantly changing. The way she remembers him is with his own strawberry-blonde hair; his lids some shimmer of blue, silver, gold; his lips a pop of pink glitter.

Late one Friday night, Randall had tried to convince Billie to walk to the store with him, to get some Jolly Ranchers. They were stoned, and once he decided he wanted something, he didn't let go. The football game had been earlier that night at nearby Eureka High—not that they ever went. Randall wanted to get to the store before it closed.

"Come with me!" he said to Billie, trying to pull her up from the hay bale she was lying on, listening to music at top volume. She can't remember, now, what it was, but whatever it was, she'd been obsessed.

He couldn't convince her. *The Wall* was in the VCR, the sound muted. Body in a bloody pool. Dragon bird crossing the sky. Bare foot smashing wine goblet. Two flowers fucking.

With the music playing, Billie hadn't heard Randall's screams from a half-mile away.

He had appeared in the door of the barn, his face dirty, dripping blood—leotard ripped at the crotch. He told her it was two guys from the visiting football team who attacked him.

Billie had jumped into action. They went in the house and she cleaned his wounds; Randall's parents were who-knows-where. Randall had asked Billie to shave his head and brows—like Pink did, in the movie—and she did that for him. She would have done anything he'd asked, given another opportunity.

But a month later, Randall was gone, to stay with his older sister in Seattle. He'd mentioned that he was leaving to Billie casually, and she'd assumed he would be back before school started. But he never returned, and they lost touch a few years later.

In all the years Billie lived and worked in Seattle, she never stopped looking for him. Everywhere she went, she was always scanning for Randall. She tried finding him on the Internet, even found some reviews of performances in Berlin, and emailed with her congratulations—but he never wrote back.

She'd called him Radnell, on account of how rad he was. But then he went away, and he left her all by herself—the black eyeliner and curtain of hair her only defenses.

He had opened her up, showed her how to trust again. Then he was hurt, and she couldn't save him. And then he was gone.

She had never showed her feminine side again.

Seeing his house, remembering it all, she feels again the terror of his attack, the fear of being queer and vulnerable in a small town, the loss of her best friend. It had changed her, no way around it—and of course she hadn't really dealt with it then. She'd had to toughen up in order to get through the rest of high school alone, to keep going to school, keep doing her chores. When she was at her mom's house, during the week, her mom had done all of the gardening, and Billie had to do all of the housework. When she was at her dad's, on weekends, they always had at least one construction job going. She learned to put her head down and work hard, and she's been doing it ever since.

She tries to remember if she ever talked to her mom about Randall's attack. *What would she even have said?* Maybe the hate crime would have confirmed to Petra that she and Ann still had to keep their relationship secret, even once she and Joe weren't together. What had happened to Randall was proof of that. *My dad kept their secret for them, to keep them safe.*

When Lisa pulls up to the airport's tiny loading zone, Billie rolls up her window. It's starting to sprinkle. *I still have an hour before my plane leaves.* One of the advantages of the Arcata airport is that check-in and security take five minutes max. Her truck is waiting at Sea-Tac, so she won't have to wait for a ride or take public transit. She has her mask to wear, to be safe.

She turns to face Lisa in the Jeep's driver's seat. "There's something else I want to tell you," Billie says.

Lisa leaves the loading zone and pulls into the adjacent parking lot, turns off the ignition. Her big brown eyes settle kindly on Billie.

Billie closes her eyes tight, clenching her fists. "I think someone hurt me when I was little." She opens one eye and peeks out to gauge Lisa's reaction. "My dad never said anything about that, did he?"

In the driver's seat, Lisa shakes her head, her eyes even bigger now, with concern.

"I didn't think so." Billie sighs. "I want to find out what happened, but I have no idea where to start. Petra was useless. And now Dad is gone, I can't ask him anything."

"Oh, honey," Lisa says, the crease in her forehead deepening. She reaches across and takes Billie's hand, and they sit there watching the rain.

"Use your sniffer," Lisa says, squeezing Billie's hand and turning to face her. "Your dad always said you had the best sixth sense in the west."

Billie blinks. "He said that?"

"He did."

As she hugs Lisa goodbye, pulls on her mask, and walks into the terminal, Billie's bones ache with the loss of him.

Crow

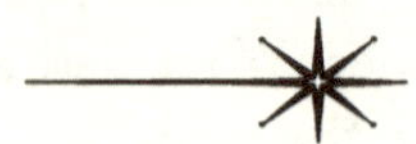

Billie gets back to the Land just before her fiftieth birthday. When her Landmates ask her what she wants for her birthday, all she can think is: a bath. No small ask in a place with no hot running water; it would take all three of them to pull it off. But it's a big birthday, and they love her, so of course they say yes.

Exhausted, she heaves her heavy body onto the bed in her old cabin, while they prepare her bath. She's been plodding forward with the new cabin ever since her return. At her dad's house—Lisa's house, Billie remembers, her head spinning—there hadn't been time to rest. They had been busy with planning the memorial, making arrangements for the future, organizing her dad's things. Billie had hoped to find some family photos, not having even a single photo of Joe—she had scoured the dozens of boxes in the attic and garage, with no luck.

Lying on her comfortable bed in her old cabin, she's not sure she'll be able to get back up. Staring at the ceiling, she remembers placing the wood beams there herself, ten years ago. How much energy she'd had then. What she'd put her body through…it was amazing what it had taken, what it had given.

Fifty years old. For so long fifty seemed so far away, like a far-off shore she would explore someday when life was quiet. Now that day was here, and life was louder than ever.

Right now your job is just to feel.

A knock, and the cabin door swings open. Jane peeks her head in. "Your bath awaits." She walks over and holds out her hand. "C'mon. Before it gets cold."

Jane knows Billie perhaps better than anyone, so she knows that Billie identifies as a woman, despite her butch appearance, though she doesn't identify *with* being a woman. She doesn't express her femininity, and she hates the way it makes her vulnerable—menopause doesn't help.

But then, she does identify with all of the feminist heroes that came before, and believes in embodying their strength. It almost feels like a betrayal, like she would be abandoning them and all of their hard work if she wasn't a woman anymore. On the other hand, it's complicated, and she could see in the future wanting to use "they/them" pronouns in public, if only to create some space and privacy around the highly personal issue.

Out here, it's always been fine for her to be just whoever she is, without needing to explain it—which is why she created a community from scratch, rather than buying a place in the suburbs with central heating.

Billie lets the smaller woman pull her up. She grabs a towel and follows Jane out, fearing a barrage of "Happy Birthday to You" outside—but no one is in sight, and Jane's is the only car parked below, next to Billie's.

Jane sees her look around in surprise and smiles. "We thought we'd give you some space. I'm off to do laundry, I'll be back tonight." Billie thanks her, blushing. "Happy birthday. Enjoy your bath."

Jane walks down to her truck, slams its tailgate shut, and gets in. Then she's gone, and it's just Billie and the Land. And the water, steaming out of the long clawfoot tub like a puff of smoke concealing a magician's trick.

She peels off her clothes and climbs in. A deep moan of pleasure as she sinks into the water, closing her eyes, her head sliding under.

Sitting up, she opens her eyes, water dripping down her face. Sunlight falls on her body through the spaces between the trees, shadows of their leaves moving across her arms. Her eyes shut tight. A loud, guttural sob bursts out like a bomb of pain, knocking the air out of her.

And then, out of nowhere, she has the sense memory again: the sensation of something inside her that wasn't supposed to be there. She has never wanted to be penetrated, by lovers—it made her feel out of control. She'd always thought it was a butch thing. Her fear of doctors, she always assumed was just a queer thing. Lots of queer people are scared of doctors, for good reason.

Her sense of the trauma, till now, has been almost clinical, in fact. Hypothetical, abstract, detached; like a medical student studying a surgeon performing a procedure. What's real, and what has been manufactured to fill in the gaps in her story?

Her imagination loves this kind of dark challenge. Visuals spatter across the backs of her eyelids, gremlins of possibility, grotesque puppet shows. The black-and-white, angry Willa, her eyes like a cornered animal.

It was the face she must have made after she screamed, in the dream of the house—after the house screamed, when all the windows shattered and all the doors slammed. Just after that, still vibrating with anger; Ann's photo is of that moment, after the scream.

Sinking underwater, she invites a sense of being in the womb, pre-trauma.

Coming up out of the water, she shakes her wet hair

around her shoulders. It feels like something is ripping inside of her.

She slides under the water again, tensing her body completely, tightening as she holds her breath, clenching her fists.

As she pushes herself up again, all the tension leaves her body, and she gives herself over to sobs. In the tub, in her home at the edge of the world, she lets the grief eat her whole.

Though Joe was a strong influence on Billie, and she admired the way he did business, even as a teenager Billie understood that the rest of the world was not Humboldt County. Growing up with two parents who did work they loved, but didn't make much money at it, Billie knew she needed another model. To be a success, you had to be good at the business part, not just the art part. And she was going to be a success. When she was accepted to the Seattle Art Institute—after a few years working with her dad, developing her portfolio, saving her money—that became her way in.

As a young student living in the big city for the first time, Billie worked hard like she always had—just now it was less physical, more intellectual. She'd mostly been bored at her public high school, but in college she pushed herself to her limit: assisting professors, volunteering for community projects, making herself invaluable to teachers and classmates. In time, she learned that she had charisma (a gift from her dad) and taught herself to use it.

After she left home, Billie had stayed in contact with her dad, but by the end of her first year of art school, Joe and Lisa had gotten together. They were busy falling in love and making a life together. Petra was in her own small world.

Even though Randall hadn't been returning her calls for a while, she'd hoped that once she was in the city, too, they could be friends again. But he politely turned down all of her invitations.

So Billie made her way on her own.

Once school was under control, Billie discovered women, and sex. Her brief attempts at relationships drained her, but she found that sex fed her, gave her energy. It made her attractive to others, and gave her confidence—another kind of power.

After Billie graduated from her self-designed mural arts program, without the structure of school she soon found herself depressed, working at a coffee shop for minimum wage. After dreaming about finally being able to make whatever she wanted, she learned how hard it was to find inspiration when you were broke and unmoored, in an expensive city that was wet and dark for way too many months. Grunge was taking off but Billie couldn't be bothered, preferred to spend her money on whiskey. She tried having a relationship a couple times, but that just made everything harder.

But then all that schmoozing and working for free paid off. A few former professors recommended Billie for a teaching position at SAI: shepherding their new mural arts program—developed from her own program—and teaching two classes a semester. She was only thirty, the youngest teacher the school had ever hired.

She had to hustle for a while, to get up to speed. But within a few semesters, her classes—Street Art 101 and Public Art: Past and Future—developed waitlists. Finding a nicer but still cheap apartment, she kept her needs simple, and put most of her paychecks in her savings account.

In the summers, she took on small neighborhood mural projects, where payment sometimes only partially covered materials, but when she knew the art would bring the community joy, she was willing to take the loss. She learned to be economical and resourceful, putting what she taught in her classes to the test, and developing her style.

Her favorite subject was the coast redwoods, the world's largest trees, which she'd grown up with. The early redwoods were representational, life-size wherever possible, and incorporated the local foliage—as if planted there, not painted. They brought the vibrancy of the forest to neighborhoods that needed it. But the longer she was away from Humboldt, the more stylized they became: sometimes she painted human eyes in the eyes of their trunks, hair for leaves, bones for branches.

Eventually, her classes became easier to teach, and she was able to use her weekends to manage and plan large-scale projects she began to get hired for, often in other countries. Then when summer came, she would hit the road. Summers were for travel and making art. By the time she was thirty-five, there was usually enough in the budget to take an assistant; by the time she was forty she always took at least three, one to manage the project, one to help build scaffolds, and one to help paint. They had planted redwoods on the walls of seven countries by the time she was forty-five.

And then, in 2010, Billie got back from a job in Morocco to find herself evicted, with one week to vacate her apartment, and classes starting a week after that. Stressed at the thought of moving yet again, she briefly considered moving back to Humboldt until she could figure things out—she missed her dad, and country life.

When her dean said no to her request for the semester off, though, she decided that if she was going to stay, she needed to be closer to nature. She started looking outside Seattle, within commuting distance, but there were no properties that she could afford available for rent. On Craigslist, even the falling-down places that were for sale were outside her price range.

The Olympic Peninsula had always reminded her of Humboldt, with its epic beaches and lush rainforests. So when, after several long days combing Craigslist, the Land had come up for sale—totally undeveloped, near the Puget Sound, so she could ferry to work, affordable since the six acres were mostly hilly—she snatched it up.

Making a name for herself as an artist, while navigating the politics of the university and managing her workload, was already a challenge. Building a new home from scratch was clearly inadvisable. But Billie knew how to dream, and plan, and build. She had a picture in her head of her new home, and from that point on she kept all her focus on bringing it to life. The Land became her art.

Though everything was harder out here—not having heat or hot water, for one, could really break the spirit— it was also easier. She hadn't known, living in Seattle, how much city life ratcheted up her nervous system. Staying out here for weeks, then months, at a time, she felt her system settle; it was just her and the forest. An old knowing returned, of herself as a wild thing. Sleeping on the ground for months, in a tent next to her growing cabin, she rediscovered her animal self, began to rely on the quiet safety of the forest, filling her back up until she had to go back in.

Now, she finds herself with a whole summer off for the first time in her life—the new cabin almost finished, and no commitments beyond the Land. The empty space is taking the shape of little Willa, before she lost whatever was taken. Billie needs to go back and rescue her, retrieve her from where she got stuck. She's not going to be able to move forward until she does.

In Humboldt these past few days, she'd felt again the pain of having hardened herself, so as not to hurt anymore. And now she feels strong enough to face whatever needs to be felt. She might regret knowing whatever it is she learns, but she'll never regret wanting to make herself whole again. Starting out on this journey while also grieving her dad is suboptimal, but there's no turning back now.

By the end of her birthday bath, she is resolved. She draws a breath, and speaks aloud: "Universe. Please help me learn what happened to me. I need to know the truth. Help me uncover the darkness inside of me, and free myself from it."

She gets out of the bath feeling rejuvenated and walks to the new cabin. It's her birthday, and she has the place to herself. She remembers that a friend of Joe's gave her (and Lisa) some magic mushrooms that he grew himself, after bringing over dinner one night.

That might be just the thing. All this thinking is too much. I need to feel.

In the tiny cabin she lays back on the bed, pulling on warm, clean clothes. She pulls out the jar of mushrooms and chews a few. It's been a couple years since she's done any drugs, other than pot. As the shrooms enter her bloodstream, she pulls a blanket over her head and closes her eyes.

Spinning like the Teacups, the dervishes return, spiraling in. *What did Willa know?* they ask.

"She knew about plants, and animals," Billie answers.

Outside, Billie hears the crow that often comes by. *Caw caw caw—come on come on come on!* Jumping up, she pulls on her boots, hooks a water bottle on her belt, opens the unfinished pine door.

She steps outside hesitantly, testing the earth's stability. The sun shines down on her like a spotlight, and it's like she's been wearing sunglasses her whole life, and has finally taken them off. Everything is just right *there.* The mushrooms have dissolved the veneer she shellacked on as a kid.

These sunny June days are as good as it gets, for Billie, on the Land. It feels amazing to be in her clean body, in the sun. It warms her up. She shakes her shaggy hair, still damp, and delights at the drops of her birthday bath that she's brought with her.

Suddenly she feels like herself again, her essential self, open and unafraid. She's included in the universe, separate from nothing—like her skin has melted into the air around it. There are no more boundaries. Everything includes her. She includes everything.

It's so simple. She remembers how it had felt, as a kid: the entire universe having her back. Complete safety. Utter interbeing. *How could I have forgotten?*

The brightness of the world, its transparency, is stunning. She stands looking out at it, in the ungrounded doorframe still, mouth hanging open. She can see every molecule, every atom, and though part of her understands that it's the mushrooms that allow her to see it all, that doesn't make it any less real.

Crow is in the tree, waiting for her. Nodding her head—like Billie's with its shiny black feathers—she caws again, *Come on, come on, come on.*

And so she does. Billie steps off the ledge, leaving the front door open.

All of these connected things. The ferns doing delicate dances. The avant-garde couture of the moss shrouds. Edible Indian thistle, like a bright purple urchin. The Fibonacci-sequence head of the sunflower—not one flower but hundreds of them. The harmonizing birds and insects, their constant collaboration. The swooping, swerving lines of branches and vines.

The scent of it all, intoxicating. Billie can't get enough.

Use your sniffer. My dad said that. He said I had a strong sixth sense.

Remembering her dad makes the whole thing shimmer, the adrenaline to her heart almost enough to shatter Billie's new peace.

Accept it, she tells herself. *There's no getting around it.*

She unclenches her heart, tries it. *Joe is not coming back.*

A sob bursts out, like she's gagging. She coughs it out: a black cloud. It quickly dissolves, and she walks on, smiling. A marmot the size of a house cat glances lazily at her as she passes by.

Bright violet lupin stalks, which always reminded Billie of a Conehead. Sometimes poisonous, Lupin offers inner strength, especially in recovering from trauma. Billie spends a moment with each stalk, calling them in as allies in her upcoming fight.

Insects fight and flirt above. After following Crow for an hour, Billie's jaw starts to ache from smiling. She finds herself in a part of the forest she's never been before.

Ahead, she sees a large circle—a clearing, filled with bright green ground cover. It reminds her of a crop pattern, the perfect symmetry. She doesn't need to know why, or how; why and how are in the wind.

Crow flies to the center of the clearing and lands there. Billie pulls off her boots and socks, placing them at the perimeter. *I'm going in.*

She walks into the middle, footprints darkening the soft, tiny leaves, making clock hands at seven-thirty-five.

In the center of the circle, she breathes deeply in, and then out, releasing all fear. She turns slowly around, taking in everything: trees, dirt, plants, flowers, birds, insects. All of it kissed by the sun, and also dipped in shadow. Nothing stays in the light for long; the shadow is always waiting. It has nothing to do with her, and everything.

Crow hovers above Billie, her wings pushing down, and then up, and then down, and then up—the constant give and take required to stay in one place. It would be easier for her to fly away.

Billie sits, hands caressing the silky oxalis, and senses down into the root systems growing below her. *As above, so below.* She closes her eyes and imagines a heavy chain running down her spine, into the dirt, and down, down, down.... When it reaches the center it gives a little tug, like an anchor reaching the bottom of the sea.

She lies back on the pillow of lime-green. She stretches her arms out gently and the small heart-shaped leaves return her embrace. The sun rubs away the worry lines on her forehead. Her face loses its tension, her jaw releases, and she breathes deeply. Her body releases all negativity to the earth, where it's neutralized.

Gone is the self-consciousness that has plagued Billie since her teens—since Randall was attacked for being who he was. This is freedom, the utter contentment of being in her body without worrying what it looks like, how it's putting her at risk.

Billie is happy to break free from the patriarchy's desperate grip. Grind down to dust the idea that women have to look any certain way. Banish forever the idea that women are weak.

They were what had kept her from all of *this*. She hadn't known how hard the armor made her—how it complicated and confused things. It obstructed her clear seeing, prevented her from taking her place in the universe. It made her separate.

Her self-sureness is back, and she lets every part of herself fall open, to everything under the clouds, and above them. To every halo and aura, spirit and ghost, ether and essence. To the art of the atmosphere.

This is her center, where she's strongest. *I can do this.*

As the walls she built around herself as a child crumble into the dirt and disappear, she feels an enormous release: a sensation of lightness, like she's been resurrected from the dead.

Tears drip down the sides of her face: for all the years she lost to separation—from her father, the universe, her sensuality. The sun burns away the shame and fear she was infected with, revealing the knowing she was born with.

I am a part of every living thing. Always have been, always will be.

Gloria

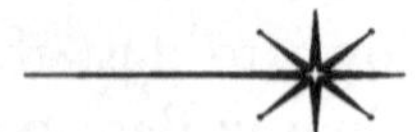

*A*fter losing Randall, and the pain of his continually shutting her out, she only ever really let one person in. In her third year at SAI, Billie fell hard for a teacher, Gloria Lance. Gloria was the only Black professor there at the time, and an established artist. She was famous for taking no shit—not from her students, not from admin, and definitely not from art critics.

Billie would never forget her first day of class with Gloria: Consuming and Creating Political Art. Gloria paced the space in front of the students, her fiery eyes watching their faces as she spoke.

"You have a responsibility to represent your community—*all* the people in your community, especially the ones who can't afford to attend a school like this. Don't ever take it for granted, that you are here and they are not. Don't assume it has anything to do with your talent. If you're not willing to study the world you live in and try to make it better, you're just contributing to the problem, and I don't want you in my class."

By the end of the second week, only six of the original sixteen students remained. That was just how Gloria wanted it.

Gloria was the first person Billie ever heard talk about white privilege, though it would become a hot-button topic in Billie's own teaching career. It was Gloria who had drilled the idea into her, and that changed everything. It made Billie want to use her privilege to help people. (And to impress Gloria.) Soon she was leading antiracism sit-ins and queer visibility campaigns. As she was older than the average student, and had a working-class pedigree, there was built-in trust among her comrades, despite her being white.

Gloria was indomitable—so of course Billie fell in love. In the freedom from someone else being in charge, she let down her guard. The exhilaration of sex with the older woman, letting G. be the top. A deep adoration developed for the woman who was her greatest mentor, everything Billie aspired to.

When Billie fell for her, hard and fast and wide open at twenty-seven, Gloria was forty-three. And while Gloria very much enjoyed their sex, she was more reserved the rest of their time together. Partly, because she was a professional—she and Billie had to continue to work together, in class and on the committees they were on, they had to keep things cool.

Billie learned a painful lesson: vulnerability makes you vulnerable. That they could recover from the ensuing mess to be lifelong friends and collaborators is one of the great miracles of Billie's life. Gloria is still a mentor, after all these years—and a figure of authority. One of two people that, even now, Billie is a little afraid of; her mom being the other. Gloria always tells it like it is. There's no hiding with her.

But the most inspiring thing about Gloria, then and now, has always been her *art*. The scale of it—Gloria did wall-size work, and she filled every inch. The authority of it—Gloria had never made even a single misstep that Billie could see, in all the years they'd known each other. But mostly, the *artistry* of it. Gloria's work had moved

Billie to tears, on many occasions. Respecting words and images equally, she used both in every piece. Her work was *always* political and *always* beautiful. Billie didn't know how she did it, and it took her a long time to finally stop trying to emulate it—to accept that no one else could do what Gloria did. That said, it had been the glory of Gloria's pieces—along with the construction and painting experience she'd developed with her dad—that made Billie want to make murals.

Gloria has been suffering this month, unable to join the revolution in her community against racism and police brutality. The success of the WTO protests cemented the city as a place where anarchy was grown and fed, seeded in the streets—setting the stage for the current protests against George Floyd's murder, and the occupation of Capitol Hill.

But Covid-19 has incited an uncharacteristic fear in Gloria, and she just doesn't feel safe to join the protesters outside her apartment, in what has become known as the CHAZ (Capitol Hill Autonomous Zone) or CHOP (Capitol Hill Occupied Protest). A police precinct was abandoned and—using the same barricades the cops hid behind during their violent standoff with protesters, which ended in their exodus—several blocks cordoned off as a cop-free zone. In solidarity, from quarantine, Gloria is doing a big piece on a wall in her apartment.

The mushrooms give Billie another important nudge: toward Seattle. The city lifted its shelter in place order a week ago—maybe Gloria will meet her in Capitol Hill, where she lives. They usually hang out together on the night of their birthdays if nothing else is happening.

In the cabin, she pulls on a stretched-out black sweater over black jeans and her best dancing boots, then floats to her truck. Blissed-out but clear-headed, and fine to drive.

On the way in, she calls Gloria. "What you doing calling my ass on your birthday?"

"I'm heading in. The universe wants me to dance. Wanna meet me?"

"Noooo thank you. Nobody's open! But stop by if you want to see the new piece—I just finished it. And definitely check out the auto zone. Wear a mask."

As Billie drives through the city, she realizes how isolated she's been, out on the Land. It's one thing to see something change slowly, over days and weeks—but she hasn't been to Seattle in months, and its late-stage sickness is shocking. Most restaurants are boarded up, messages of solidarity stenciled on the boards; lots of businesses are marked CLOSED or CLOSING. The truck's window open to the warm night, her muscled arm hanging out, Billie cruises by slowly, the windows of empty establishments reflecting her shock back to her. All of her favorite bars and clubs are shuttered.

When she was living in Seattle in the eighties and nineties, Cap Hill was a chaos of queer art, drugs, and music. Protests were staged atop bins of *The Stranger.* Someone would put a boombox in the middle of an all-way crosswalk, and people would mob the intersection, dancing in the street till the cops came. Then there were the silent, mile-long processions honoring friends lost to AIDS.

We survived another virus, Billie thinks now. In fact, the HIV antivirals have created a resistance to the coronavirus for some.

She finds the barricades delineating the CHAZ/

CHOP. The zone had been established in the wake of George Floyd's murder, when protesters squared off against police in riot gear, using tear gas. When police shut down their East Precinct, activists occupied the block around it, declaring it a car- and cop-free zone. By now it has grown to encompass a six-block radius around the vacated police precinct—the sign out front now reads SEATTLE PEOPLE DEPARTMENT.

Billie parks outside the barricades. As she pulls on her mask and walks in, she senses the safety right away. With no cars, people hang out all over the street, some on comfy couches with rugs underneath, some sitting on the asphalt. Three Black women are rapping on a small stage. Residents jog through with their dogs; commuters head home. Someone is passing out patches that say RACISM IS A PUBLIC HEALTH CRISIS.

Billie heads straight for the already-legendary BLACK LIVES MATTER mural, which fills an entire block of Pine Street, down the center of the street—each letter painted a different design by a local artist of color. Billie has seen images of it but it's stunning up close: the detail, the variety in styles, and how well they all work together. Other cities copied the idea soon after: Bed-Stuy and D.C. both did bright-yellow versions.

A "No Cop Co-Op" is set up on a nearby corner, providing donated food and medical supplies, including masks and antibacterial gel, free of charge. Signs are propped up: REMEMBER WHO WE'RE FIGHTING FOR and THIS IS JUST THE BEGINNING.

In the street, an indigenous group, some of whom are wearing traditional garb, are drumming and chanting. People of all colors circle them, in protection and solidarity. One young-looking person with a bandanna covering their face holds high a sign that reads THIS IS A PROTEST NOT A PARTY.

In Cal Anderson Park, a community garden has been planted in the social distance circles the city had mowed to promote social distancing—reminding Billie of the clearing she found in the forest earlier. What looks like about a hundred tents are set up around the garden.

There's more free food donated by local businesses, a medical tent, free clothes, a hand-washing station, even volunteer-provided mental health support. People sit chatting on the grass, reporters interview people. A man and woman that look like they dressed up for the occasion are sitting on a blanket watching it all, their baby sleeping in a portable crib beside them and their dog at their feet. TRAYVON WOULD BE 25 RIGHT NOW, reads a sign someone has staked into the grass.

Billie wanders, marveling now at the transformation to this neighborhood that she knows so well. And yet, what it reminds her of is the Capitol Hill she landed in when she arrived in her twenties. When the tech boom happened in the 2000s, artists, musicians, and revolutionaries had been driven out of the city—no longer able to afford it, no longer feeling like this was their home. Now, it's like *that* Seattle, which so many thought was dead, has come roaring back to life. Billie is surprised by an overwhelming wave of nostalgia and relief, at rediscovering something she had given up on looking for, thinking it was lost forever.

Headed for Gloria's place, Billie sees an enormous altar to George Floyd on a sidewalk, with about thirty candles burning, and a guy randomly sitting in the middle of it all. A woman is sitting at an easel in front of it, a brown-skinned face emerging on the canvas.

WE CAN'T BREATHE is projected high above, on a wall covered in graffiti tags.

Hanging from a flagpole, an American flag has been reenvisioned: the stripes are black and red, while the rectangle in the upper left features black stars on a green background. As Billie stares at it she feels proud to be an American, for the first time she can remember.

At Gloria's building, G. buzzes her in. At her door, Gloria sees that Billie is crying under her mask. They don't hug. Gloria just leads her straight back.

She's calling the new piece "June Teeth," a play on Juneteenth, June 19, which marks the day the last slaves were finally freed. It covers two walls of equal length, fifteen feet wide and seven feet high. In the center, in the corner where the walls connect, Gloria has painted George Floyd, all six feet and seven inches of him standing tall. A halo made of lightbulbs is lit around his noble head.

To his left, on the left wall, is the beautiful, shining face of Ahmaud Arbery. To Mr. Floyd's right, on the right wall, is the bright, happy face of Breonna Taylor.

Ahmaud Arbery was chased down by two racist white men in South Georgia, who hit him with their truck, then shot and murdered him in February of this year. Breonna Taylor was shot eight times by police, in a botched raid on her home as she slept, in March of this year. George Floyd was murdered by police, who detained him with a knee pressed down on his neck, after a convenience-store employee reported him for using a counterfeit $20 bill, in May.

Surrounding them, almost covering the background—which is that same African green—are the faces of hundreds of Black protesters, reflecting the racial justice revolution that has broken out around the world.

In Gloria's version, though, rather than face masks, they have mouths and teeth. Some yell, some smile, some laugh, some cry—from babies to the elderly, and lots of young adults, of all genders. She has documented the Black faces she sees in the media, and outside her window, imagining what's under their masks, memorializing their beauty. Celebrating their voices and their bite.

Starting from the far left end of the left wall—as if protecting the protesters, keeping them safe—red letters span ceiling to floor, spelling JUNE. On the right wall, at the far right corner, in the same tall red letters, is the word TEETH.

Randall

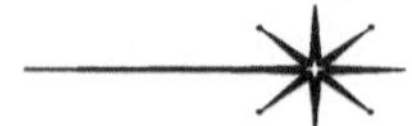

*A*fter Randall was attacked, it was a long time before Billie was able to dance again like she had in the barn—like the survival of the species depended on it. It just wasn't safe to be that open anymore. When survival is the goal, you just do what you have to do. Survival beats integrity every time.

As she leaves the noise of the CHAZ/CHOP, Billie turns off her brain and lets herself be guided. Turning a corner, she crosses the street on impulse, then backtracks in the other direction—no one is around to notice her disordered movement, or get in the way of it.

She's ready for a drink. But nothing is open.

And then finally, after walking for a while, she sees an open door. It leads down some narrow, red-carpeted stairs. From the bottom, she hears some faint guitar come floating up.

The fact that they're open seems reason enough to go in. *I'm fucking fifty years old. This virus can't stop me.*

At the bottom, after some negotiation, she's able to convince the bouncer that she's not a cop; it's her birthday, after all. He finally gives in and she pays the cover.

Walking in, she sees it's an old theater, which she never knew was here. As she wanders toward the music, she thinks she hears Pink Floyd—*The Wall?*

Rounding the corner, she beholds a majestic space, complete with chandelier and ornate Deco embellishments. In the low light, she sees a small standing-room-only crowd.

The massive stage is occupied by one petite performer—behind whom video plays, on the back wall. It is in fact footage from the film of *The Wall*. The song is "Another Brick in the Wall, pt. 2" and the scene is one she always loved, when the kids riot, smashing the shit out of their oppressive school. The expressive, melodic guitar sounds just as thrilled and breathless.

The performer rages across the stage as if urging the rebels on. Their hair is a dark shag, like Pink's in the film, and their lithe, androgynous body, in tall silver boots and a snakeskin jumpsuit, shimmers in the spotlight.

Getting closer, she can see that the jumpsuit is made of white sequins, with green slashes. It reminds Billie of the costumes Randall used to make in high school—times a hundred.

Randall…?

Oh, my god.

It's him. It's totally him.

She walks toward him. He looks amazing. Behind him, on the back wall, the kids are destroying their school, lighting it on fire. She laughs, and then cries, and then waves, yanking her mask down, shaking her head.

It's her Randall. After all this time, she has finally found him.

The song ends, and another begins: "Is There Anybody Out There?"

As a teen, Billie always thought of this as the witchcraft scene. The music starts quiet, builds slowly. Pink's belongings are arranged ritualistically on the floor, like a mandala—records representing all phases of the moon. Guitars, candy bars, cigarette packs, pills. Pink is making spells from the detritus of his life. Randall, however, is nowhere to be seen.

And then the music stops, and Pink starts to shave. First his chest. The only sound in the entire theater is the dripping of blood into the water, splashing against him to wash away the blood. The close-up of the razor is giant in the projection and terrifying, and it's uncomfortable in the dark, quiet space with no guide. But Pink looks so fucking good up there: those dark, wild eyes. Billie's body wants to move.

The now-bald Pink puts his face against the glass door—through the glass, he looks gloriously extra-dimensional.

And then, as Pink slides open the door to reveal his new hairless self, Randall steps into the light, revealing his own bald head as Pink does the same behind him. Randall unzips the jumpsuit a few inches, revealing his hairless chest; gyrating gracefully, he runs his hand down his side, the green sequins glowing white in his wake. When he closes his glittery green eyes, Billie clocks that even his brows are gone—just like in the film, but without the blood.

Just like we shaved Randall, after his attack. Oh, my fucking god.

And the screen goes black. The lights go dark.

Billie gives a whoop of excitement and somebody else hollers "Yes!" and they all go crazy, yelling and clapping in the dark.

She's fully crying now, slightly disturbed by the reference to Randall's trauma (and her part in it, however pathetic). She stands in the middle of the crowd among the other stunned audience members, and as the house lights slowly come up, she pushes away the images of Randall's bloody face (and ass).

Walking to the bar, which appears to be in the coat room, she finds herself trembling, and sweating. She orders a gin and tonic and removes her sweater, plucking at the black tank top underneath to get some air flowing through.

I finally fucking found him.

Surely he'll come out and say hi, she hopes, and decides to sit in one of the seats that used to be in the center of the space—but were removed for a dance floor and are now staggered around the outside of the space. As a DJ starts spinning, she drapes her sweater across the plush red seat next to her.

Tears come to her eyes again and she swipes at them, tired of crying. The mushrooms seem to want to pry her open as far as she'll go. She shakes her head again in disbelief.

In all this time, she hasn't had another friend like him. Not even close. She has finally accepted that maybe a best friend is something you only get once in a lifetime.

And then there he is—in lower-heeled boots, but still in full makeup—and he sees her and walks toward her, and then suddenly he's here next to her, close enough to touch, and so alive. Crawling, Gollum-like, onto the seat two away from hers, he takes her sweater from the chair between them and drapes it dramatically around his shoulders. The bartender brings him a large glass of water, and he kisses them on the cheek in thanks.

Randall's hair, she sees, is the same strawberry-blonde it was when she knew him, but shaved on one side and long on the other, falling over one eye then flipping up at the end. And his brows are intact—he'd been wearing a bald cap and had very convincingly glued down his brows, with the shag wig over that. She thinks all of this but says nothing, not sure how she feels, speechless.

Randall takes a long drink of water, peeking out the side of one eye at Billie, with a flutter of luxuriously long lashes. Setting the empty glass down on the carpet, he turns to face her.

"Billie Knight," he says, reaching across to wipe at the eyeliner smeared on her cheeks. "I see you still like black."

He moves into the chair next to her then, and they hug, all the years melting away as their bodies remember the other. They hold each other tight. Billie is afraid to let go.

As they pull apart, he takes her sweater from his neck and puts it around hers, and for a moment they're linked by it.

He sits up straight then. "Today is your birthday! It's fifty, too, isn't it?" He's quiet. "I was hoping you'd find me. And now you have." His voice cracks, and as he looks up at her, tears fill his bright green eyes, reminding her of the oxalis that held her in the forest that afternoon.

"It worked," he says, smiling.

She nods shyly. *So he's been looking for me, too?*

There are so many questions to ask, she doesn't know where to start. She reminds herself, *I know this person. I have his stories in my bones.*

"Let's dance." He takes her hand, pulling her up. "It's your birthday!"

And then, like they're back in the barn, they pogo all over the dance floor to New Order's "Bizarre Love Triangle." Billie shakes her hair side to side like it's 1999, Randall voguing in a circle around her.

"I thought you hated *The Wall*!" she yells.

"I've mellowed out a bit," he replies. "Wait here, I'll be right back."

And so she does, dancing by herself, eyes closed. *This is just what I needed.* The shrooms have relieved her of all self-consciousness and it feels amazing to be among like-minded people, after so many months alone. She had almost forgotten that she needs this, too.

But a few songs later, Randall still isn't back. She goes to the bar for a glass of water and asks the bartender if they've seen Randall, but they shake their head no.

Billie drinks her water, pondering. She doesn't have his number, so can't call him. He wouldn't have left her here, would he? She's starting to feel rejected again.

She heads to the bathroom. After using it, she continues down the hall, dread growing in her with every step, until she reaches a door that reads DRESSING ROOM. She opens it.

At the other side of the empty room, with its line of vanity tables and lit mirrors, she sees Randall's body, spread across one.

Rushing over, she shakes him, his body falling to the floor. She kneels next to him and, holding his shoulders, pulls his head up and props it on her leg. His head slumps and she shakes him.

"Randall!" she shouts. "What the hell!"

She thinks she feels a pulse, but it's very faint. A needle hanging gruesomely from his arm falls to the floor. "No, no no no no." Pulling up his jumpsuit strap from where it's fallen off his shoulder, she calls 911.

I can't lose him again.

She starts doing CPR, but encounters a stiffness in Randall's chest that's nothing like the dummy they used in class. It feels like if she pushes too hard, she'll break him. She persists, though, yelling for help in between breaths.

It seems like a very long time before the two EMTs, one male and one female, come. She points out the needle and a baggie of white powder on the table, among scattered makeup and brushes.

They quickly move to treat an opioid overdose and squirt Narcan up his nose, but Randall just convulses.

The woman checks his pulse. "Hypoxia. Probably Fentanyl."

"Again?" the guy asks.

"Try the injectable," she replies, and he quickly readies a dose and injects it into the arm that isn't already bruised.

This time it's immediate: Randall gasps for air, eyes cartoonish with the dramatic lashes, blood trickling from the Narcaned nostril. The EMTs get to work checking vitals.

His silvered lids are at half-mast, as if the lush false lashes are almost too heavy to lift. His pretty green eyes—which always reminded her of sea glass—find her next to him. Looking into them is dizzying.

"You're back!" Randall says affectionately to Billie, touching her cheek. Like she just went home for lunch and is back for afternoon classes.

"*You're* back." She smiles. Taking her sweater from around her waist, she very gently pulls it over his head, one and then the other arm, and rolls up the sleeves.

When the EMTs prepare to take Randall to the hospital, he protests. "I feel fine, and I don't have health insurance. I don't even live here! Please just let me go?"

"You need someone monitoring your vitals," the guy says. "Heart rate, respiratory rate…"

"He can come home with me," Billie offers.

Randall looks unsure about that, and so do the EMTs.

"He'll need to be watched," the female EMT says, "to make sure his breathing doesn't slow or stop."

"I can do that," she responds right away. She feels sure that if they take him away in an ambulance, it will be the last she sees of him. She nods to the baggie on the vanity, then looks to the EMTs. "Can you guys get rid of that for us?"

"Uh, no," the woman says. "We have to report it."

"We aren't required to report schedule ones right now, if they don't end in death," the guy says to his colleague. "Cops are too busy with everything else."

"Thanks," Billie says. "I'll go get my truck. Can you help him up the stairs and I'll meet you out front?" They nod. "Randall, is that okay?"

He nods and she leaves, before they can change their minds.

Pulling up behind the ambulance, Billie hops out to open the passenger door. The EMTs struggle getting Randall up and in, and she goes around the other side to pull. Randall—loopy from the Fentanyl/heroin/Narcan cocktail—giggles at being pushed and pulled, his body out of his control. He took off his makeup while she was getting the truck, and he looks like a kid, in her big truck, wearing her too-big sweater.

Finally, he's situated in the passenger seat. The male EMT stretches his seatbelt across and Billie takes it from him and fastens it.

"Thanks," she tells him, taking a breath.

"No problem. So, watch him for two hours, to make sure his breathing doesn't slow or stop. If it does, you need to take him to the emergency room right away."

She nods, calculating that they'll be on the road home for about two hours—but once they are, the nearest hospital is about forty-five minutes away. She probably should mention that to someone.

The female EMT comes around to Billie's window, on her way back to the ambulance. "He'll probably be sick for a day or two, like a bad flu. Plenty of fluids. Keep an eye on him, bring him in if anything seems seriously off."

Billie nods, and thanks her, then starts the ignition and pulls out into the quiet street.

Worrying about the lack of hospital proximity on the Land, and whether she's bitten off more than she can chew, Billie navigates toward the closest highway onramp. As she does, Randall asks casually, "So what have you been up to?"

She laughs. In high school, whenever he found her, Randall would link arms with Billie and start up again wherever they had left off. Their conversation had started when they met looking at art books in the school library, and it didn't stop until he left.

She merges onto the almost-empty I-5, headed south, and starts filling him in. "So, we're headed to my Land—queer community, six acres, off-grid. Northern tip of the Olympic Peninsula. We're going the long way. It's faster to take the ferry, but it stops running in the evening."

He looks over at her and smiles weakly. "Please continue."

"I'm a muralist. I also teach, at the Seattle Art Institute. But I have the summer off. I'm building a new cabin." She remembers then. "Also my dad just died."

Randall gasps. "Oh, no! I loved your dad. I'm so sorry."

"Thanks. Heart attack. We had his memorial at the Logger Bar and sprinkled his ashes in the Mad River. Next time you go home, you can go to the river and say hi."

"Yeah…that's not my home anymore, Bill. I live in Mount Shasta. I haven't talked to my parents in years."

They're silent for a few moments, and then she sees him cup his nose, blood flowing out.

"Glovebox," she says, pointing, one eye on him, one on the dark freeway. "Napkins."

They drive in silence for a while as he mops up the blood. He sneezes, then pulls the bloody napkin away to look at it.

She looks over at him with worried eyes. "Are you okay?"

"I'm fine," he says quietly.

"Listen, the nearest hospital is almost an hour away from my place. Do you want to stay at a hotel or something, just in case?"

He shakes his head, then rests it on the window.

"Don't fall asleep," she says, feeling like a nervous nag.

He just nods. He pulls the sleeves of her sweater down over his hands.

She turns the heat up higher, adjusts it until it feels right. She's wearing just a tank top, and now that the adrenaline has worn off, she's chilly, too.

They're quiet for a while as they get off the I-5 onto the smaller, quiet Highway 101. She doesn't know how to bring up the drugs without sounding preachy.

"Fuck," he says then.

"What?"

"My car. It's in a resident zone."

"Shit. Is it safe?"

"It'll have to be, I guess."

After another prolonged pause, she says, "In mother news, Petra has Alzheimer's. Oh, and guess what?" Billie says. "She's fucking *gay.*"

"Wait, what?"

"That's right: the ice queen has been having her ice creamed all this time, by her bestie, Ann! I just found out. Do you remember Ann? Tall, dykey-looking…? I really should have figured it out sooner."

He shakes his head, his mind clearly elsewhere. He's definitely coming down.

She's afraid if she doesn't keep talking, he'll fall asleep. She tries a different subject. "What did you do for quarantine?"

"Got out of jail." He smiles at her, sickly sweet. She knows he's serious, and that he wants her to know it.

I don't give up that easy. "Can we talk about the drugs?"

"Arrrrrrgh."

"Listen, I won't judge. I took some mushrooms today, to celebrate my birthday."

"Happy birthday again." He hums a few bars of "Happy Birthday to You," and she remembers Gloria singing it to her around this very same spot, on her way in. Now, just a few hours later, everything has changed.

Randall continues, "I'm sorry I fucked it up. I was just so excited to see you…and this is really stupid, but sometimes when I'm excited about something, I feel like I have to use, to match the intensity of the situation or something…. Anyway. Thank you for saving me." His voice breaks on the last bit, and he clears his throat.

"Shush. You are the best birthday present I could ever have dreamed of. The thing I wanted most in the whole world, actually. I've been looking for you." She's quiet as the vulnerability of that sinks in. *Apparently I was the only one looking. I would have been easy to find if he'd tried.*

"What's really sad is I had five years sober until tonight," Randall says.

"Shit."

He shakes his head mournfully. "Not looking forward to telling my sponsor. Turq was my cellmate at Folsom. When I got out, he hooked me up with a place in Mount Shasta—and he agreed to stay my sponsor if I visited him once a month, and called once a week."

She says quietly, "You can always start ag—"

"No, I know," he interrupts. "So yeah, that's what *I've* been doing for the past couple decades. Now do you get why I didn't want to see you?" He catches his reflection in the window and moves his mouth open, closed, open, closed, watching the deep lines framing his mouth and chin.

Billie waits.

"Thank you, Billie. Thank you for taking care of me, and I want to see your Land. But I don't want to put you through my shit, not after we just finally found each other again." He can't stand the thought that she saw him like that—so ugly, after all this time.

Billie decides not to push. They're quiet for a while. She picks up her phone, toggles to Spotify, and *Ziggy Stardust* sparkles out of the speakers. They sing along.

When they were kids, Bowie's assertion that Earth was dying and they had only another five years had felt correct. Now, thirty-five years have passed, and they're still here, but the lyrics never sounded more true.

The Land is covered in darkness, no lanterns burning, and the stars are so crisp they seem frozen up there, drawn with icicles. Billie goes around to the passenger seat and helps Randall slide out of the truck. Remnants of glitter on his cheeks shimmer in the moonlight as they walk to the lodge, holding hands. Randall shivers, his eyes bright and wet in the dark.

Billie puts her arm around his shoulder. "Don't worry," she whispers. "It's three a.m., everyone's probably asleep. Hopefully Tulip won't bark." Her Landmate's dog sleeps with her owner on the second floor of the lodge.

Guiding Randall into the lodge, Billie grabs her headlamp, hanging by the door, and switches it on, careful not to look Randall in the face. She pulls off her boots, and Randall unzips his Chelsea boots and places them neatly by the door, with nervous hands, deep gray pockets under his light-green eyes. He seems sober now, or maybe just wiped out.

She leads him to the Captain's room, on the ground floor; they call it that since the bed is shaped like a ship, with a steering wheel on the side. She changed the sheets after the last visitor left and is now very glad she did. It's cold in the small room but there are several blankets on the bed. She lights the lantern, goes to the kitchen for a water bottle, fills it up. It, too, is icy cold.

Randall sits on the bed, already starting to nod off. She hands him the water and he drinks. *Now he looks his age.* He has blood crusted under his nose. She gets a hot washcloth, and wipes it away.

"You need sleep. It's been two hours, I think you're in the clear. There's a bathroom right outside; I'll explain the toilet situation tomorrow, but for now go ahead and go in there. Take the lantern if you need light. Are you hungry?"

He shakes his head forcefully. She kneels and hugs him. He feels just like he did when they were young: slight, almost half her size, but wiry. She pulls back and looks into his eyes. "You're gonna be okay. I'm glad you're here. My cabin is just up there"—she points uphill—"if you need anything. I'll introduce you to everyone in the morning."

She pulls the sheets and blankets back. "Everything's clean." He climbs in in his jumpsuit and her sweater, shuddering at the cold shock of the sheets. She pulls a couple more blankets over him and tucks him in tight.

Kissing his forehead, she turns the lantern low.

She sits and watches him for a moment. Seeing he's already asleep, she opens his tote bag and checks for drugs, finding only makeup, neatly organized in colorful bags.

In the morning, Billie finds Jane and Rabbit making breakfast and tea at the stove, wearing headlamps in the low light. She tells them the story of her birthday, until she sees Randall come out of the Captain's room and go next door to the bathroom—quickly.

He comes out a few minutes later, looking miserable in the jumpsuit and sweater. Tulip barks at him from a few feet away, then slowly walks over to him. As he pets her head, she leans against him.

Billie says, faux cheerfully, "Hey, guys, this is Randall!

My best friend from high school." She goes to him and takes his hand, so clammy it's almost wet.

Jane and Rabbit introduce themselves. "My girlfriend, Helene, is upstairs still, sleeping," Rabbit says, pushing their glasses up their nose.

"I'm making coffee," Billie says.

Randall staggers outside and onto the deck before vomiting. Billie watches, concerned, but decides to give him some space and focus on caffeine and food.

He's suddenly drenched with sweat. Realizing this is the start of what is going to be a long day, Randall starts to cry. He sits down on the edge of the deck, and puts his head in his hands, sobbing. He yanks at the arm of the jumpsuit angrily, trying to rip it, but the stretchy double-sided sequins are durable as hell and nothing happens other than some minor sequin cuts to his fingers.

His head feels like someone is scraping it from the inside, scooping out his seeds and guts.

Randall looks around and sees three cars parked out front: two small sedan things and a truck. The truck looks almost exactly like the one she had in high school, just bigger.

Barefoot, he walks behind the lodge, past the outhouse and henhouse to the vegetable garden. He admires the boxes, feeling envious. On the way back, he wanders the path, following signs to the outhouse. A handmade sign in front of a small wooden structure reads W.C. Inside, he lifts the seat and averts his eyes as he sits gingerly over the open pit below.

What am I doing here? Without a car, he's stuck here.

He's not sure now why he agreed to it.

Finishing up in the bathroom, he washes his hands and pushes open the door with his foot.

Tall, skinny trees are blowing in the wind. The air is refreshing, and he sits at the side of the path, lies back on a pile of leaves. Above him the trees dance a wild tango. He closes his eyes, shaking, and tries to stay calm, watching them.

Billie finally found me. He'd known she would, eventually. He'd tracked her whereabouts for decades, had always planned to find her after he quit—too ashamed to show her what he looked like as a druggie.

Oh, the irony. It just went to show that we really have no control over how things play out.

And now suddenly here he is in her strange world, with no way home. He had misplaced his phone at some point in the mayhem after the show. He can't stand the thought of going back inside, however kind Jane and Rabbit might be.

After a bout of vomiting and diarrhea, the shakes are back. Shivering violently, he goes back into the lodge, leaves stuck to the back of Billie's sweater.

Jane and Rabbit are sitting in the living space, reading and working, Tulip in her bed by the fire. She looks up at him and considers getting up, then settles back down. He glances over and sees Billie cooking in the kitchen.

"I put a T-shirt and hoodie on the couch for you," Jane says.

Grateful, Randall thanks her and pulls them on, leaving the rest of the jumpsuit still hanging down, and Billie's sweater on an ottoman.

"Come over and warm up," Jane says.

He sits in front of the hearth and stares into the fire,

pulling the black hood over his head and warming his hands and feet over the fire. But the shakes don't stop.

Jane goes upstairs and comes back with some socks. Seeing him shaking, she puts them on for him, then grabs a quilt and settles it over his shoulders.

Randall stares into the fire. After a while, he seems to forget where he is.

And then, Billie asks loudly from above, "Do you want something to eat? Coffee? Tea?"

He shakes his head miserably, then rolls onto his back and looks up at the ceiling of the wooden cabin. *Billie made this,* he thinks.

He closes his eyes against the spinning. The sweat cools on his skin. Tears fall from his eyes, and he shuts them tightly.

Jane sits on the floor next to him, Tulip curling at his feet. Rabbit goes into the kitchen, preparing some medicinal herbs for him. Helene comes down and introduces herself, stokes the fire.

Randall's hair clings to his face. He looks, to Billie, sitting on a chair near him, like a wet cat.

"It's okay," she tells him, and pulls him up, leads him back to the Captain's room. She helps him out of the jumpsuit and into a fresh T-shirt and sweats; as she does she sees all the raised scars on his arms and legs. They show her every attempt he made, to hit that high, to make it stop, to be someone else. She's glad he's too out of it to notice her seeing them.

Day two is worse. He wakes up shivering, but she's right there with him. She holds him, tells him he's okay. All day long Randall feels nauseous and then vomits, sweats and then gets the chills, has diarrhea even though he's eaten almost nothing. He cries out like a baby in pain, and she soothes him. It's as bad as quitting heroin had been, the couple times he'd kicked.

Billie is with him for all of it, minus the diarrhea. That night, she climbs into bed with him. Luckily the bed is big and she can mostly sleep through him thrashing in his sleep. If he needs something, she wants to be here. She keeps her hurt feelings to herself for now and simply meets his needs.

When she wakes up on day three, Randall is sitting up, looking at a zine he found in the living room. "Morning." He's still super pale, but he's smiling. He shows Billie the cover: a drawing of a black cat that she realizes now has always reminded her of him.

When he hasn't been excreting fluids, they've continued their conversation in the quiet spaces, remembering things together.

"You remember Black Cat?" he asks her now.

Billie remembers the cat dying, and Randall heartbroken. She rests her cheek on her arm to keep her morning breath to herself and does a sleepy circular nod that means "No, sort of, it doesn't matter, go on."

"She died right before I met you, that's right. She was big as fuck, that cat. Biggest cat I ever saw. When I was in middle school, Black Cat would chase away these brothers who used to bother me, hissing. She would even leap at them, bit them both more than once.

"They kept getting more and more pissed off. I worried that they would hurt her, but all they did was throw rocks at her, which she easily ducked. Every day it was, could I get to Black Cat before they got to me."

Billie can't believe she's never heard this story, but

knows she would remember it if she had. It happened before they'd met, and Randall never was much for backstory.

"And then this cat—Bill, she started meeting me at *school*. A *mile* away. School got out at three and she'd be there, lounging in the sun, waiting for me. Like I had a butler or something, she'd walk me home.

"But once I got to high school, it was too far for her to walk, and she got old—and then, you know, Black Cat died.

"But you know what I just realized? When Black Cat died, you became my new Black Cat. You had my back. I knew that you would have done anything you could to protect me."

Not go with you to the store for Jolly Ranchers, she thinks.

"You couldn't stop the brothers from hurting me, though. 'Cause it was them who hurt me, Bill—not some other team's football players, like I told you." He sniffs, and laughs. "And they had been doing it for a long time—that night was just the worst of it. I knew you'd go after them if I told you, so I didn't tell you. But it was my neighbors who raped me, Billie."

She closes her eyes, falls back on her pillow. The room spins.

"I didn't tell *anyone* the truth, though—except my sister, eventually. I was scared of them, and humiliated. That's why I left—it didn't have anything to do with you. But..."

He takes a breath, looks over at her. It's easier with her eyes closed. He speaks quietly. "I was angry at you, for a while—that you didn't come with me that night. It wasn't your fault, what happened—not *at all*—but I was sixteen and...this is silly, but I was resentful that you were just lying there listening to music while I was being…you know. Chased, violated. I couldn't walk after. I don't know how I made it back to the barn.

"And then later, the anger went away, and I was embarrassed, that I had lied to you about what happened. I was afraid you'd be mad if you found out.

"So I pulled away. It was just easier. I appreciated that you would reach out and invite me to do stuff, and those couple times seeing you at shows, that was great. Honestly. I just couldn't do the work of keeping in touch. The hole between us got wider and wider, until I couldn't get past it. I let you fall away from me."

She knows she should say something, but no words come.

"But I never had another friend like you, Billie. You need to know that."

Tears leak out of the sides of her eyes. Her chin quivers.

He stands up. He brushes Billie's bangs out of her face, then gets up to make coffee.

The Land

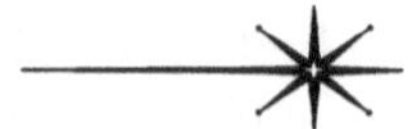

*L*ater, Randall feels okay enough to walk with Billie to the cell phone vista. He wants to use her phone to take care of some business, get in touch with his work, and Turq. They bring Tulip on the walk.

Billie has often wondered what her life might have been like if Randall hadn't christened her Billie—if she hadn't had a friend who understood her that deeply, early on. An adulthood as Willa is impossible to imagine. Not only did Billie suit her better, the more boyish she became—it also helped her to leave behind her childhood, the things that had happened to her when she had no power. Not just the mystery trauma coming back now, but also the basic indignities of being a child—less than, weak, with no defense against Petra's vicious disregard. Her mom could be vicious; some of the things Petra said to her still sting after all these years. But by the time she was fifteen, Billie was taller than her mom, and stronger. The new name made it easier to forget that she had ever been a victim.

And, she realizes now, walking quietly with him along the sunny path, that Randall left her with something important: an identity.

Randall was always big on names. He loved making up songs about people featuring their name. He'd learned that Dolly Parton had happened upon the melody of her song "Jolene" while walking to her trailer after a show—

having met a fan named Jolene, she wanted to use the name in a song, and didn't want to forget it. Randall sometimes uses a name as a sort of chorus, too, while he thinks up the rest of the lyrics.

The child of intellectuals who taught at Humboldt State University, Randall didn't grow up close to nature like Billie did; his parents chose a country house with a barn because it was a novelty to them. But Billie had pulled him into nature with her. They went on long walks along Humboldt's seven rivers, built driftwood sculptures and traipsed through tidepools.

They rode their bikes everywhere—throughout the Arcata Bottoms, where Billie lived, to the marsh, and even to the larger town of Eureka, where Randall lived, ten miles south. The trail along the 101 took them straight into Old Town, where they snuck in, through the back patio, to a dive bar called Fat Albert's. By the time Billie was fifteen she could drive on back roads, to parties or to other small towns nearby.

They also loved being creative together. Randall was a talented hairstylist and makeup artist even then, and he was always experimenting on himself and Billie. Sometimes Petra even let Randall do her face and hair, if she and Joe were going out. She was quite extraordinary-looking, and it suited her to have people acknowledge that—which was part of Randall's skill. Making the person he was working on feel like the center of the universe. Petra liked that.

The path to the vista from the lodge is wide and easy, unlike the claustrophobic one from Billie's new cabin. They pass a tall Pacific willow tree, its skinny yellow leaves embedded in the dirt at their feet. Tulip runs ahead, peeking back to check on them now and then. She's very much a people dog, motivated to stay close to her humans.

"I just started a new project," Billie tells Randall. "To find out what happened to me when I was a kid. I can't remember, but I know someone hurt me. And now that my dad's gone, I can't ask him."

"You don't think it was him, do you?" Randall asks.

"No. For a while I thought maybe, but now I know he would never have hurt me. Though he might have known something, even if he didn't understand what it meant."

She sucks air in, lets it out. "My mom is an outside possibility, or her childhood friend, Ann, who's her caregiver out in Petrolia, and, like I said, apparently her longtime lover. I had a weird experience the last time I was out there." She tells Randall about asking Petra what she remembered; about the photos of Ann and young Petra; about the wild thing poster of Willa in Ann's bedroom. She shows him on her phone.

"Oooh, that *is* weird," he says. "But I mean, you *were* a pretty cute kid."

"Yeah, I was. It's a good photo." As they walk, she shares the sun-dappled Petra pics that look like an ad for lesbian sex circa 1965. "Whether either of them hurt me, I kinda don't think so. Not ruling it out entirely, but—"

Randall stops walking. She stops, too, and looks at him. Grabbing her arm, he says, "I remember you telling me your doctor had hurt you. Could this be about that?"

"What?"

"You told me a doctor hurt you when you were little. I remember it clearly. We were out in the field at school, eating lunch, so it was pretty soon after I met you. You don't remember?"

"No." Billie's face is pale under the shifting shadows. "I didn't have a doctor."

You were special, she hears Petra say. *That's what he said.*

"You said that was why you didn't have a doctor," Randall replies. "You had, like, a bad cut on your leg, and I was asking you why you didn't go to the doctor. You said because a doctor had hurt you."

Billie starts walking again. "Did we ever talk about it again?" Her eyes are wild as she scans for the ridge.

"No, never. I'm sorry, I should have asked you—"

"It's okay. I didn't want to talk about it, obviously, or I would have. I mean, I trusted you—I told you. I just don't understand what I meant. I literally have no memory of ever being seen by a doctor."

But then the smell of bleach fills her nasal cavity. *That's it.* Something bad had happened to her in a medical facility. So bad she wasn't able to deal with it. After she told Randall, her psyche must've buried it.

He remembers, "When you told me about it you started to cry—but then you kind of froze up, like you wouldn't let yourself go there."

And then you left me, and I've been frozen ever since. "I think you're the only person I told," Billie says quietly.

"Wait," Randall says. "I remember, I actually asked you that. That day at lunch. I asked if anyone else knew and you said your mom knew. Right—that's why I never felt like I needed to tell anyone. 'Cause your mom knew."

Nausea fills her belly, at the thought of her mom knowing a secret about her body that Billie doesn't even know. She feels a burst of anger toward her dad, for not helping her.

Seeking these answers now—this is dangerous. Whatever happened, it was bad enough that Billie buried it deep. *Am I better off not knowing?*

They emerge out of the trees and there's the wide

valley below, and the sea beyond.

She stops. "See that land, across the water? That's Victoria Island, Canada." She points to the right. "That's Port Townsend, where we get the ferry, and then Seattle is fifty miles east."

As he takes it all in, she walks over to her log, sits down against it. Tulip darts out of the trees, then goes off exploring again. Randall sits next to Billie, and takes her hand.

She closes her eyes. It's just like all those years ago. Holding hands with Randall was the first intimacy she ever had, with anyone outside of her parents. There had never been anything sexual between them, so the hand-holding was pure affection, care, closeness. She feels all of that jolt back to her in the present, as she holds his hand, squeezes it.

The sky is turning colors. Despite all the time that's passed, watching the sunset with Randall is the most familiar thing in the world. Looking into infinity together. They've been reunited to help each other, in this strange balance: her moving toward something danger-ous, and him away.

"How are you feeling?" she asks.

"Nauseous, still. Headache. But not too bad." He looks in her eyes. "It's wonderful here. Thank you." He smiles and sweeps his strawberry forelock behind his ear. He's wearing Billie's big sweater again and some of Jane's leggings. "I'm sorry that I've been so…much. Your poor Landmates. How can I make it up to them?"

"Don't worry about it. We can make them dinner one of these nights."

Her stormy dark-blue eyes settled on the sky, she takes her hand from his, pulls up her knees, and rests her chin there, trying to remember. The smell of bleach. Now that she knows what it was, she's sickened by it. Petra never kept bleach in the house, so it had to come from somewhere—someone—else.

I'm not gonna sleep tonight.

The truth is like a feral animal, not wanting to be caught. The more she finds out, the deeper it hides; the more it hisses, and scratches.

Billie sleeps in the new cabin that night, for the first time since Randall arrived, and Willa appears in her dream again. Her bangs hang in her eyes and her smile is wicked like always.

On the trail to the vista, Willa runs from side to side in front of her, laughing. Blocking Billie from going forward.

Finally she skips away, off the path and into the woods. Billie peers into the tall, skinny trees. Far in front of her, she sees a jolt of something electric. She moves toward the flash, then sees it again, much further ahead. She begins to run now, afraid of losing Willa.

Running fast and hard, she scans around for the girl, and then—

She goes over, just barely catching the edge of the cliff; the woods have given way to the valley beyond the vista. She clings to the edge of the earth for dear life.

Above her stands a man with glasses. He's pulling on latex gloves.

She calls to him to help her, and he shakes his head. He towers high above her, seeming taller than the trees, and pries up her two index fingers with his rubbery hands. Then the two middle fingers. She can't hold on anymore, and she falls, falls, falls....

This time, she sits up in bed but doesn't wake up.

Standing, she sleepwalks outside and into the earth in her socks. Something is pulling her away, into the night. Fog obscures the path. She walks through it slowly, like a zombie looking for the man in her dream.

Who was he? She looks for him but her view is obstructed by the fog, she can't see anything. Her head pulls her forward, to find him, but her body holds her back, wanting to be back in bed. She stands still, turning in circles in the fog, looking up, out, around. On her dream-screen she sees now not the clouds surrounding her but the kaleidoscope of spinning children, around and around as she turns, losing all sense of direction, all sense of herself.

Eventually, her exhausted body falls to the ground.

A couple hours later, she wakes up to find herself curled up on the forest floor. She sits up quickly, shoulders hunched around her head as she scans her surroundings.

She's alone—in a large ground nest, so big it's like it was made for her. *I must have sleepwalked.*

Though she can't remember it yet, as a young child, asleep, she had sometimes walked from her bedroom to her mom's studio, her body seeking maternal warmth in the night, drawn to Petra by biology. She had, more than once, come upon her mom and Ann moving together in the dark, on the window seat across the room. The moonlight shone on them, moving like animals, and unconsciously Willa witnessed queer love.

She would try opening the studio door, but it was always locked. Her body would give up then and find its way back to bed.

116

As she walks back to the new cabin, just outside she sees a little black pouch, wrapped in a yellow ribbon. Billie picks it up, goes inside, and closes the door. She takes the tiny bundle to her messy bed, pulls off her wet socks, gets under the covers, and drops back into a heavy sleep.

A few hours later, she wakes. Seeing the little bundle in bed with her, she remembers it all: Willa trying to block her path. The man with the latex gloves, who tried to kill her. Waking up in the nest.

Could it have been a Sasquatch nest? she wonders, remembering she's heard them described very similarly. Lots of people think Sasquatch live in these woods.

She unties the ribbon and pulls open the heavy black paper to find a satchel of dried rose petals (from Helene, who's an herbalist); a THC truffle (Rabbit works in a dispensary and gets lots of free samples); a tiny bone of some small creature, which has been painted a shiny gold (by Randall, with eye shadow, she bets); and a postage stamp of Frida Kahlo (Jane's greatest hero), cut from a heavy gold envelope. One of them has written "Happy 50th Billie" in gold on the inside of the paper; someone must have dropped off the little bundle while she wandered the woods in her sleep.

She wraps up her treasures and sets them on the rough wood floor, sliding back under the blankets. Her pillowcase is sticky with sap.

Leaving for the lodge a half-hour later, she ties the silky yellow ribbon around a branch of the silvery spruce next to the cabin. She pees in the leaves along the way and drops the toilet paper in the fire pit, heads in the southern lodge door.

She calls quietly, "Morning." No one's in the living area. She looks up at the wall clock: 8:22.

In the kitchen, she gets the water boiling. She goes down the hall to Randall's room, knocks and listens. He opens the door with messy hair, yawning.

"Thanks for the golden bone. That was you, right?"

He nods and smiles. He looks good, rounded out a little, healthy. "We felt bad you didn't really get a birthday, with everything."

"Aww, that's not true," she says, cocking her head, embarrassed.

"Sleep okay?" he asks, to deflect her discomfort.

They walk into the kitchen and Billie makes coffee. They take their mugs to the couch, pull their knees up, and face each other.

She says, "Last night I dreamed Willa was blocking me from something. I was running and I fell off a cliff but grabbed onto the edge. Then a creepy guy tried to kill me. He was wearing latex gloves."

"The doctor?" Randall asks.

"Maybe. Why can't I remember him?"

"Trauma is a mystery. There are things from my attack that I don't remember. Maybe it would be too much to process, so the mind just blanks it out. Until you're ready to deal."

Maybe I'm not ready. Billie remembers the man touching her with his gloved hands, and her skin crawls. She rubs her arms, sits up, and puts her feet down on the rug. *Breathe,* she tells herself.

Sunlight is coming in through the kitchen windows. He pulls her up off the couch. "Come and sit in the sun with me."

She follows him and they sit in a patch of sun, their backs against cupboards, facing each other like they used to when they parked after a drive, under the camper shell of Billie's dad's truck. For the first time she sees, in the spotlight of sun, that his strawberry hair is dyed. His roots are starting to show—and they're gray, like hers.

Her heart cracks and she smiles at him. He smiles back. He looks tired. She wishes she could give him a bath.

"I'm grateful you remember so much about back then—so much more than I remember! It's really helpful. And, I mean, it's good we're talking about this now because soon we may both have the Alzheimer's."

"No!" Randall says, covering his ears.

Billie laughs. "Actually—speaking of. I have a favor to ask. A big one. Will you drive down to Humboldt with me, to try talking to my mom again about this stuff?"

Their eyes meet—she sees curiosity in his, and fear.

"Wait. Would this be the first time you'd be going back after…since you left?"

He nods, tracing the grout between the tiles with his finger.

"Shit. I'm sorry, I wasn't thinking about that. But, you know, we would only need to pass through Eureka, not stop there. We wouldn't be anywhere near…what happened."

"Sure, yes. When do you want to leave? I'm free anytime." He smiles at her cheerfully.

"Tomorrow morning!"

"Road trip!" he says. "Can we get my car from Seattle on the way out, get it back to Shasta? I can show you my place—it's simple, but it has a view of the mountain."

"Good idea," she says. "I have a tow hitch, we can put it behind us." Her throat aches with emotion as she notes the double entendre, hoping it's true. "Thanks, man. It'll be *so* much easier with you there. Petra always liked you. Even if she doesn't remember you, I'm sure she'll be much less hostile to you than she is to me."

"Okay," he says. "Can we make dinner tonight then, for everyone? I can raid the garden, use up some of those veggies, maybe make us something for the road too."

"Sure, that sounds great. I have some work to do out at the new place, but I'll meet you back here. What time?"

"Six?" he asks.

"K." She gives him a sideways smile and scoots across the black-and-white tiles to hug him, then pushes herself up.

The light fills most of the space now. The love in this place makes her proud when she remembers to notice it. Next to the door is a large framed sheet of paper detailing every project they've completed together over the years—notes, names of people who helped—and it's so long, it runs off the frame and onto the wall.

The River

*A*fter working for a few hours, hot and sweaty, Billie decides to go for a swim. At nearby Gray Wolf River, she strips off her clothes and wades in. She forces herself to dunk her head then jumps up, shocked by the icy cold.

Wading through a shallow part, Billie gets to her favorite spot and stretches out naked on the large, flat rock, which reminds her of a tortoise shell. Her feet are in the water, carried out in front of her by the strong current. The water is deeper than usual for this time of year.

This spot has always reminded her of the Mad River. *Dad River,* she thinks. She clenches her jaw. Billie will be the last of the line.

After warming up, she dunks a little more of her body into the water: legs, knees. The cold takes her breath away. The river washes over her long, strong body and rages on. A sharp wind picks up suddenly, lifting her hair.

The physical, physiological, psychological—she wants to feel it all. *If I don't let in, if I don't feel it, it will never go away.* Billie doesn't want a life like that. She wants to look in all of the dusty old cupboards and exterminate whatever's been hiding there.

She's ready.

She lowers her naked body all the way in and dunks her head. Coming up and shaking her wet hair, she feels like a creature of the water—like a selkie, a seal that can remove its skin to walk on land like a human. If its coat is stolen, though, it gets stuck on land forever.

Her body is being pulled away, into the deep. She holds on to her rock, imagines letting go.

The wind rips through the trees above her. It fades in, then out, undulating like a magic spell. Billie wraps her arms around the tortoise rock behind her as the river attempts to pull her away, into the deep.

And then the wind screams—through the river, sucked into the trees above, whistling into her ear. The same sound that has been echoing through her since she was five.

Willa's scream. The sound of fear, rage, frustration. She feels it in her body, reverberating through her—coming out of her body then going back in, like a tornado spiraling through her. She wants it out of her.

She screamed because she couldn't stop it, whatever had happened—she couldn't make it stop. Her hands and feet were restrained, she knows now, so the only ammunition she had was her voice. Billie can remember now, in her body, the terror of no power.

The people who should have been protecting her weren't. Did they not know they needed to? Did they not know how?

She thrashes like an angry bear in the cold water. She can't stand having this terrible thing inside her anymore. She needs it *out*.

All of the elements are screaming: howling wind, raging river, suffering earth, burning fires. The animals, too, make that sound when they're scared. Billie screams with them, loud and hard, until she's hoarse.

Her lower half is numb in the water. The feeling

is familiar—it reminds her of something. Her eyes pinch shut.

Then.

Stills of Willa flash through her head, the glimpses Billie's gotten as her inner child fled and hid, in the dark forest, on the far bank of the Mad River, the path to the vista. She wasn't running from Billie—she was enticing her to follow. Leading her to where she needed to go, to find what she needed to know.

Billie closes her eyes, fighting the images that come.

The bright light of some room. It feels foreign. She tries to see details but it's too bright.

Why did no one hear me scream?

Her hands find moss at the sides of the rock and hold onto it. *This is too much.* In the water, she wrestles against the memory growing in her body, against knowing too much.

The feeling of being held down makes her flail, makes her want to never stop moving. Because when she stops she feels the stuckness of it, the fear of no agency. It's the worst thing she's ever felt in her life. The sensation of helplessness, of no power, of no options, of all that's left to do is disassociate. When she doesn't fight against it, in real time in the river, Billie feels it come for her in her memory.

The sensation is one of being taken: the soul being taken out of her. She can't stop moving or it will get her.

She doesn't think any of this. She only knows; an animal in survival mode.

Of course she hasn't felt all of this, all this time. It's too much. Billie is afraid now—she has found much more than she wanted.

Because the feeling of absolute powerlessness—who

could survive remembering that? In a world where rape and abuse are rampant, there's no way she could have functioned so well all this time, knowing what she knows now: how it felt. The feeling of being taken against your will. And it could happen again. *That* is what she's been fighting against for the last forty-five years.

Now.

Billie dries out on her rock in the middle of the river. The sun warms her numb, red legs. The last place to defrost is her pelvis.

And then there it is: something cold inside of her, something metal. The feel of it. That's why she's often felt a coldness inside her—it wasn't some metaphor, some lesbian thing; it was a very literal memory. She can feel it now. Cold, metal. A pinch on her insides. Some device inside her.

A speculum. Growing up with a mom who didn't take very good care of her, she never went to the OB-GYN when she was a teenager. When she was a little older and on her own, she didn't want to go then either. She had an aversion—for good reason, she realizes now.

So she's never seen a speculum, or—she'd thought—felt one in her. She saw them used in an art installation once, and as soon as she remembers the cold, silver contraption, the machine opening, getting wider....

That happened inside her. That was what she had remembered as something growing in her, exploding.

It couldn't have been Ann then. Why would she have a speculum? Petra despised everything medical. Billie knows Petra has specified that she wants to not be resuscitated, if she ever loses consciousness and ends up in a hospital;

she would never let herself be taken to a hospital if she was conscious. Billie grew up hearing her complain about doctors. No way would she ever have had anything to do with a speculum.

She turns over onto her stomach. Feet dangling in the water, she turns her head to the side and watches a red dragonfly fly around her, then land on her arm, in the sun. Billie watches it: moving, then still, moving, then still.

She hears Crow caw nearby. The crow is known for its intelligence, she knows, even helping to solve puzzles.

This is the only way to do this, she thinks. *Discover, incorporate. Go in, and then come out.*

As she wades through the water to her clothes, and the cold water hits her genitals, it gives her a shock, which she now understands. "*Fuck!*" She shakes her head, droplets flying like sparks.

Reaching the bank, she finds a sunny spot to warm up in. Holding out her arms, she opens her body to the warmth.

She puts her clothes back on—*my human suit,* she thinks: black jeans, black hoodie, worn gold high-top Vans—and, seeing it's almost six, decides to go straight to the lodge to meet Randall.

On the way, she feels some relief at having cleared Ann. It feels right. *It wasn't that, what I felt from her. It was her discomfort about me not knowing about her and my mom.* Billie's distrust of the woman had come partly, too, from her inherent suspicion around her mom's intentions—guilt by association. *But she would never hurt me.* Billie imagines a future world in which she and Ann talk openly about her and Petra's relationship, and her mom's health.

And that picture of me in her room—it's just a good photo.

Thinking of the big black-and-white of Willa looking fierce, she has an idea. *I'll paint Willa. I can start when we get back from Humboldt.* She brightens at the thought of a new project.

She imagines Willa in a wide oak tree, spread like a panther across a branch.

Willa holding something behind her back, looking mischievous.

Willa riding Crow, high up in the sky.

Hang tight, girl. I'm coming for you.

Turns out Randall isn't the only one who wants to celebrate. As she ambles up the hill and nears the lodge, Billie's friends jump out from behind trees, yelling "Surprise!"

Randall looks pleased and beautiful, his hair teased up and back. Rabbit made a big banner that says HAPPY 50TH BILLIE! and hung it high, from a couple trees. Jane is sitting on the deck, tearing lettuce from the garden into a salad bowl. Helene walks out from the kitchen with a couple more big bowls, giving Billie a cheery "Bonjour."

Catalina—Billie's ex-mentee, now good friend—is swinging Gloria in the hammock. Gloria is laughing and telling Catalina to stop. Tulip is with them, crying with excitement.

Randall tells Billie, "I didn't actually make dinner. You know my ass can't cook. But everybody brought stuff." He gestures to the deck at a table covered with food.

Billie introduces Randall to Gloria, even though they already met while they waited for her. Catalina, he had met when she dropped off a pot of vegan soup and homemade bread, after Billie had texted that they were having trouble getting Randall to eat. Cat and Randall had bonded over being vegan.

Billie grabs a beer from a cooler on the deck. "You don't mind?" she asks Randall, who shakes his head. He's already said he doesn't care if people drink around him, but it feels insensitive to assume; he's off all drugs again, even alcohol.

Randall and Billie sit on the edge of the deck. Looking around at her favorite people, Billie smiles. "Thanks, man. This is nice. You even got Gloria to come out." Billie knows Gloria hasn't left her apartment since quarantine started; she's touched. That the whole Olympic Peninsula only has fifty cases—compared to almost ten thousand in Seattle—surely made it an easier ask. But even out here in the forest, Gloria wears a mask.

Billie flashes to what she found in the river. The metal machine looms in her mind, opening and closing like a duck's beak. Thinking about it, she feels a chill enter her groin.

Billie yanks her damp hair toward her face. "Hey— want to have a fire?"

"Oooh, yeah," Randall agrees.

"Let me get something to eat and I'll meet you over there." She needs a moment.

As she serves herself some delicious-looking food, Helene walks up with utensils. Helene rarely speaks French, preferring instead to improve her English, but Billie spent a recent summer in Paris working on a mural, and likes to practice.

Helene asks, "Quoi de beau?" which generally means *What's up?*

But Billie takes it literally, as meaning "What's beautiful?" and answers "Tu, bien sur." *You, of course.*

"Which is yours?" Billie asks with a nod to the table. "The raiti and the cauliflower gratin. *Bon anniversaire.*"

As Billie sits to eat, Helene and Randall carry some logs from the stack on the deck to the large fire pit. Catalina gathers kindling, Rabbit and Jane get more chairs. Helene crumples newspaper, and Randall finds a bunch of dried pine needles. The others meander over, chatting; Gloria almost tumbles out of the hammock and shrieks.

Watching her friends, Billie drinks the last of her beer. A cognitive dissonance sets in: the new knowledge she discovered at the river doesn't fit in this scene. She considers telling them, then quickly dismisses the idea as TMI. *No one wants to know what happened inside you.*

Randall, across the pit from her, meets her eyes and strikes a long match, then lights a few pieces of toilet paper. When they were teenagers, he was always the one to walk around the fire, tending to the big picture, while Billie managed the detail work.

"Should we sing?" Rabbit asks, and they all break out into the happy birthday song.

"Happy Birthday, dear Billie…happy birthday to you!" Randall points his tending stick at her and trills "And many more!" with an awkward pirouette.

"Cheers!" Billie says. She finds a stick of her own and casts it around the circle like a magic wand, blessing each of her friends in turn. "I love you guys. Thanks for being here."

She looks down at the fire, spiraling upward, going strong thanks to the group effort, and with no work needed on her part. She thinks about what she remembered today. *Should I tell them?*

Rabbit passes around an assortment of weed edibles, beer caps are popped.

Later.

Wilhemina

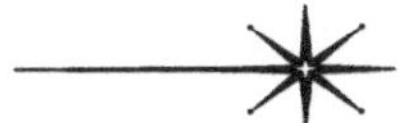

*A*fter a couple hours of catching up with friends, drunk and a little high, Billie sits down next to Gloria, in an antique chair brought out from the lodge. It's her grandmother Wilhemina's, from Joe's childhood home in Mobile, Alabama.

Suddenly she makes the connection. The old house with the staircase at its heart! *This chair came from that house. Which I've never been in, but dreamed of so vividly.* It's like she knows the house now, because of the dream, because of the chair—she feels connected to her grand-mother through it, even though she never got to meet Wilhemina, who died before she was born.

She stares into the fire. The pain of a million survivors burns there, an eternal flame. The pain of being penetrated against one's will. The pain of the people doing the pen-etrating. The fire wants to eat it all, burn it to the ground.

Billie looks around, assessing the vibe. She senses Willa nearby, but the girl is hard to track, skipping between the shadows and light.

Her dad is here, too, sitting on the edge of the deck. Joe had helped build the deck, too, which extends the western half of the lodge by ten feet. It's weathered well, good as new after six years. Willa sits next to Joe at the side of the deck, swinging her legs. Billie can't see them exactly, but she intuits that Willa is being cared for, and that her dad has her back. Wilhemina, Billie's namesake, sits behind them on the deck, in a rocking chair.

Billie clears her voice, calls everyone over. "You're gonna wanna sit for this."

Jane moves to stand behind Billie, one hand on her shoulder. Catalina sits on Billie's other side and takes the fire stick from her.

Her friends settle in. Crow lands nearby, on top of Billie's truck.

Billie holds tight to the arms of her chair. "So, I've mentioned to most of you that I've started having memories about something that happened to me when I was little. It's starting to feel more urgent that I figure out what happened. And since I have the summer off...I have a couple leads I want to follow.

"Also, I have a partner now." She makes a ta-da/jazz hands gesture in Randall's direction, and he does a little shuffle step. He's been circling the perimeter, keeping himself moving, to manage his urges. Catalina isn't having any marijuana or alcohol either, in solidarity.

Gloria has her legs crossed elegantly in her camp chair. Arms crossed, she stares at Billie, brow furrowed and one eye half-closed under her glasses, gray silk mask over her mouth and nose. Rabbit sits on the other side of Gloria, Tulip at their feet.

Billie closes her eyes. "I think I made a promise, to whoever hurt me, not to tell. Right now, I want to say out loud, I reject that promise. They have no authority over me anymore."

She stands, looking into the fire. She takes a deep breath. *Is it too much?*

Fuck it.

"I remembered something else today: he used a speculum on me."

Everyone freezes, staring at Billie. She starts pacing in place—rocking forward, then back, like she's warming up for something. Randall walks over and stands behind her, next to Jane.

Billie stops moving. She stands still, seeing how that feels. She makes a fist and holds it in her other hand. "Yeah. So, Randall is going with me down to Humboldt, to talk to my mom before she loses her mind completely…maybe find some stuff out. We leave tomorrow morning."

Billie looks behind her at Randall. He was hurt, too. But Billie also knows that he hurts because of what happened to her. It's why he's still here, why he hasn't gone home. He will do whatever he can to help her get better.

Gloria yanks her mask off and, angrily pointing a finger toward the fire, she says, "*Fuck* that guy. Fuck *him*. No one gets to hurt you and get away with it." She shakes her head. "Oh, hell no. If you need backup, any one of us will be happy to go down there and provide it. You go get him, Billie. You go."

Billie chews her cheek, trying not to cry. As she looks around the fire at her friends, she knows that Gloria is right—every one of them will do anything they can to help her.

She sees a light flicker like a firefly by the deck; she hears a giggle.

She nods at Gloria. "Okay." *Okay, I will. I'll go get him.*

Billie walks over to the clearing—the first work she did on the Land was to clear the vegetation here, to begin building on. It's the best place on the Land to see the stars; there's a pile of sleeping bags there. Billie lies on her back, pulls her hood over her head, and looks up at the stars. The sky is covered with them.

Catalina lies back next to Billie, and then Jane does the same on the other side, and then Helene, until they surround her—heads at the center, feet pointing out, like a star, an asterisk.

When she was a kid, someone was always giving Billie a sparkler on her birthday—so close to the fourth of July. Her favorite thing to do with it was always to draw a star. If you drew a star with the light, over and over, it started to look like the star remained, like it lived on in the air.… She was forever making a star, another star, an infinite star that never ended, even after the sparkler died.

All those stars had burned into her brain, and as she looks up at the solar system she can still see it. Up, down, left, right, down. Connecting the dots.

The Redwoods

*O*n the morning, Billie and Randall drive into Seattle, to get Randall's car. It's parked just a few blocks from the Seattle Art Institute and there are three tickets behind the windshield wipers, but at least it's still there.

As Billie is finishing attaching the old Honda to the hitch, and Randall is retrieving some things from the car, a former student of hers walks by, recognizes her truck from when they went on an errand together. "Hey! Remember me?" she says to Billie, grinning.

Billie remembers the girl from her Mural 101 class the year before; she had thought she might have had a crush on her. She can't remember the girl's name now but she's so cute, and clearly interested—but Billie just feels like she has zero game left. She's already exhausted and they haven't even left Seattle yet. She doesn't even remember how to flirt.

As they make awkward small talk, Billie realizes she's become a hermit, and is severely out of practice. Between the virus, the new cabin project, and then Randall, she's been off the map for months.

She's relieved when Randall announces that he found his phone. When she goes to introduce them, it becomes clear that Billie doesn't remember the girl's name, and she feels her cheeks flush red. The girl saves her, inserting her name, Gabby, and backing off to maintain some social distance from Randall, who does a charming mimed handshake, then climbs up into the truck.

After Billie makes her exit and gets behind the wheel, Randall looks over at Billie and says, "Cutie!"

Billie just rolls her eyes, then quickly heads for the closest freeway entrance. They aren't supposed to be on the road; Washington, Oregon, and California all stopped sheltering in place recently, but only essential travel is officially permitted. Billie can always say she's needed to take care of her mom in Petrolia, though, and the job of getting Randall's car back home explains his presence. She stays closer to the speed limit than she normally would, matching the speed of the other cars on the road, which are few and far between.

For a long time after they get on the I-5, it's just subdivisions and strip malls. Randall offers to drive, but Billie is more comfortable driving her truck. She drives, and he plays with his phone, happy to be reunited with it. He appears to be texting with someone, and Billie wonders who, but she doesn't want to ask.

Finally, she can't stand it anymore. "Who are you texting with?" *Ugh, you sound like a jealous lover.*

"Oh, just a friend," he responds distractedly. His phone keeps pinging, and then he types, it pings, he types—the back and forth of a conversation.

She's annoyed, then reprimands herself, *Give him some space.*

But the pinging and typing continue till finally she can't stand it anymore. "What friend?" she asks again, irritation in her voice.

"Oh." He looks over at her with surprise. "Um, well a friend of mine from Seattle is in Humboldt, it turns out."

This makes it worse. She doesn't know if she'll ever get over this feeling of rejection, of Randall not wanting her as badly as she wanted him—choosing strangers, over her.

"Oh, yeah? Who's that?" *Chill. Jesus. You're not his mother.*

"Her name is Ariel."

"Is she someone you used with?" The question pops out before she can stop it.

He glances at her, his brow furrowed, then looks out the windshield. She knows he's considering what to tell her, which can only mean one thing.

"Kind of," he says eventually.

"What does that mean?" she fires back, wound up from having to wait for an answer.

"Billie!" he responds, shooting her an angry look. "I am not your problem to solve."

"Wrong," she says. "It's like you said—I'm your Black Cat."

He just shakes his head. "You need to trust me."

"I don't, though. I mean, I don't really know who you are anymore." As soon as it's out she regrets it.

He blinks. She looks over at him searchingly but he won't meet her eyes. "I—"

He cuts her off. "No, you're right." He looks at her with eyes she doesn't recognize, then looks away. "You don't know me."

"I want to," she tries.

"Do you, though?" he explodes. "Or do you just want your old Radnell? You want me to be who *you* need me to be. Not who I really am."

"That's not true," she says quietly.

He looks away, out the window.

⌇

They ride in silence for hours, until Billie starts nodding off. She pulls off to get gas and sees a little motel next to a truck stop. She had planned to drive the full nine hours to Mount Shasta and sleep at Randall's, but all the tension in the car has drained her.

"Want to stay there tonight?" she asks Randall, pointing.

He nods okay, and they drive over. When they walk into the lobby together, pulling on masks, the Indian guy at the counter looks them over with concern; he stands a foot or so back from the counter, and so do they. "Good evening. One room or two?"

"Um…" Billie isn't sure if Randall is okay to stay in his own room; she remembers hearing that drug dealers often hang out at truck stops, to sell to truckers. On the other hand, she doesn't want to force him to stay in a room with her when he's upset with her. Maybe they need some space for the night, to cool off, since they have another long drive tomorrow. She can't handle another day of that oppressive air in the truck.

Randall raises his eyebrows and looks at her in anticipation of how she will handle this—resentful, she can tell, that she'll be the one making the decision. Like she *is* his mom.

After a few uncomfortable moments of silence, the man says, "Our double rooms have two beds on separate floors." He points out the window at them: funny little two-story houses with sharp V roofs, like something out of a fairy tale.

She looks at Randall, who nods, then she pays for the room. They drive over, grab their bags, and go inside. Billie starts to apologize. "I—"

He cuts her off again. "I'll sleep up there." He nods

toward the stairs, which lead to a separate space, like a little attic. He waits a second, and when she doesn't say anything he goes up.

Not knowing what to say, she sets down her bag and uses the bathroom, then flops down on the bed, which squeaks under her weight.

If he were down here with me, we'd giggle at that. She refuses to giggle. She turns on the TV and turns the volume down, flips through the channels until she lands on a bad comedy, which she watches till she falls asleep.

In the morning, she wakes early and goes next door to the truck stop for breakfast, to let Randall sleep; he doesn't eat breakfast anyway. She brings him a coffee. When she gets back he's in the shower.

By nine, they're back on the road. They've arrived at an unspoken truce, not talking about what happened yesterday but moving on to a civil chill. She plays music on her phone; he watches videos with his headphones in.

By noon they're in Mount Shasta. Billie pulls off the I-5 and follows Randall's directions. She's never spent much time here and, as they near his place, the mountain grows larger in the background. Even after all her years of living near Mount Rainier, and the Olympics, she's never seen anything like it.

"I'll just run up and get some stuff," he says. He doesn't invite her up, and Billie doesn't ask, even though she needs to pee from the coffee; she can pee at the gas station on the way out.

It's a basic apartment building, but she can see what he meant about the view. Mount Shasta is so tall, it makes its own weather: lenticular clouds circle its peak, looking like spaceships, or haloes. She unhitches his car, sweating in the dry heat, and then spreads out in the truck bed to cool down.

A few minutes later, she hears, "Oh, thanks, I almost forgot about my car. I'll just park it and be right back."

She pushes herself up, hops out, shuts the tailgate, and meets him in the front. She starts the truck and they get back on the road, the majestic mountain shrinking in the rearview mirror.

When they hit the coast, and head south, then cross over into Humboldt County, they're welcomed by the redwoods and fog—a balm for Billie's skin and soul.

Randall says, "I forgot how pretty it is."

"Oh, yes," Billie says. "Most beautiful place on earth."

Randall makes a noncommittal noise and gazes out at the ocean. She can't see his face.

She wants his reentry into Humboldt to happen in the best possible light. She wants the sun to come out; she wants him to love it like she does. She's worried it will hurt him to be here again.

He's crying. Shit. She waits.

Let him have his tears. We don't have to process everything.

The largest trees in the world. As always, they're like coming home. She loves how small they make her feel. And as much as she loved them when she was a kid—and then tried to paint that love around the world—her love for them now feels even more overwhelming. They're like family, practically, or something even bigger.

A religion. Mystic, mythic. An ecosystem unto themselves—like Shasta. Growing their own defenses—like her.

She glances over at Randall, then back at the curvy

road, which hugs the ocean. She wants to turn on some music, but can't look away from the road for too long. *What to play?* Something nostalgic, she decides. She goes to Spotify and jabs at the Smiths' *The Queen Is Dead.*

As the title track starts to play, he turns to face her. He blinks heavily, mouth slightly open. "You don't remember?"

"What?" she asks.

"This is what was playing, that night. It's why you didn't want to go with me."

Her heart sinks to the floorboard. *Fail. Epic fail. Fuck!*

"How could you remember," he muses, pushing past the awkwardness, "when the memory doesn't hold the same resonance for you? It was so long ago!"

"I'm so—" she starts.

"Don't worry about it. Just—give me that." He takes her phone and turns on Depeche Mode's *Black Celebration,* which also came out in 1986, instead, then sets the phone back in its holder. "Listen. Ariel, the person I was texting with yesterday, was my dealer in Seattle. I did use with her sometimes, after I bought from her. But we were friends, too...."

He trails off, looking out at the ocean.

He's lost so much, she realizes. He's told her a little, about the worst of his drug use in Berlin; how he was extradited to the US and had to leave everything behind.

He continues, "This trip is about you. Yesterday, I was so excited when I found out Ariel lives down here, we were making plans to hang out.... But I don't know if I'm ready for that. I miss her, but I also still really want to use." He sets his jaw and looks ahead.

"But listen, Billie, these are my decisions to make. I have to learn how to make it stick this time. You can't do it for me." His eyes search her face.

"Okay," she says quietly, her eyes on the road. "You're right, I know."

"I want you to trust me. I do. But the truth is, you can't trust a junkie. I mean, I *desperately* wanted to go to the truck stop last night to score."

She's holding her breath.

"It took every ounce of my willpower not to. I just couldn't stand the thought of how disappointed you would be."

Looking over at him, she says, "Well, thanks, I guess. I would have been disappointed, that's true—but not in you, *for* you. I just want you to be happy."

She leans into a curve. "And listen, I truly am sorry, for forgetting about that record. I'm so sorry. And for choosing Morrissey over you that night—worst decision of my life. I'm just lucky you forgave me."

That's a pretty big assumption. What if he hasn't? She braves a glance his way, eyebrows rising questioningly above her sunglasses.

He nods and reaches for her hand, squeezes, then releases.

The Ocean

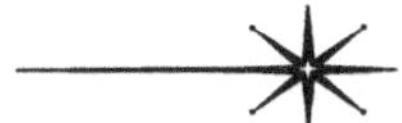

An hour later, Billie pulls over to a vista point overlooking the ocean, and parks. Below them is a beach they went to together once.

He says, "I just remembered something. When you got your period in high school and were having such bad cramps, I said maybe you should see someone. 'They're always men,' you said. I just remembered that. I guess there probably weren't very many female gynecologists, back then."

Billie remembers, "Petra said, when I asked her about who hurt me, that he said I was 'special.'"

"Maybe he told her you were special and he wanted to study you, or run some tests or something."

"That would explain why she would have left me with him."

She feels it again: the speculum. The terrible cold inside. She can feel it in her still, breaking her open.

She shakes her head and pushes open the door, goes to sit on a bench overlooking the ocean. The fog is coming in, so Randall grabs Billie's hoodie from the car. She puts it on, pulling the hood up over her head.

"It could have been a woman," she says. "Now that we know it was actually a speculum inside me, not a dick.… Not my mom or Ann, but it could have been another woman."

He shakes his head. "Honey. No. A woman would

never use that on another woman. Unless they were a gynecologist."

"No, you're right." Billie looks out at the fog below. "Do you remember when we came to this beach?" She laughs. "We were in a cave, and a rogue wave came in, and we had to climb up the walls? Remember? We got soaked. We were like twelve or so, one of our parents must have dropped us off."

"No, we got a ride with your neighbor. It was summer and we were bored so we hitched a ride. We got her backseat all wet on the way home."

"Oh, yeah, that's right." She smiles. "I don't remember being scared, though, when the water came in, do you? I don't remember ever feeling afraid, when you were with me."

Randall looks at her sadly. "I'm sorry I left so suddenly. I just couldn't deal."

As his seafoam-green eyes alight on her, she feels a powerful love for him.

They arrive at Mattole Beach Campground and by three o'clock they've pitched a tent. Billie had distracted Randall as they drove through Eureka, where he was attacked, and he hadn't even noticed they passed it. Later today they will go up the hill to interrogate Petra.

Here, the Mattole River meets the Pacific. It's one of Billie's favorite places, but Randall has never been. They walk out on the beautiful black sand to the water, then north to where the river comes in, powerfully joining with the ocean. They lie down in the sand above the mouth and feel the energy of the convergence move through them.

The knowledge growing in Billie is like a circling tide: it comes in, then retreats, giving her a break between waves of insight. It seems to approach, gauge her readiness, and back away when she's not there yet. Expanding, and contracting.

She opens one eye and looks at Randall, who is looking at her. He flares his nostrils. They laugh, and she tosses some sand on his leg.

"Let's go get sandwiches and bring them up to Petra," Billie says.

He nods, and she stands and pulls him up. He looks out at the foggy sea. She looks into the tall bluff above the river, wondering if her mom can see her.

They get the sandwiches—along with some drinks, chips, freshly baked cookies, and a bouquet of wildflowers—and Billie texts Ann to tell her they're bringing dinner and would like to spend some time with Petra, just the three of them.

Petra is in her usual spot on the deck. She has her back to them and is looking out at the ocean, where they just were. Seeing her, Billie remembers that she's gay, for the hundredth time since she talked to Lisa about it.

Focus, Billie. Be assertive.

"Mom," Billie says, not up for a game of pretend. She tries to take a deep breath but gives up halfway through. "Mom, it's me, Billie. And this is Randall. Do you remember Randall?" She forces some joy into her voice. "Randall was my best friend in high school. He used to do your hair and makeup—remember?"

Randall kneels next to her chair and says conspiratorially, "Hello, Petra."

"We brought you some food, Ma," Billie says, taking the bag into the kitchen and laying everything out on the table, putting the flowers in the same Mason jar as last time. She looks up and sees Randall leading her mom in.

"Great," Billie says. "Come and see. We got all your favorites. Joan down at the store made you a ham sandwich. We're hungry, too, we drove in from up north today."

She briskly pulls out a chair for her mom, who sits delicately. Petra is pale today, despite spending most of her day outdoors. *I hope she's not getting sick.* None of them are wearing masks.

Billie says, "Actually, let's wash our hands first."

All three of them wash their hands, then sit down at the table to eat. Joan is a good sandwich maker, and Billie enjoys her veggie sammy, Randall his vegan one. They are quiet, looking out at the trees.

"See the magpie?" Petra asks, pointing at the window. The pretty little black-and-white bird has just landed outside, on a little table, Billie notices. Ann must have built it for Petra. "I leave him things. And he leaves me things."

"What kind of things?" Randall asks. His eyes look to Billie. *Is this a true story, do you think?*

Billie goes to the window, but she moves too fast and scares the magpie away.

"Now why did you do that?" her mom says angrily.

"I didn't do it on purpose. I'm sorry. I just wanted to see the perch." It's a few inches square, with a little bowl that has some sunflower seeds in it, and a larger bowl of water.

Her mother glares at her, eating a chocolate chip cookie very slowly. Chip by chip.

Randall asks, "Petra, may I make you some tea? Maybe the bird will come back if we stay away from the window."

"Mm-hmm," Petra says, agreeing like a little girl. "Who are you?"

"I'm a detective." He fills the kettle and puts it on the stove. "We have a very challenging cold case and we need your help to solve it."

Genius, Billie thinks. *He remembers how much Petra loved detective novels.*

Petra looks interested.

Randall gives Petra a big smile. "We call it 'The Case of the Missing Memory.'"

Billie smiles and nods. Her mother's jaw drops a little, as if to say, *You have brought me my very favorite bone.* Billie couldn't have thought of a better way to engage her.

If Randall's the good cop, that makes me the bad cop. I can handle that.

Randall brings Petra her tea, and pours them some, too. Leaning back against the kitchen counter, he crosses his ankles, then his arms. "This case is from quite a few years back. It's a cold case—the department had stopped investigating it when it landed on our desks."

Billie's eyes get big but she looks casually at the floor. *He's really going for it.*

"It has to do with a doctor." He peers into Petra's eyes for any recognition. There's none there.

"Go on," Petra says impatiently.

"Sorry. Yes, so this doctor was known to have hurt little girls."

Her mom's forehead furrows, and Billie looks to Randall with surprise. He raises his eyebrows, like *You said you wanted this. Let's go.*

"Do you remember this case now? It happened not far from here."

Petra shakes her head slowly. Billie can see Randall considering where to go next. She decides to jump in. Work every angle.

"He called one of these little girls 'special.' Does that ring any bells for you?" Her mom shakes her head. "This guy was not a good guy. We heard he used a *speculum* on five-year-old girls." Billie sees confusion on her mom's face. "A speculum is a metal lever that opens up vaginas for gynecological exams. But it's not ever meant to be used on a woman younger than thirteen."

Billie glances at Randall, then continues. "He used that on these little girls. We think he may have been doing some kind of study. With the *special* little girls."

Billie sees something light up in Petra's eyes. Quickly, she says, "You remember this case, don't you? Do you remember what kind of study this doctor said he was doing with these special girls?"

Petra's mouth opens as she considers this. She has a little mustard on her chin, which Randall goes to wipe off, until Billie shakes her head. *Don't distract her.* She is learning that with Alzheimer's one fact has to be built upon another. Petra might not remember where they started, but she would usually remember the last thing that was said.

She tries again, "Do you remember this guy, or what he was studying with these special girls?"

Her mom looks conflicted. Randall is watching, waiting.

"I was the special one," Petra says.

Randall and Billie glance at each other and then back to Petra.

Petra looks confused now. "I only know his name."

"His name?" Randall jumps back in. "Well, that would be very helpful indeed."

Billie freezes, her eyes on Petra, trying not to let her mom see how badly she wants this.

Petra says, "Mars."

"Dr. Mars?" Billie asks quickly, and Petra nods. "You sure?"

Petra nods her head firmly yes. "I could never forget that name. It was my favorite planet. Used to be."

"Until what?" Billie holds her breath.

"Dr. Mars," Petra says.

Billie lets her breath out, and stares at Petra. It takes all of her willpower not to pull out her phone and start Googling. She remembers that there's no service up here anyway.

"Well," Randall says, "that is a huge help, Petra. We will put this new intel in place right away. Should we head back to the station...." He pauses, not sure what to call Billie. "Chief?"

Petra actually raises an eyebrow at this, and looks at Billie, impressed. Billie just nods authoritatively, not trusting her voice. *A name. We have a fucking name.*

"Thank you for your help, ma'am," Randall says. "This has been a most lucrative visit." Petra looks up at Randall with hopeful eyes. "We couldn't have done it without you."

Billie starts to clean up the sandwich wrappers, and Petra—some ingrained decorum kicking in, thinking Billie is the police chief—pushes her hand away. "I'll get it. You get back to work."

Billie pulls back and pauses, surprised. Out of the corner of her eye, something black streaks by—the magpie is back. She walks slowly to the window. It's a black-billed magpie, with bright blue tail feathers. It sets something down on the little altar, some small shiny thing.

Officer Randall and Captain Billie head back to the station.

There's no Wi-Fi or cell service at the campsite. Exhausted, they crawl into the tent without making a fire. But there's a savage wind outside, and it feels like the tent is going to blow away. When Randall gets cold, and starts to shiver, Billie rubs his back to warm him up; once you get a chill in this damp climate, she knows, it can be hard to shake.

Billie decides, "Fuck this. Let's sleep in my truck." She thinks for a second. "You go sit in the front and run the heater, get warmed up. I'll put the bedding in the back." The back of her truck has a camper shell, and Billie keeps a futon mattress back there for times like these. She gives him the car keys.

In the car, Randall gets the heat going, then leans back and opens the window from the middle cab to the back, to let a little heat migrate back there. "Good idea," he tells Billie. "Thanks."

"We'll be safer, too, locked up in here."

They had seen some rednecks on their initial circle around the campground. In southern Humboldt, you never knew when someone would make your unconventional gender presentation their problem. Best not to risk it.

Billie realizes on her last trip to the tent that nobody else in the campground is sleeping in a tent. It's too windy.

"Okay, your bed awaits," she says brightly.

Randall goes to pee behind the tent, which Billie has secured for the night.

The howling wind has blown away all the fog. They brush their teeth looking up at the stars.

Mars, she thinks, looking for the planet and not finding it. She remembers Jane saying, when they were stargazing, that in the summer Mars is only visible in the dawn. *I hope the man will be easier to find.*

After falling asleep by ten p.m., Billie wakes at seven to kids playing at the neighboring campsite. She gets up and makes tea, taking Randall's to him in the truck bed while she carries hers out to the ocean. It's bright and clear out here.

Having a name feels both nauseating and empowering—it was the greatest gift her mom could have given her. She would never have gotten it without Randall, though.

Thank you, universe. She scoops up the soft black sand and lets it fall from her hands.

She considers praying. Usually, if she wants something she just sets her mind on it—but there have been times when she realized that the thing she had asked for maybe wasn't the best thing for her. Holding on so tightly to one specific dream or plan or person left her unavailable to other opportunities that might come her way.

Today, Billie asks for something more general. She needs to be stronger than she's ever been, so she asks the ocean to bless her with some of its power.

They pack up quickly and stop as soon as they have service, in the small town of Ferndale. Next to the historic Victorians lining the main street, the café they find is weirdly modern. Inside, armed with coffee, they hunker into a corner booth and pull out their phones. A guy at a nearby table moves—either social distancing, or afraid their queerness might rub off on him. Other than him, there are only two other people in the café.

"I'll look for news stories about a Dr. Mars," Billie says. "Maybe we'll get lucky and he's a known offender."

"I'll see if I can find out where he lives," Randall says.

"Okay, thanks. I'm so glad you're here, by the way. There's no fucking way I would have gotten the name from my mom without you. You're good at this."

"We're a good team." He smiles at her. "And please, after everything you've done for me? Plus, you need all the help you can get. This is big shit."

She nods and goes back to Googling:

Seventies Humboldt doctor abuse

Humboldt doctor Mars molest

Mars scandal

He starts in with:

Dr. Mars

Dr. Mars Humboldt

Dr. Mars Eureka

He doesn't find anything. "What kind of doctor was this guy?"

"Probably a gynecologist, right? If he had a speculum. Unless he just used it for prying open little girls."

Randall looks up at her, wrinkling his nose.

"Sorry," she says.

He tries:

Dr. Mars gynecologist

Gynecologist Humboldt

"Who knew there were so many gynos in Humbo?"

"Not me. I only ever saw this one."

This is too much for Randall. He retches, and runs

to the bathroom, then to the counter for the key, and back again.

The locals are really staring now. The coffee shop is all sharp angles and cold, reflective surfaces that seem practically medical.

All of a sudden she remembers something. Something else cold, against her neck.

A blade? She remembers a stickiness, too—blood?!

She shakes it off. *Breathe.*

Randall, returning, sees Billie's ghostly face and takes her hand under the table.

"This is hard," she says, her voice breaking.

"Yes, but you can do it. It will be worth it. Once we see our shadows, they lose their power over us."

"But what if we can't find him?"

"Well, maybe we can't find him, but we find what you need. Enough to understand. Whatever that looks like." He catches her eye, squeezes her hand. "Who else do you know who was here in the seventies?"

"Lisa. My dad's wife. She would've been a teenager."

She picks up her phone, checks the time. It's almost nine. "What day is it?"

"Wednesday," he says, smiling.

"She'll be headed to work." She dials Lisa.

Lisa picks up. "Hey, Billie."

"Hey Lise. I have a question for you. It's for…that project I mentioned. Me and Randall just got a break in the case." She winks at Randall, and he sticks out his tongue.

"Where are you?" Lisa asks. "The connection isn't great."

"Freakin' Ferndale," Billie says quietly. She holds the phone on her palm and speaks into the speaker. "Can you hear me now?"

"Kind of."

People are staring. Billie looks toward the door ques-tioningly, and Randall nods. "Hold on, Lisa. One sec." They grab their coffee, head for the back of the truck, and climb in. Billie makes a desk from a couple pillows, puts Lisa on speaker, then grabs the black notebook Lisa gave her out of her backpack. "Lise? Is that better?"

"Much better."

Randall pulls the back hatch closed. It's warm in the back of the truck, and the sleeping bags smell like camp-fire, from Billie's party a couple nights ago.

Billie and Randall sit facing each other, backs against the sides of the truck, just like they had in high school. They smile at each other, happy in their safe place. Her feet almost reach his side of the truck; his, only a little past her knees.

"Okay, Lisa. You're on speaker with Randall and me."

"Hi, Randall." Lisa hasn't met him but knows who he is, having heard stories about their high school esca-pades. "Joe told me a lot about you."

"Hi Lisa. That's sweet. I'm so sorry for your loss. He was a wonderful man, and there aren't enough of those." He pauses, looking at Billie. She nods, and he continues, "Right, so we have a question for you. We're looking for a guy named Dr. Mars, or something like that. He would have practiced medicine in Humboldt in the seventies—maybe gynecology, but that's a guess."

"How would he have seen little girls, though," Lisa asks, "if he was OB-GYN?"

Billie says, "Apparently he was doing some kind of study, or said he was." She pauses. "Lise, this guy may have been the one who hurt me. He may have hurt oth-ers, too. We need to find him."

"Can I ask around? My rez friends, some of them

have been here since the seventies. Some family, too. And a couple people at work."

"That would be great," Billie says. "Thanks. It would have been like '73. Dr. Mars, Petra called him. Probably he worked in Eureka, or nearby."

"Okay, got it," Lisa says. "I'll send some texts before I head into work."

Billie thanks her and presses end.

"What was in it for Petra, do you think?" Randall asks. "Could she have been having an affair with this guy?"

"Jesus, Randall. Ew. Also, she was gay, remember?"

"Sorry, but…I mean, why would she have left you alone with him? There had to be some incentive, knowing Petra."

"Maybe he was one of her art students," Billie says.

"Or maybe she was dropping you off with this guy so he could run tests, or give you some kind of treatment. Or, wait—what if the study he was doing was on her? A psychology thing, or who knows? Maybe he was testing her, or treating her, and she brought you with her."

"Narcissistic Personality Disorder would have been a new thing back then—maybe he was studying her." Catalina had suggested, a few years ago, that from what she'd heard of Petra, she might have NPD. "But how would he get access to me if she was there?"

"Maybe he put her under," Randall says. "Or maybe it was someone else who hurt you. In the hospital he worked in? Like, maybe he left you with someone and *they* hurt you?"

DING DING DING DING DING! An alarm goes off in Billie's head.

She nods. They're getting close.

"You're good at this," she tells him weakly. She picks at the knee of her black jeans; it's about to rip. "That would explain a lot. If they were a team it would be much easier to pull off. Which could mean I'm not the only one it happened to."

"So maybe Dr. Mars is a bigwig in charge of the study," Randall posits. "He's studying your mom…or sleeping with her. Maybe both. She leaves you with his assistant, say. She doesn't know what he's doing with you…. But then maybe you told her."

"She remembered his name—he must have made an impression on her, even if it was ultimately a negative one. Maybe sex, or some kind of attention he gave her, for her to remember all these years later, even through the Alzheimer's. He made her feel good about herself in some way. He fed her ego. If it was all about me, it wouldn't have stayed with her like that."

Billie's phone vibrates on the pillows, and she jumps. *Jesus.* She reaches for it.

Billie reads the text from Lisa: *"My friend Jenna remembers a Dr. Mars. He was a shrink, kind of a local legend. She thinks he lives in Manila."*

"He's Filipino?" Randall asks.

Billie says, "No—she must mean the Manila here, out by the dunes. You know, we used to go to the beach there?"

He nods, but clearly doesn't remember. "How far is it from here?"

"Half hour," Billie says, chewing on her cheek.

They climb out of the back of the truck and get in the front, and get the hell out of Ferndale.

Vinnie

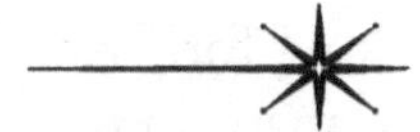

$\mathcal{B}$illie has no idea how, but as they near Manila, she starts to think she might know where the doctor lives—muscle memory, some knowing in her limbs.

When they get there, they stop first at the community center, to use the restroom. Billie remembers being here when she was little, more than once. *What was I doing here?*

As she walks out, she sees a group of kids sitting in a circle on the grass, spaced six feet apart from each other, their teacher or parent in the center. They stare at her as she walks out of the bathroom, pushing her hand through her hair. They're the same age she was when she was hurt.

I definitely spent time around here when I was little. And if I had to use the bathroom, we must have stayed a while.

Billie drives them to a quiet residential street. It's beachfront property, but it's still Humboldt, so many of the houses are humble beach shacks. Driving slowly, with the windows down, déjà vu overwhelms her.

"I remember coming here with my dad," she tells Randall. "Now that I think about it, he was looking for someone. Like we are. I didn't understand then...." She remembers, "He called it 'taking a drive.'" *But he had to have been looking for Mars, too.*

"Fuck! I should have talked to him about this." Tears

of frustration prick her eyes and she grabs at her hair. She peers out at the mailboxes they pass, looking left and then right. The dunes in the near distance block the ocean from view.

"What are we looking for?" Randall asks.

"I don't know," she snaps in response. "Mars?"

"Why don't I drive? Pull over."

She does and they switch places. In the passenger seat, she has the same point of view as on the drives with her dad. Midday, the streets are quiet; a couple locals out walking look suspiciously at the big black truck driving slowly by.

I was out here when it was foggy once. It's dreamlike in her memory. She can remember being afraid. There was a tightness in her dad—some tension or darkness—and it had scared her.

It seems unlikely that Mars is still here. None of the mailboxes and gates have names; it's hard to even find a number on most of these old, ramshackle houses. People come to Humboldt to hide, not to be found. *No one who did what he might have done is going to advertise where he lives.*

And then. She tells Randall to pull over and rolls her window the rest of the way down, peering out ahead at a Moroccan-style house with a red-tile roof. It stands out from the rest of the homes, with a heavy wooden gate and a tall fence. There's a camera above the gate, pointed at the driveway; they're pulled over about fifteen feet before that.

"I remember this house," she tells Randall quietly. It feels familiar. She remembers her dad's tension, can feel it here still. And though the fence and gate aren't familiar, everything else—the broad hedges, the palm trees on either side of the property—are as familiar as if she's studied them.

Beyond the camera's view, Billie sees a mailbox. *If the mail hasn't been picked up yet, we could look in there and see if anyone named Mars lives here.*

She looks at her phone—almost two p.m. The doctor would be retired, but he could be out running errands and come home, or he could come outside and find them there. Kids will be coming home from school soon…. If she and Randall are going to make a move, they need to do it now.

"I want you to park over there," she tells Randall, pointing to a dark spot under a tree, past the house and across the street. "But don't drive past the camera. Let's go around the block."

Randall turns around, makes a left onto a small dirt road and then another couple lefts, till he's headed down the same street from the other direction. He parks under the tree, a few houses down from the blue house, and out of camera range. Billie's black truck blends into the shade and they have a perfect view of the driveway, but are far enough away that no one in the house could see their faces. From this view, the whole scene feels even more familiar, and she realizes that this is why she directed Randall here: because this is where her dad had parked, watching.

Once he's parked, without thinking, she opens the door and slips out the passenger side. Randall looks over and she puts her finger to her lips, closes the door quietly, and walks behind the truck. She looks around and, seeing no one, quickly crosses the street. Next to the dark fence in her dark clothes, she's barely visible. She ducks down behind the bushes and heads for the mailbox.

The camera stays fixed on the driveway, doesn't move toward her. These people aren't worried about their mail; they just don't want intruders.

Nearing the mailbox, she can see that it has a lock on it. *Though it may not be locked.*

She looks back at the truck, can see Randall watching her, biting his nails.

She creeps closer, looking all around her. The street is quiet. And the fence is so high, there's no way anyone in the house could see her. The manicured shrubs cover her so that no one driving by would see her either.

Just do it, she tells herself.

Where the landscaping ends, nearing the driveway, she takes a second to breathe. *It's only ten feet to the mailbox. No one's watching. Go!*

Like an orangutan, she stays low to the ground. At the mailbox, she reaches up and pulls on the little brass handle. It's locked.

She can see something inside, a magazine maybe. Sticking a finger in the slot, she tries to pull something out, but her fingers are too big, the angle too awkward.

Fuck!

She crouch-walks back to the bushes and quickly back to the truck.

"Did you see me?" she asks Randall, cheeks flushed as she climbs back in the passenger side.

"I did. You're my hero."

"Pretty sure no one saw me. It's locked, but there's mail in there." She looks at where she just was, adrenaline charging through her. *Stay cool,* she tells herself. *Don't go getting a migraine now.*

Randall asks, "You know anyone here who knows how to pick locks?"

Racking her brain, she remembers, "Wait, I do, actually. An old student of mine." Vinnie had picked Billie's truck lock once, after she'd locked her keys inside, rushing to get to class. They bonded over both being from Humboldt and became friends. Vinnie had dropped out of SAI when he had to come back to Humboldt and help with the family pot farm.

She texts Vinnie: *Hey man, I'm in town and could use a hand. Any chance you're near Manila?*

Vinnie buzzes back: *30 min. where u at?*

Cool, thanks, she writes, then looks out her window to see the address of the house they're in front of, and texts it to Vinnie, telling him where to turn so he doesn't pass by the camera. *Park a ways behind me and get in cab on passenger side.* "He's on his way."

"Cool. Seems like you have an ex-student for every occasion."

Billie just nods. Her head is pulsing with energy. She downs half a plastic water bottle and looks over at Randall. He looks elfin in the driver's seat of her big truck. He changed out of his camping clothes at the community center and is wearing a green button-down with white polka dots, buttoned all the way up, and some skinny jeans. *Even now, the outfits are perfect.* He looks healthy; they'd stopped on the way for juice, and he chews on his straw, smiling at her.

"You seriously look, like, half your age," she tells him. "What's your secret?"

"So do you! Did you see the way those kids looked at you, back there? Such a rock star. I bet half of them have seen your murals and know who you are."

"Ha ha." They haven't spoken much about her art, but Randall had seen a lot of her early paintings in high school and had even sat for her a few times. With the greenery behind him, he looks so beautiful she wants to paint him again. *It's been too long,* she realizes, since she made something. Normally, a month into summer, she would be finished blocking out the new mural and would've started painting; she finds herself flexing her hand like she does when it's sore from working all day.

She remembers her plan to paint Willa and desperately wants to be back home, doing that. Pulling out her little black notebook, she starts to sketch Randall with a pencil.

"I have a bunch of your paintings," he says.

"Old stuff. You haven't seen the murals."

He nods sheepishly. "Seen pictures of all of them."

She stops, blinking at him, and registers what he's saying. *Wait—he's followed my career?*

Just then Vinnie pulls up behind them, and soon he's opening the door to the extended cab of her truck, pulling on a mask. "Yo, teach! Y'all are coming from Seattle? You aren't sick, right? I can't get no coronavirus right now."

"Not that we know of," Billie says, turning around in the passenger seat to see Vinnie. "We've been pretty safe, and we don't have symptoms. But anyway, if we stay up here and you stay back there, you should be good." There's a few feet between them and the cab, plus the barrier of the front bench seat. "No one's sat back there in months. Want us to put our masks on?"

"Nah," he says, climbing up.

She introduces Vinnie and Randall, and says to Randall quietly, "Let's talk later." He nods.

The truck's cab is just big enough for Vinnie's six-foot-two, 250-pound frame. He looks good, with some new tattoos since she last saw him: a bear on one hand and a wolf on the other. She recognizes his drawing style and admires them.

"Okay." She claps her hands together and turns back to Vinnie. "You good?"

"Yup. Whatchu need, sis?"

"You see that house there, with the high fence?" He nods. "We think a very bad man might live there." She laughs nervously.

"Word," Vinnie says, nodding.

"There's a camera, there." She points. "It's focused on the driveway, doesn't extend to the mailbox, doesn't track movement. But the mailbox is locked."

"It'd be easy to pick."

"Great. How long would it take?"

"Less than a minute," he says.

"Okay. So, if you're down, you open the box, look through the mail—I saw some in there—maybe take pics with your phone of the address line, or whatever looks important? The guy we're looking for is called Dr. Mars."

"Yeah, I can do that. Now?"

"Yeah, I think so. Right?" she asks Randall.

"No time like the present," Randall says.

"Cool," Vinnie says. "I'll be right back."

"Damn, he's all business," Randall says after he leaves, impressed.

She nods, still upset that Randall has known all along where she was, what she was doing. They could have had more time together. As with her dad, they can never get that time back.

But unlike her dad, he's sitting next to her now.

They watch Vinnie, who has reached the mailbox. He

has his back to the house, to block his actions from any-one who might be watching, but unlike Billie he's not all in black, and there's no missing the football player–size person doing something he's not supposed to be doing, if anyone were to drive by.

"Hurry," Billie says under her breath. She sees the mailbox open, and Vinnie shuffling through what looks like a big stack of stuff. "Jackpot. Lucky for us, he's lazy. Or on vacation."

Vinnie jogs back to the car, gets in the back passenger side again. He pulls something out of his hoodie pocket: an advertising circular. He hands it to Billie.

It's addressed to Jerzy Marszalek.

"Is that your guy?" Vinnie asks, showing them pic-tures of other mail addressed to Dr. Jerzy Marszalek and Mrs. Maria Marszalek. "Looks like just him and his wife."

Billie shivers. "It's him," she whispers.

"Buddy," Randall says to her. "You okay?"

Billie's face has gone white and she's staring at the house. "I can't believe we found him."

"This guy hurt you?" Vinnie asks.

"Maybe, when I was little. Or knows who did."

"So should we ask him?" Vinnie proposes.

"What do you mean?" she asks.

"Wait for him, grab him, take a drive."

"How do you know he's here?" she asks. "There's hella mail in the box, and it's June, they're probably out of town."

"Lots of doctors travel in August," Randall says. "Es-pecially shrinks. I dated one."

"He's here," Vinnie says confidently. "If he's not, all we lose is a few hours of sitting."

"Okay, so, what?" Billie asks. "We wait here?"

"Yeah," Vinnie says. "He pulls up. We can see whoever's in the driver's seat perfectly from here. If it looks like him and he's alone, I run over. I make sure he's Mars, then have him move his car and come with us."

"How will you convince him?" Billie asks. "What if he hurts you?"

"He won't," Vinnie scoffs. "A fucking pedophile? Please. They're the most chickenshit of all."

"But what if he carries a weapon?" Billie says.

"I'll have mine on him first." Vinnie pats a bulge at his waist.

The thought of a gun there makes Billie nervous. But they may need it if they're going to do this. "I can pay you. This is asking a lot."

"Nah, man. How many times did you have my back when admin wanted to kick me out? Nah. If this guy had any part in hurting young girls, he has no rights, far as I'm concerned."

Randall looks at the circular, tries Googling the name, but can't connect to Wi-Fi.

"Randall, what do you think?"

"I think it's a good plan," he says calmly. "I can drive."

"How will we make him talk?" she asks Vinnie, who again lays his hand on his waistband. "We can't hurt him, though. That's not what this is. If we do this—*if*—it's just to find out what he knows. To get him to talk. With three of us—and a gun—and only one of him, maybe he'll tell us something."

She imagines the doctor in her truck. "I don't want to sit next to him, though. I'll stay here; Randall, you drive, that's great. Vinnie, can you sit in back with the doctor?"

"No probs," he says.

"I can question him from the front. Oh, god—what if I recognize him? What if he recognizes me?"

"You look very different from when you were five," Randall reminds her.

"Yeah, but maybe he knew me when I was older, too. We don't know."

"What *do* you know, so far?" Vinnie asks.

"Not a lot. My mom gave us his name—Dr. Mars, she said. She also said something about me, or her, being 'special.' We think there may have been some kind of study—either me or my mom could have been involved. I remember a speculum inside me, so we think maybe this doctor or someone in his office was a gynecologist?"

"Jesus," Vinnie says.

"Yeah. Sorry." She's quiet. She drinks the last of her coffee. "Shit. Does this mean we can't go get more coffee?"

"Nope," Vinnie says. "It's a stakeout. We stay until he goes in or comes out."

"Right, he could be coming out," Billie says. "What do we do if that happens?"

"Well, it looks like a manual gate. So he'll have to get out to open it, whether he's going in or out. I'll quickly get to him before he drives off, make him move his car, bring him to you."

"What do you think?" she asks Randall. "This is a lot to drag you into."

Randall waves a hand like it's nothing. "We'll take a leisurely drive along the bay. We used to do it all the time, right? Nothing to it."

She nods hesitantly, blinking.

They look back at the driveway. "It's good it's a quiet street," Vinnie says. "No one has been by since I got here."

"I wish we had more coffee," Billie says.

❧

Randall and Billie talk quietly, watching the house, while Vinnie snoozes in the extended cab.

"Okay, so I forgive you, for not being in touch," Billie says. "After all, if you hadn't scheduled that show on my birthday, I never would have found you."

He nods.

There's so much about his life that she wants to know. *This, what he's doing now…this is some serious good-friend karma.*

Shadows and light stripe the truck. Billie glances into the back. Vinnie is snoring a little.

Biting her cheek, she stares at the house. "Is this a good plan? Being on a stakeout isn't helping my anxiety."

"What are our other options?"

"I don't know. We Googled him and couldn't find anything, right?"

"But we didn't have his full name then," he says.

"That's true. We could go somewhere and look him up. Maybe find a phone number. But then how would we get him to talk to us?"

"We could also just wait and watch," Randall says gently.

"But we have to talk to him to know if he's the right guy."

Randall says, "Unless you remember something. Anyway, there can't be that many Dr. Marses in Humboldt County—"

"But we don't know for sure that that's our guy's name, or if this guy has any attachment to what happened to me. I mean, our source is *Petra*. She's not exactly what you'd call a trustworthy witness." Billie's eyes are bright in the dark car. "Will we be kidnapping him if we drive around with him in the car?"

"I mean, legally, I suppose. But I'm not worried about that." They had discussed Randall's jail time, for a botched robbery, on the way down. "Are you? If this guy has done what we think he has—and we'll make sure right away we have the right guy—if it's him, he is not going to want this getting out. We'll convince him it's in his best interest."

Billie blinks, picking absently at her cuticles. They've only seen two cars in the three hours they've been sitting and waiting. Soon, though, people will be getting off work, picking up the kids, and coming home.

A black sedan rounds the corner.

"It's him," she says sharply, and Vinnie wakes and sits up quickly.

"How do you know?" Randall asks.

"I just know."

As they watch the car approach slowly, Billie feels her heart rate double. She turns to Vinnie just in time to see him slip out the back. As he crosses the street and slinks through the shadows toward the car, she wants to reach out and bring him back.

The car has dark tinted windows. "It looks like something out of *Goodfellas*." She moves forward in her seat, trying to get a better look. "Can you see?" she asks Randall, rubbing her sweaty hands on her jeans.

"He's rolling his window down to get the mail," Randall says.

"Can you see what he looks like?"

Vinnie walks in front of the mailbox just as the guy reaches for it—blocking their view of him. He gestures toward his waistband and points to the spot where they want the guy to pull over.

And he does. The guy parks the sedan and gets out,

looking scared. He's short and swarthy. Billie wasn't thinking about how old he would be, until now—doing the math in her head, she guesses he must be nearing eighty, though he has a surprising amount of hair. They are about to take this guy on the wildest ride of his life. What if he, too, is heart attack–prone? *Would that be murder?*

Vinnie hasn't pulled his gun, that she can see; he's just implied it. She thinks there's a distinction there when it comes to the law.

And then she thinks about who this guy is and the pain he may have caused her—pain that could have been avoided were it not for him—and she doesn't feel guilty anymore.

I need this. I need to know.

As the two men climb into the extended cab from the passenger side—the doctor first, then Vinnie—Randall turns to her. "You okay? You want to do this, Chief?"

"I don't know. What do you think?" she asks quietly.

"I was a heroin addict, dude. My whole life was illegal. This doesn't scare me."

She nods, and as she turns to the back a charge moves between them—what they are about to do is not safe. But they're going in eyes wide open.

The back passenger door opens. "Dr. Mars?" Billie asks.

He doesn't answer, but his dark eyes say yes. They understand. *He knows something.*

Mars says, "I don't have a mask. Is anyone sick?" He pronounces it *seek*. Billie can't place the accent. *Russian?*

She shakes her head in answer to his question. He struggles to climb in, and Vinnie pushes him forward.

I need to know, she thinks as she turns to face front.

We made it this far, there's no way I'm stopping now.
"Drive," she says to Randall.

Mars

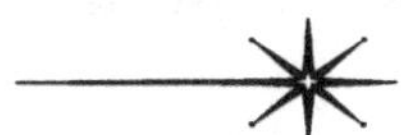

*R*andall remembers to turn around, to avoid the camera, and they make a right onto Samoa Boulevard, the rural highway connecting Eureka to Arcata. Billie and Randall had driven it a million times as teenagers—to get to each other's houses, or the beach, or sometimes just cruising while they worked out some problem and/or got high. She knows the road like an old record, its scratches and grooves. They're headed south, toward the Samoa dunes, where people go off-roading. There are many more cars out here than there had been on the doctor's quiet street.

Billie turns to face the man in the back. "Do you know who I am?"

He shakes his head. He seems unsure what to do with his hands, and places them in his lap politely.

"You're a doctor, right?" she asks. "Dr. Mars?"

Sweat beads on his forehead. He glances at the door handle.

"Child-lock his door," she tells Randall, showing him the button. "Don't even think about it," she tells the man. "We are not afraid to tie your hands if you try anything at all. Don't fuck with us, and we won't fuck with you."

Billie sees a defensiveness kick in. The doctor's shoulders tighten, his wide forehead unwrinkled, dismissive.

Vinnie lunges across the space and slaps him hard, across the jaw. Billie looks at Vinnie wide-eyed but doesn't say anything. She notices that Vinnie's mask has little pink and yellow flowers on it.

"Sorry," Vinnie says. "He was askin' for it."

"What do you want?" the doctor asks, holding his cheek.

They pull into the parking lot with the wooden tower, which had been one of her and Randall's favorite spots. He catches her eye and nods; finally he's remembering, too. They had imagined a lot of future scenarios, up on that platform, but this wasn't one of them. How she wishes, now, that they were back then instead, dreaming up glittery futures as the sky changed colors.

From the parking lot, the dunes block the ocean from view, but she can hear it, can feel it rumbling out there. Billie guides Randall back onto Samoa, where they came from.

She turns to the back seat and decides to take a risk. "So, Dr. Mars. Dr. Marszalek, who ran tests on 'special' little girls in the seventies?" The man's guilt is practically seeping through his pores. He wasn't just some middle-man—this guy participated in whatever happened to her. *He may have been inside me.* She gags at the thought, afraid she'll vomit.

Don't think about that. Just focus on getting answers.

She looks at him, and he meets her eyes. "I was one of those little girls. Willa. Remember her? A little wild, big for her age? Which was *five*. Five years old."

The doctor looks upward, seemingly searching the files in his brain. When he doesn't find the one he's looking for, he shakes his head and looks at Billie dismissively. "What do you want?" he asks again.

Vinnie makes a fist and stops just short of the man's face. "Talk to her like that again and I'll come for you."

Mars hears him, looks over at him and then away, disdainfully.

"I want to know more," Billie says, snapping her fingers to get his attention. "About what you were doing. Who you were doing it with."

His eyes find *that* file, quick. She can see that he knows exactly what, and who, she's referring to. But will he say?

The guy closes his eyes. Vinnie takes the opportunity to look up at Billie questioningly. *What's next, boss?* his eyes ask. He reminds her of her dad, how he takes up almost the whole back cab himself, how comfortable he looks with a potential child rapist. He flattens his hands on his thighs, his bear and wolf ready for war. Both tattoos are black—just their faces, with fine detail and fierce eyes.

They pass the bridge to Eureka. For a while it's mainly cow pasture, the bay beyond at their right.

She looks into Vinnie's gray eyes. Mars still has his eyes closed. She shakes her head. *I don't know what's next.* They pass a sign for the Arcata Marsh and Wildlife Center.

"Hey, dude! Wake up!" she says angrily to Mars. Vinnie claps in the man's face, and his eyes open wide. "Did you fuck my mom? Remember her? Petra. Did you guys rape her, too?"

"No," the man says. "Did she tell you that?"

"It's just a guess," Billie says. "Why don't you tell me, so I don't have to guess. What were you doing with her? What were you doing with me?"

"I was with her, not you," he says tightly.

"Who was with me then?" she asks.

"Someone helping with the study, perhaps an intern. Your mom, she came in for electroshock treatments. We were studying the results, on her and others with mental illness."

"Were you treating her for Narcissistic Personality Disorder?"

The man shakes his head. "Bipolar. Though back then NPD was often misdiagnosed as bipolar; they have a lot in common. Or she could have had both. I wasn't the one who diagnosed her. Her psychiatrist referred her, and she volunteered to try electroshock, to be part of our study."

Billie suddenly remembers being afraid, driving home at night, that her mother would drive off the road—once she almost did. That was why her mom had been so out of it: she was getting shocked with electricity. Petra had been a zombie, even more withdrawn, not available to Billie when she'd needed her most. *Maybe that's why it took her so long to figure out what was happening to me.*

"Was this some underground operation?"

"Oh, no," he says confidently. "We had federal funding, many participants. The study was conducted in a medical office, everything."

"Oh, really?" she asks, rolling her eyes. "Did your intern get busy with all of your patients' toddlers, was that part of the study?"

Randall calmly crosses over the 101. There's a turnabout ahead and he's about to drive all the way around it and back over the highway, but Billie stops him. "There's a drive-up coffee place up here." She has a headache coming on; coffee might keep it at bay.

They pull up to the little coffee shack. "My treat," she says to the car. "We may be at this for a while if the doc doesn't start spilling."

"That's okay, I can do this all night," Vinnie says. He points at the doctor. "You shut up, alright? Don't forget, I have a weapon." He pulls his hoodie up casually, lets the doctor see the outline under his shorts. The older man just shakes his head disapprovingly.

"You better fucking respect me—us," Vinnie says. "We won't hesitate to throw a bitch in the marsh."

Billie cough-laughs, as Randall pulls up to the counter. The young woman working there smiles at them. She can't see into the back seat from where she stands.

Billie leans over and tells her, "I'll have a cappuccino. Double shot please."

Randall smiles and says, "Small decaf coffee with almond milk."

Vinnie barks out, "Cold brew for me, black. Doc wants a strawberry smoothie."

"And four vegan doughnuts," Billie adds, handing her card to Randall, who passes it to the woman.

When their drinks are ready, Randall passes them out, careful to hold the cups from the bottom, just in case. Passing her card back, the girl leans around Randall to tell Billie, "Hey, I'm real sorry to hear about your dad. Allie is my best friend—Joe was her boss. He was always super nice to her—and me."

Billie smiles sadly at the girl. *I almost forgot he was gone.* "Thanks. Is Allie doing okay?"

The girl nods, with a small, sweet smile. Billie smiles back. "Will you give her my best wishes?" The girl nods again and waves as they drive away.

Randall pulls over so they can get situated. Billie takes a few sips, feeling more confident now that she has coffee.

She turns to the back seat again, cup in hand. "So, doc, it's up to you—we can do the whole Humboldt tour: the marsh, like my friend said, maybe even Old Town Eureka. *Or* we can head west on Samoa and drop you off at home, since you will have given us what we need. It's up to you."

"Samoa!" he shouts.

"Good choice," Billie says. "You might even make it home in time for dinner."

"Listen, fucker," Randall says, looking back at the doctor before pulling out of the lot. "If I get back on Samoa, I want you to *tell* us what we need to know. We are not fucking around, and the trip to the marsh is always on the table." He spreads his hands out to encompass the extensive marshland in front of them. "Not a bad place to hide a body…"

"It wouldn't be the first time," Vinnie says.

"Okay," Billie says, as they get back on the road. "First question—who was your partner, in this electroshock study?"

"I had a few part—" he starts.

"Do *not* even fuck with me right now. You know who I mean. Who hurt me? You might as well tell me, I'm going to find out anyway. I already practically know everything. And I *will* know if you're lying."

"There was a young pediatric intern who worked in the medical building where we were doing treatments. He volunteered to help with the young kids that would sometimes come in with their parents. He'd take care of them, give them a snack and something to color. It seemed like a good idea at the time."

They'll be back in Manila in about six minutes. Suddenly she's afraid. *What if someone has reported him missing, and the cops are there when we pull up?*

"Take the bridge to Eureka," she tells Randall.

"Wait!" Dr. Mars cries out. "You said you were taking me home!"

"I said," Billie growls, "I'll take you home when you tell me what I want to know. I want a name, and location, for this intern."

"Oh, I have no idea! You can't expect me to keep track of him all these years...."

"What was his name?" Billie demands. "I know you know it. Tell me now."

"Klein," Mars says. "Colin Klein. We used to call him Calvin Klein, because he looked like that, very all-American type boy."

Fucking Calvin Klein, she thinks, her stomach turning. *Of course it's a fucking white boy, getting away with this shit.*

She looks out over the bay as they cross the bridge. The sun is just starting to think about setting; it reflects, orange, off the strip of blue stretching to the horizon. Her mind goes to her mom—looking at the same sun going into the same sea.

Alone, she always imagines Petra. Now, though, she thinks, *Or with Ann.* Looking out at the water, she sees the picture at the center of Ann's main collage, in her living room: of Ann and Petra in love. Her mom had that, maybe still does.

Don't check out, she tells herself. *You got this. This is what you came all this way for. This is what success looks like.*

"Where is Colin now?" she asks, having no desire to look at the man in the back. She nods her head to the right and Randall pulls onto Broadway. Up here is the police station and there are always lots of cops around. She keeps an eye out as she finishes her coffee, then directs Randall to a quieter waterfront road.

"Where are you taking me?" the doctor asks, trying to insert some authority into his voice.

"Good question, doc—where, indeed. *Where* is Colin now?" Billie asks loudly. "Is he around still?

"How would I know?" Mars asks.

Vinnie slaps him again. "You better have respect. Think about where you are right now, motherfucker."

Billie turns around. "Speaking of. Did you fuck my mother?"

"No," Mars says, shaking his head, trying to break free from her dark eyes.

"Liar!" she yells at him. "Tell me the truth. If you lie to me, I told you, I'll know. All you have to do is tell the truth, and we'll take you home. Lie to me once more, we'll take you down to the waterfront and throw you in. The tourists will love it, some authentic Eureka flavor."

Billie is sweating. She pulls the neck of her hoodie away from her skin. Randall rolls her window down, and the funk of the bay creeps in.

Her eyes on the water, her mind travels back, trying to understand. "You fucked my mother. And my dad knew, didn't he? That's why we always took those drives, over by your house. He wanted to see you." Billie has thought of her mom differently, since learning she was gay; now they have being queer in common. *But if Petra was fucking this guy, she was bisexual.* Not that there's anything wrong with being bi—but still, Billie feels something she thought she'd gained being yanked away from her.

Of course, Petra was with Joe, too, but that now seems like something she did just for looks; as a cover almost, with Joe her beard. Affairs are the opposite of that: something that happens in the dark. *Maybe she liked the power of it, having control over a doctor.* Petra was always dismissive of the medical establishment in general.

Broken-down buildings edge the outskirts of Old

Town. *Dad might have been willing to look the other way about Petra's relationship with Ann—but he couldn't allow an affair with a* man. *That also could explain why Petra took me with her, because she didn't want Dad knowing where she was going. But he found out anyway.*

She turns around to face the man again. "Just a fucking affair, huh?" Petra's mythology sometimes feels almost exotic to Billie, like she has an extinct bird for a mother. But this is just bargain-basement straight-person behavior. "That's pretty sad."

"No, the study was real," Mars says, his pride puffing up. "We were ahead of our time. People weren't ready for it, but electroshock is still the most effective treatment, for many."

"You ever do electroshock on kids, doc?" Billie asks.

"No, no, no," he says.

"Oh, sorry—wouldn't want to offend your code of ethics. So my mom—was she the only one you slept with? Was she 'special'?"

"She was special," he says quietly.

"Oh, really? How so?" Billie asks.

"She had a remarkable regard for herself. Unflappable."

"Pretty sure that's called NPD, doc. Story of my life."

They reach the end of the industrial road, and return to busy Broadway. "Which way, boss?" Randall asks.

"Left!" the doctor shouts pathetically.

Billie catches Randall's eye and asks, "You good to go a little deeper into Eureka?" He nods, and makes a right on Broadway.

"What else do you want to know?" Mars asks, his voice cracking. "I told you everything!"

"Hmm, I kinda doubt that." Looking out the window, she gazes at a series of chain restaurants, then sees an old Denny's. *I was there with my mom.* She has a sick feeling, looking at it—something about the bathroom.

Blood. I went to the bathroom and saw blood in my underwear. And I was afraid to tell her....

We were coming from the doctor....

She gestures for Randall to get in the left lane. The car is quiet as she has Randall take a sharp left turn, uphill onto Harris.

"What are we doing up *here* now?" Dr. Mars asks.

"I think you better text your wife," Billie says. "It'll be dark soon."

"Give me a break!" Mars says. "I am not texting my wife."

She turns toward the back again. "Compose a text to her on his phone, Vinnie. '*Sorry, honey, I got hung up.*'"

Vinnie takes the phone and writes it, presses send, then hands it back and rubs antibacterial gel over his hands.

The doctor takes it back and squints, reading the text. "'Hi honey, sorry I got hung up. What's for dinner?'" He looks at Vinnie, shaking his head. He peers out the windshield at the busy one-way road. "Where are you going?"

"Why, you know someone up here?" She senses they are getting close and tells Randall to slow down, peering out at the buildings they're passing, mainly homes.

Pointing out a small parking lot to the right, she asks Randall to pull in. In front of them is a medical practice, in an old house, and instantly Billie knows: *This is where it happened.*

"Look familiar, doc?" she asks, looking back at Mars. "You hear back from your lady yet?"

His phone dings. Vinnie grabs it and reads the text. "Lasagna!" he says loudly. "Oh, man, that makes me hungry!"

Billie holds the bag of donuts open to Vinnie, who takes one. She offers one to the doc, who shakes his head; Randall doesn't want one either. Billie takes a glazed blueberry.

"You Italian?" she asks Mars.

"No!" the doctor says, sounding offended. "I'm Polish."

"You got a problem with Italians?" Vinnie says.

"No! Jesus. My wife is Italian."

"Niiiice," Vinnie says. "Yo, can we get some of that lasagna, when we drop you off? I bet it's bomb."

"Sure," the doctor says, in exasperation. "Just take me home, and you can have as much lasagna as you want."

"Great," Billie says, mouth full of doughnut, "dinner is solved." She looks out at a sign between them and the small pink house. "Dr. Richard Belvedere," she reads aloud. "Wow, that's fun to say. You know what else is fun to say? Gy-ne-col-o-gist."

Dropping her mouth open in faux surprise, she looks back at the doctor. The color has drained from his face—all the proof she needs. She guesses that he probably normally avoids this street at all costs, from how uncomfortable he looks.

"I wonder if Richard Belvedere knows Colin Klein? I bet he does." It's all falling into place: just as she fits one piece in, the next arrives.

Harris is a major street, for Eureka. What had happened to Billie had happened with cars driving by right out front, all day and night. That feels right.

She looks at Randall, across the truck from her. He's quiet. She realizes they're less than a mile from where he was raped.

Vinnie hands Billie his phone. It's a page of Google results for *Colin Klein Humboldt*. Scrolling down, she sees a business page for Dr. Colin Klein, pediatrician, Fortuna.

He's not hiding at all. He's practicing medicine—treating children—twenty miles from here.

She feels sick, pushes out of the truck, and puts her hands on her knees, bending over; then slams her door and leans back against it, suddenly exhausted. She puts her hands in her jean pocket, where she put her dad's pipe. She rubs it, closing her eyes.

What if I wasn't the only one?

Opening her eyes, she looks over at the building. The pink façade looks wrong somehow, kind of gross for a gynecology office…. *It was another color then.* Here, in the parking lot, she feels all of the queasiness and fear that little Willa felt, brought here by her mom, scared to go in. Petra acting put out, having to bring her daughter to meet her lover. That tightness she would get, like a rubber band—the slightest pressure could make her snap.

Billie walks over to the building and looks in the window. It's tiny, couldn't possibly fit more than two small exam rooms. Maybe an office, too—but they would've all been right next to each other. Which means her mom definitely would've heard her when she screamed. Until now, she's imagined her mom being way down a long hallway—in another wing of a large medical building. But seeing it, she realizes: while Petra was fucking this guy, Billie was *right next door* being violated.

Also, someone, likely Petra, must have told Billie that Colin Klein was a doctor, since Billie told Randall that a doctor hurt her. Whether Petra knew he was only an intern, she'll never know.

She breathes in the cool air from the bay. *This is ridic-*

ulous. We need to get the fuck out of Eureka. Take this guy home and find somewhere to sleep.

On the way home, Billie takes over driving. She's focused and careful, so they won't be pulled over by the cops. She asks Randall to make sure Humboldt isn't sheltering in place again—that's how few cars are on the road.

They get back to Manila unscathed, and there are no police waiting for them there; she pulls into the same spot they were in before, across from Mars's house and his car, again avoiding the camera.

Before Mars gets out, Vinnie grabs his phone. "Bring us out some lasagna, and I'll give you your phone back."

Mars shakes his head, getting out of the truck and into his car, then going through the gate. A couple minutes later he walks back out, carrying a disposable baking pan covered in tin foil.

"That's all you, Vin," Billie says.

Vinnie rolls down his window and takes it from the doctor with awe, pulls back the foil, smells it, and smiles.

"She made an extra," Mars says. "She doesn't know I brought it to you. You have to go now."

"Doc," Billie says. Mars stands at the passenger window, looking past Randall at her. "You can't tell anyone—not your wife, and especially not Colin Klein—about our little drive."

The doctor hesitates. "And you won't tell my name to anyone?"

She looks down at him. He seems to have shrunken in on himself, like the drive has drained his life force. *He wasn't the one who hurt me.* He hadn't laid hands on her—

that she knows for sure. He had played a part, then; but he had played a part now, too. The scales feel balanced, and she decides to let him off the hook.

"I won't mention your name to anyone," she says.

He nods. Vinnie hands his phone through the window.

Mars starts toward his house, then stops. Walking to the driver's side, he looks into Billie's eyes. "I'm sorry," he whispers. "For what happened to you." His shoulders relax then, seemingly relieved of their burden. He nods again and turns to leave.

Pulling open the heavy gate, he looks so small— not even half its height. He slips through, and it closes behind him. Billie stares at the gate for a few moments, stunned. She swallows back tears.

She turns to Randall and Vinnie then, blinking until it's them she sees. "You guys, that was some beyond-the-bonds-of-friendship shit. Randall, nice driving—you can be my deputy anytime. Vinnie, man, I feel like I should pay you."

"This lasagna is payment enough. Trust." He laughs. "Y'all wanna see something funny?"

"Yes," Billy and Randall reply in unison.

Vinnie pulls up his hoodie. Stuck in his waistband is a banana.

"A snack for the drive home," he says, sticking out his tongue.

Billie's jaw drops open. Randall cracks up and she joins him. After all the tension of the past couple hours, laughing feels exhilarating. Like her heart might bust out of her chest and fly away.

Vinnie laughs, too. "Works every time. I don't carry a damn gun! You really think I'd carry a gun?"

"Well, I don't know! I thought the underground biz

was getting crazy after legalization."

"We have business to take care of now and then, at the farm, sure…but I don't take that out into the community. I live with my girlfriend, yo! We're expecting a kid. No guns."

"Got it," Billie says. "Sorry. And thanks. We couldn't have done it without you and your banana. And congrats! On the baby. Can't wait to meet it, and your girlfriend."

"Lizzie. She's out of town right now, with her family. Last trip before the baby comes."

"Where to next?" Billie asks Randall. "We should get out of here."

"I don't know. Food? Motel?"

"Nah, man," Vinnie says. "Y'all come to my crib. You can help me out with this." He holds up the pan. "It's been lonely, with Lizzie away."

Billie looks at Randall questioningly, and he nods. "Sure, why not?" she says. "We'll follow you. Flip around, though. Don't drive past the camera. Just in case."

The Crown

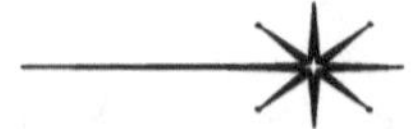

$\mathcal{O}$n the morning, Billie takes her coffee out to the front porch. Vinnie's place is nice, up by the community forest where there's lots of sun. Randall is still sleeping, and Vinnie just left for work; he wouldn't allow her to pay him the $500 she'd pulled from her bank, as thanks for helping the night before.

Billie sits on the porch swing to call her lawyer, Hank, who was also her dad's best friend. After Joe hired Hank to represent him in a skirmish with a client—a case they won—over the years they became close friends. Hank was an uncle to Billie, growing up, gay and proud of it. She'd seen him at the memorial, but they hadn't had a chance to really talk.

She tells Hank what she knows: this guy Colin Klein hurt her when she was five years old, in the Eureka office of Peter Belvedere (or whoever was in that office then; this is something she wishes she had asked Mars while she had him in the car). He used a speculum on her, while her mom was fucking Dr. Mars, who was doing a study there involving electroshock therapy, and for whom Colin Klein was supposedly interning. She doesn't tell Hank how she got the info; he wouldn't want to know.

"Did you know about any of this?" she asks him.

"No," he says solemnly. "Bill, I'm so sorry." She can hear the pain in his voice.

"And the guy now has a pediatric practice in fucking

Fortuna. I want to blow this guy up, Hank. He needs to not be able to even *touch* a little kid again."

"I understand," Hank tells her.

"But I know coming down on his head at his office is not the most practical approach. I need to get home; I can't be getting thrown in Humboldt Correctional right now."

"Good, yes, you're right," Hank says.

"So what are our options?"

"Let me call a colleague and get right back to you."

Thanking him, she hangs up, looking into the trees outside Vinnie's place. *This happened because my mom was fucking Mars. If she hadn't been so distracted, if she hadn't been so self-obsessed, desperate for attention, if it hadn't always been all about her...*

A headache is lurking, and Billie's staving it off with Excedrin—the strongest thing in Vinnie's medicine cabinet. She'd checked when they arrived last night, knowing opioids are a danger to Randall.

I can't drive with a migraine. Jane will handle her chores for another couple days, if needed. But Billie wants to be home, where it's safe. Where it *had* felt safe, anyway.

She'd assumed that when she learned what happened to her, she'd feel better. But instead she's sickened by it, and very, very angry. And confused, still—she understands less than she ever did.

Walking down the front steps and onto the earth, she's soon surrounded by forest. She walks through it for a while, to get out of the sun, out of her head.

Soon she sees a big red trunk, double-wide, covered in lichen. The tree is delightful, its bark falling off all over—it's scruffy, like an oak playing dress-up.

She'll have to leave the redwoods when she heads home, and she may not see them again for a while. She lowers herself with care to the tree's base, closes her eyes and rests against the ancient being, hands on its bark. Breathing in the terpenes—the trees' pheromones, their breath—Billie remembers being in the forest like this as a child, feeling like a part of all of it. But then the connection was cut, and she's spent the rest of her life looking for it. Wanting to be part of the *we* again.

When she was shrooming, she had rediscovered her oneness. But in ordinary reality, it's harder. She has to let go of her need for control—and how can she ever do that now? How would she keep herself safe?

Her hands find moss at the tree's base; it reminds her of Gloria's hair, when it was close-cropped, back when they first got together. She sees a banana slug among some leaves.

Interbeing can't be accomplished intellectually. It's not an idea.

It's a decision, she decides. *An attitude.* She just *is* all of this. The beetle is the bark, the quail is the ferns, the large butch woman is the lichen.

Billie misses the days when her body could be pushed to its limits on a regular basis, but she would never trade that for this knowing, which is so hard-won, after a lifetime of programming. The deprogramming, it turns out, is as simple as remembering what she knew before she was hurt.

But with unity comes fear of separation, she realizes. *If I am all of this, then I need it all, which makes me vulnerable.* Was that what had kept her from knowing nonduality all these years? The risk of losing it all again? The danger of caring?

Being hurt at a young age, she learned that it's not safe to care. Because it *isn't*. Caring will hurt you time and time again. And a little hurt child wants nothing but to never be hurt again.

I was separated from all of this because *I was harmed. My connection with all of it—banana slugs, Crow, the moon, stars, ocean, rivers, sun—was taken from me. I lost my place in the universe.* Though she feels at home on the Land, she has still remained separate from it, not fully belonging there. Some part of her has felt other, outsider, invader, has resisted calling it hers, instead just calling it the Land. Honoring the autonomy of the place, she has also detached from it.

Grabbing a dead branch, she breaks it in half. She rolls its leaves in her hands and crunches them to dust.

The inner part of the branch, she imagines as his backbone. She clears off all the other leaves and branches and focuses on the backbone branch—his spine. She breaks it in two and then cracks them again, and again, until all of the pieces are only a fraction of what they were. Small, and separate.

A web of light beams down from the canopy of trees, like lace—delicate, intricate rays of energy that connect near her head. It's something of this that she can take with her. She feels a subtle, soft buckling, of the crown to her head, then a sensuous tingle spreading across her scalp.

She's going to need all of this, to confront the monster. She has to remember that she's part of a force powerful enough to take down a million molesters, more. It's the only way she can do it—and now she knows she can.

She heads back out into the sunshine—head still pleasantly buzzing, headache gone—and up into the house.

Hank

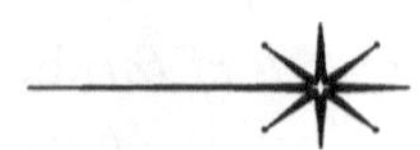

"*I* trust my intuition," Billie says to herself as she makes more coffee.

Charmed by the idea of it being true just because she says it aloud, she says again, "I trust my intuition," as she walks two mugs back to the sunroom in the back of the house. She knocks, and Randall calls her in.

The room has a greenhouse window, and the bed is tucked under it. She ducks and hands Randall his coffee, sits on the floor. She stretches out her body and faces him, lying on her side. Randall looks well, his cheek marked with sleep. She sees his phone at his side and wonders if he's texted Ariel yet.

"Good morning. Thanks for the coffee." He sits up cross-legged, the greenhouse's silver seams running vertically and horizontally, like a picture frame, behind him. He sips the coffee. "About the case. What do you need to feel whole—or at least to know how to get there?"

She sets down her mug and closes her eyes, rests her head on her forearm, wishing she could just sleep like this, right here right now. She wants to know *why* Colin Klein hurt her, why he went inside and took something from her, but she also doesn't feel ready to take on something so dark. That question is going to take time to answer. She needs to move slowly now, to get through this.

She answers Randall, "I need to feel like his patients are safe."

"So that's what we do today," he says. "We work on that. Can we work from here?"

"Sure. The Wi-Fi is good. I'll text Vinnie and make sure it's cool."

"Okay. I know you wanna get home, but I agree that the little ones' safety is most important right now. And we might need to be here in Humboldt, to make that happen. Once we're sure, *then* we head north."

"Sounds good," Billie says, pushing herself up. "I'll see you out there."

She pulls the door closed and texts Vinnie to ask if it's okay that they stay, forcing herself to breathe. "I trust my intuition."

Pulling a page out of her notebook, she folds the money for Vinnie in it and leaves it hidden under the TV remote, just as he texts her back: *whatever u need, sarge.*

She sits down on the front steps. The trees line the horizon, an infantry at the ready.

Her phone rings in her pocket. "Yo," she says to Hank.

"Hey," Hank says.

Randall comes out and sits next to her on the steps.

My gay Watson, she thinks. "My lawyer," she tells Randall, and puts the phone on speaker. "Hank, you're on with me and Randall. You guys remember each other, right?"

"Hi," Randall says. He shakes his head at her, mouthing *He doesn't remember me.*

"Randall," Hank says.

"Whatchu got?" Billie asks.

"Not a lot," Hank says.

A screw inside her tightens.

Then he says, "But what I do have—I think you're going to like it."

Hank says he'll pick up some lunch and drive out to Vinnie's place in a few hours.

They hang up, and she asks Randall, "You've met Hank, right?"

He nods, a funny look on his face. "Don't you remember? I had a huge crush on him."

"Oh, fuck. Did you?" She tries to remember. "Did anything ever happen?"

"No, because I was fifteen, and he wasn't a pedophile." His cheeks turn red. "Sorry. I didn't mean…."

"It's fine." She shakes her head. "Is it okay that he's coming? I can text him, meet him somewhere else…." She picks up her phone.

"Don't." Randall puts his hand on top of hers. "It's fine. Is he…?"

"He's single, as far as I know. He was married, to a guy, but they broke up a few years ago…. Wanna take a bath while we wait? Vinnie has a clawfoot. Enjoy it while you can."

Billie sees Hank pull up, and meets him on the porch. He sets down the pizza boxes and she lets herself melt into his arms. He's the closest thing she has to a dad now, and she lets go of her resistance and cries.

They fall to the steps and hold each other for a while. They both miss Joe dearly, deeply.

"Thanks, Hank," she says as they pull away, swiping at her tears with a little smile. It had been a thing of theirs when she was a tween. "Thanks, Hank," she would say, snapping her fingers and pointing a fake gun at him. She does it again now, remembering Vinnie last night and his fake gun. They laugh. She feels lighter with him here. *If I can't have my dad, Hank is the next best thing.*

"It's weird without Dad here," Billie says. "But it's good to see you, Uncle Hank." She smiles affectionately.

He smiles back, handsome as ever in heavy-frame glasses, crisp shirt, beautiful shoes. She thanks him for bringing food and leads him inside to the kitchen.

"Whose house?" Hank asks, looking out at the bay through the living room window.

"My friend Vinnie. He may be back later."

Randall walks into the living room, wet hair tucked behind his ear. He's wearing a gray sweater, with the green polka-dot collar peeking through.

"Hank, do you remember my best friend, Randall?" Billie asks.

"Of course," Hank says, smiling at Randall. "You've grown a little though."

Randall smiles shyly, puts out his hand. Hank takes it, and holds it rather than shaking it. They stand there almost holding hands until Randall drops his. Hank pats him on the back, as though there was nothing awkward about any of it. "Food," Hank says, pointing to the kitchen.

Randall goes in and come back out with a plate full of salad.

"No pizza?" Hank asks.

"Vegan." Randall smiles through some lettuce.

"Oh, no! I'm so sorry," Hank says. "I didn't even think…."

"It's okay," Randall says. "Fresh veggies are the hardest thing to get, away from home." He sits down on the couch, feet folded under him.

He's been away from home all this time. Roughing it with me on the Land. Eating whatever he's given.

Hank gets a plate and joins Randall on the couch. Billie offers them coffee, and they decline. She gets more coffee for herself and sits in a chair across from them, folding her cheese slice like a New Yorker.

Hank says, "Okay, so media attention is one route we can take. Add what we know to the Me Too conversation. Apply pressure. Even if it's just social media, which might then get picked up by a bigger outlet, it's the most strategic thing, but it's probably not enough to shut him down."

"We *need* to shut this guy down though," Billie says. "He works with kids every day."

"I hear you," Hank tells her. "But you don't have enough for a criminal case. And the statute of limitations ran out a long time ago."

"Yeah, no, I don't want that anyway. My name can't be associated with this. We're way too vulnerable up on the Land."

"You could file a complaint with the medical board," Hank says. "In conjunction with a media story, that could create a lot of movement. And it would be the quickest way to protect his patients."

"Yes! Can I go do that right now?"

"They're in the Eureka courthouse. They close at four," Hank says. "It's 3:15 now."

"Back in an hour," Billie says, screen door slamming behind her.

⚘

Speeding down the safety corridor along the bay, Billie sees a cop ahead and slows down just in time to cruise by him at fifty-five. Getting anywhere in Humboldt in a hurry is a challenge. This is a place where people wait for you to reach the stop sign before they go. It drives her crazy.

You can always come back in the morning, she tells herself. *Calm down. Breathe.*

But Billie doesn't want to come back in the morning. She wants to file this complaint, and then start their long trip home. Feeling stuck here, away from the Land, is making her anxious.

She passes some people standing on a corner holding BLACK LIVES MATTER signs, and honks as she passes them, pumping her fist. Then, risking it, she speeds the rest of the way to the courthouse, and swoops into a spot right out front. She rushes up the steps two at a time, asking at a desk for directions, noting that it's 3:30. Who knew how long the forms would take, or what info they'd need from her—it could take a while.

Up on the third floor, she can feel that she's getting close. *I trust my intuition.* They're moving in the right direction. She needs to pee, but that's a low priority.

She reaches the medical board office and explains to the woman at the desk that she wants to file a complaint against a pediatrician; the woman gives her a form. "Then we just need your photo ID and proof of address."

"Proof of address?" Billie asks.

"To make sure you live in Humboldt and can legally file a complaint here."

"Got it," Billie says and takes a seat, thinking, *Shit.*

Maybe Lisa has something. She texts her, then starts filling out the form.

Just as she's about to finish it—at 3:48—a text comes in from Lisa: a photo of a recent water bill with Billie's name miraculously on it.

She keeps it open on her phone as she walks up to the desk, handing the woman the form and pulling out her ID. The woman checks that the three match and nods distractedly; Billie puts away her phone and wallet.

"Everything looks to be in order," the woman says gently, holding very sensitive information about Billie in her hands.

"Thanks. Seriously. Thanks so much. Wait—one more thing. Let me get a picture of that."

She snaps a pic of the two pages and hands it back, looks up. The clock reads 3:56.

She smiles and thanks the woman, then leaves the office, running down the stairs and out the front door just as someone is coming to lock it for the day. "Thanks!" she shouts to the man as she leaps outside, races down the front steps, and jumps in her truck.

She texts Lisa a thank you. *Oh, Humboldt,* she thinks. Down here, everyone is an artist or a rebel or both.

Back at home base, Vinnie is eating pizza and drinking a beer on the porch. "They told me about the complaint. Did you make it in time?"

"I did." She smiles. "It felt good. Even if it's just bureaucratic, I am on the record saying that man is a pedophile. His patients' parents will be notified. And they have to protect my identity by law, so no one will come for me."

"Good job, you."

"Thanks." She smiles, wanting to sit next to Vinnie

on the porch swing but still needing to use the bathroom. "Thanks for letting us use your house today. I had a religious experience out in those trees…."

Remembering, her crown chakra tingles in a way that feels almost sexual.

"I gotta pee," she tells him. "Then I'm hoping to get on the road. You know, before rush hour." She winks.

"You'd be surprised, these days. These Bay Area motherfuckers are movin' in. They're gonna come fuck our shit up, too, you watch."

Sitting on the toilet, she closes her eyes, suddenly completely wiped out. All she wants is to be under the covers at the funny motel, watching a bad comedy.

In the living room, Hank and Randall are cozy on the couch, but move apart when they see her coming. Randall does his innocent butterfly routine, fluttering his eyelashes, while Hank clears his throat authoritatively. Billie tries not to show her surprise. *That was fast.*

"How'd it go?" Hank asks.

"I filed the complaint. Just in time." She grins, cocky. "You should've seen me. Being a local pays off."

Standing above them, she pushes her hair out of her face. Now that she's set her mind on leaving, she can't sit or she might lose momentum.

Vinnie comes in, closing the front door and ambling over to the living room, where he kneels at the fireplace to start a fire.

"So what's next?" Billie asks. "I'm itching to get on the road. Randall, how about you?"

"Oh," Randall says, surprised. "I didn't know. But yes, of course…"

"Wait, but *you* don't need to go," she says, picking up on his hesitation. "I can totally just go back up on my own, if you want to stay...." At the thought of driving home alone, she feels lightheaded. She sits on the arm of the couch.

"It might be good to have you here, in case any other local stuff pops up," Hank says to Randall. "I have a trailer behind my place that's vacant. You're welcome to stay as long as you like."

"Yeah, that would be helpful, having you here." Billie nods. "I'll head back and you stay here. How's that? Whenever you're ready, I'll get you a ticket back to Seattle, or Shasta. Yeah?"

As Randall nods, looking embarrassed and unsure, she has a rush of anxiety about whether he'll be able to stay clean here on his own. *I'll talk to him before I go, make sure he's ready.*

"So, okay, next steps," Billie says. "I go home. You three are here...."

"I want to do some more research on Mars and Klein," Randall says. "Even just online—I bet there's a lot more there if I spend some time digging. And I have connections at *The Stranger*, the alternative weekly in Seattle...maybe they could put me in touch with someone at the *North Coast Journal*, down here? Get some of this in print?"

"Ooh, yes," Billie says. "Just don't forget, we promised we wouldn't use Mars's name." She pats her back pockets, pulls her notebook out of her pocket. "Got a pen, Vin?"

Vinnie tosses her a Sharpie, then settles into the armchair next to the fire.

Billie pops the lid off the pen. She's in her comfort zone. These guys care about her—that she knows for sure. And it helps, it calms her.

She writes:

<u>RANDALL</u>
Internet research
NCJ article?

Hank says, "I can keep looking into civil liability and negligence law, and assault. And if we find any other cases, whether they might be actionable."
Billie writes:

<u>HANK</u>
civil liability
negligence law
assault
new cases?

"If you want to try again with that Mars guy," Vinnie tells Randall, "I'm down. That lasagna is bomb. There's more in the fridge, by the way."
"But we have to be careful." Billie chews the inside of her cheek. "We all need to stay safe. Dirty men don't like their secrets out in the world. I don't want any of us encountering any accidents."
"Nah, but he knows more than he's saying," Vinnie says. "Maybe he's had a change of heart and realizes it might be worse for him if he doesn't talk. Especially if we're getting the media involved."
"We could request an interview with him," Randall says. "Couldn't hurt."
"Well, but it tips our hand," Billie says.
"Not necessarily," Hank says. "Your name wouldn't need to be attached."
"Right," Randall says. "He doesn't know my name, or Vinnie's. The request could come from one of the weeklies."

Billie says, "So he grants the interview and then one or both of you show up to interview him? He knows it's us."

"I could do the interview, in that case," Hank says.

Billie nods, thinking. "Okay, that could work. So Vin and Randall, you'll try and get an interview with Mars?"

They nod, and she adds:

VINNIE/RANDALL
Mars interview request

Vinnie says, "You need any help up there, I got my friend Matt in Tacoma. He can ride backup—whatever you need."

Billie nods. "Thanks, Vin. Good lookin' out." She writes:

VINNIE
Matt – Tacoma – backup

She sits back and looks at the page. She writes:

BILLIE

She knows she doesn't want to confront Colin Klein yet. She feels sick at the thought of seeing him. And she doesn't want him knowing who she is. She's known around here; with a big butch build like hers, you get noticed. No, she needs to lie low, while they work on next steps.

"Remember what I asked you this morning?" Randall says.

This morning seems so far away. She shakes her head.

"What do you still need?" he reminds her. "Now that you've done what you could to protect his patients."

For the first time in her life, she's fresh out of ideas. *I trust my intuition.* "I need to get home."

She can't think any further than that. Sometimes it's good, not knowing what's next.

As she heads into the kitchen to make tea, she catches sight of a calendar. She looks at it, trying to figure out what day it is, feeling brain-dead. *I can't even add.* Finally she determines that it's Friday, July 3.

Wait—it's Randall's birthday. He didn't say anything, and she spaced it. *Shit. I can't believe I forgot. He turned forty-eight today.*

She really wants to get on the road tonight, but it's almost dark. *I can leave in the morning.*

Vinnie calls into the kitchen, "Bill, need anything from the store?"

"Yeah, come here a sec," she calls back to him. When he gets close, she says quietly, "I just remembered it's Randall's birthday today. I totally forgot. I feel terrible."

"Well, you remembered now. I was just gonna hit up the co-op, get some deli stuff for dinner."

"You know what, that's perfect. They have vegan pies there. Will you get one, whatever looks best—and some candles? And get whatever vegan deli stuff looks good. No meat. It's on me." She hands Vinnie her debit card and writes the PIN on a piece of notebook paper.

"No prob, sis," he says, and heads out.

I need a bath. She makes tea for the three of them, stokes the fire, and takes her tea to the bathroom.

After a hot bath, Billie feels much better, resolved about staying one more night and excited to celebrate Randall.

Back in the kitchen, Vinnie is unloading grocery bags. They make up a tray of various salads, popcorn tofu, and fruit. Vinnie got a beautiful peach pie. She puts four candles around the top and eight around the bottom, and lights them. Vinnie turns off the lights in the living room and they walk in, Billie holding the pie and Vinnie the food, then start to sing.

Vinnie has a beautiful singing voice, which balances out her warbly one. As Hank joins in, Billie watches Randall, sees his surprise and joy.

She missed so many birthdays. Sickly sweet cupcake at his sister's, that first year after he left. Practicing a libretto, his final project at opera school. Club kid on the dance floor, bouncing in the dark. Doing makeup at a drag show, all the queens singing to him backstage. Eating crème brulee for the first time in a Paris restaurant. Making out with a stranger in a dark alley. Sleeping through it—wanting nothing more than oblivion. One birthday he was so fucked-up he forgot his own birthday.

"Happy Birthday, dear Randall…happy birthday to you!"

Smiling at him in the candlelight, Billie wants nothing more than Randall's happiness.

He smiles back at her. His hair falls into his face as he pulls himself forward on the couch, away from Hank. The curl at his cheek is deeper than usual, having dried behind his ear. He leans in to blow out the candles, then closes his sea-glass eyes to make a wish.

It's going to be hard for Billie to leave Randall, early the next morning, having been with him almost 24/7 since she brought him home with her. It helps knowing he'll be with Hank. She wants to talk to Hank before she leaves, make him promise to take care of Randall, not let him score.

Instead she talks to Randall. After they eat pie he comes with her to the new baby's room, where Billie is sleeping. Fabrics are hanging and draped over everything, creamy flannels and cottons—Lizzie is making a quilt for the baby, Vinnie said. A gentle yellow and white polka dot is folded on the dresser/changing table. Billie holds a soft, delicate plaid of lavender and gray between her hands; its softness assuages some unmet need in her. There's something so soothing about it. Billie has the sense that this is what it would feel like to be a parent, this goodness, this softness.

Billie sits on the full-size bed and pulls her feet under her, pats the mattress beside her. Randall climbs on, turns to face her.

He takes his time raising his head, and by the time his eyes meet hers he has the biggest grin on his face.

"You look proud of yourself," she says.

"Fulfilled a lifelong dream," he says. "Kissed your dad's best friend."

They giggle like high schoolers. Hearing his little hiccup of excitement, she cocks a crooked grin at him. "You are so sprung," she says, and they laugh again.

"I'm going to miss you!" she says then. "Will you be okay?"

"Yes," he says. "I will. I could use a little alone time. I've enjoyed every second of our adventures. Probably be good to slow down a little, though."

She nods, watching him.

He says, "I want to follow this and see where it goes. You know, the case, but also..." Here he does a comedic head-point toward the living room, where Hank is still on the couch.

She laughs. When they had discussed exes, she got the impression that he'd never really found someone he wanted to make a life with. *Maybe now he has.*

I have to learn how to make it stick this time, she remembers him saying. *You can't do it for me.*

"I trust you, Randall," she tells him gently, reaching out and hugging him tight.

Sleepy and happy in the foggy dawn, he stands with her at the truck's driver side, dusty from Humboldt's dirt roads.

It's hard to say goodbye. They start to, and stop, and come back together. She takes his hand in hers, places the heart-shaped lava rock in it.

A promise that they won't ever lose each other again.

The Survivors

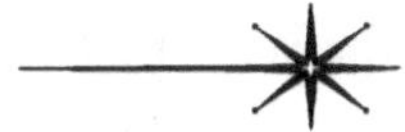

Once she's on the road, Billie feels weird about leaving. She remembers, around the fire, Gloria saying "You go get him" and Billie saying she would. *And now I'm just running home with my tail between my legs? Should I stay and fight?*

She feels infected with the new answers, the how and where; her skin crawls with them. She had hoped that leaving the scene of the crime would help, but it's not. *I want my body back, without any ghosts in it.*

Maybe telling the story aloud will help me get it out.

Once she's out of Humboldt and on the I-5, she calls Gloria. Gloria picks up saying, "Do you *know* that it's seven a.m.?" Gloria sleeps till ten, left to her own devices. But Billie had texted the night before, to say they had found him and she was heading home today. *She left her phone on in case I needed her this morning.*

Billie is fighting back tears. Gloria hears her and says, "You did it, man. You fucking did it. I'm so proud of you."

Her phone on speaker in her right breast pocket, Billie gets out of the fast lane, fingers swiping at her eyes like the windshield wipers, intermittent in the light rain.

"You solved it, Billie. This was what you needed. No matter how dark it is, now that you know, your life will be better. Now you know all the parts of you. Your shadow side only has power over you when it stays in the shadows."

Billie snort-sobs. She stretches for a napkin in the glovebox.

It's like Gloria is there in the truck with her. The connection is perfectly clear, G.'s voice at her shoulder. "Now all you have to do is bring it out into the sun, and watch it dry up and die. You can do this, Bill. You got this."

Soon Billie's chest is heaving with the awful, lonely sobs she associates with childhood. The kind where it's hard to breathe. She pulls off at a rest stop and parks away from the other cars, turns off the ignition, hyperventilating through the tears.

"Breathe," she hears Gloria tell her.

So she does. She forces herself to breathe in deep and lengthen her exhales.

"You got this, Billie," Gloria says again. "You're strong. Just breathe."

After a few minutes of G. talking her through it, she's breathing normally again. She opens her eyes and sees a sad little oak tree, its leaves already turning yellow. *On the freaking fourth of July.*

"You okay, puss?" This is Gloria's pet name for Billie. It had started as an endearment to her clit, when they first got together. Since Billie didn't like being penetrated, Gloria had focused all of her skillful attention on Billie's clitoris, and the word *puss,* said aloud, created a rumble that felt amazing.

Gloria had been more than twenty years older than Billie when they first got together. The authority Gloria had over her, from the beginning, had been total; Billie turned herself over completely, with a courage and strength of spirit that fifty-year-old Billie is proud of, thinking back. *Gloria was the only one who got to know that me,* she realizes. Billie has never been able to go that deep with a lover again. But she had a master for a teacher, and she would not have changed that for anything.

It had made her resilient, clawing her way up from that low, when G. left her—the deepest hole inside herself that she had ever fallen in. The *deep* dark, in which living felt unbearable.

She can remember even now how it had felt to turn everything over. To let it all go. She wants that again. To hand it all off to whoever's next in the race.

"Billie, you still there? Where you at, pussy cat? Want me to come get you?"

Billie blows her nose, gulps the rest of her coffee. She watches a couple kids running in the distance, kicking the rainy leaves. "I'm on the 5; I pulled into a rest stop. I feel like I'm fleeing the scene of the crime."

Billie feels suddenly afraid, and locks the doors, scanning the parking lot. No one is near her. "He's a pediatrician. I don't know how to live with that." Her voice is feral, frantic, and she hits her head against the steering wheel. The horn goes off and she stops. The two kids freeze, looking her way.

"You've done your best, for now, filing that complaint," Gloria says. "You can't save all of them, Billie. Only Willa." This last, she says thickly, emotion frogging her husky voice. She clears her throat.

"He was the intern for an electroshock study my mom was part of," Billie says. "He took care of me using a speculum, while my mom was fucking the doctor."

"*What?!*" Gloria pinches the word high and tight. "Let me guess: he's white."

"You got it."

"Motherfucking—" Gloria stops, realizing what she's saying.

"Right, no—that was the doctor. A psychiatrist, getting it on with Petra in the room next door. She didn't hear me scream because she didn't want to. She was busy."

"You know what this means?" Gloria asks her. "You have your own army. All of the other survivors. And they—we—are *pow-er-ful.* That's you now, Billie, and it's me, too. It's a lot of us; you get to join us now. You dove into the fire and you came out the other side a billion times stronger, crystallized. The rest is gonna be easier, because we got you."

Billie sits up in the passenger seat. She straightens her back. "Okay."

"Don't go forgetting, now. You don't have to do this alone."

Billie nods. "Okay. Thanks, G. I'm gonna get back on the road."

"Alright, puss. Be safe and I'll see you soon."

Billie hangs up, plugs in her phone, puts on some Nina Simone. She has to pee but doesn't want to deal with restroom drama right now. She takes a deep breath in, and out. She feels into herself, as if mentally checking her body for scratches, bruises, thorns caught in her skin.

Head? Check. No headache today, hallelujah.

Chest? Bruised, but beating.

Pelvic floor? Defrosting. She feels cold inside when she remembers the speculum. The seat warmers help.

Legs? They're sore, and she doesn't know why. She will never admit it out loud but getting old really does suck sometimes.

Feet? She flexes them in her gold high-tops. Comfy. Good to go.

Stomach? It'll hold, with trail mix, till Portland.

I'll pee on the side of the road, she thinks, starting up the car.

Catalina

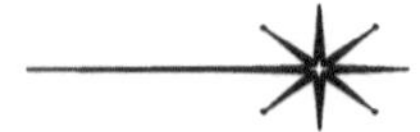

When she gets back from Humboldt, Billie catches up with her work on the Land for a few days. Jane cleared away all the sawdust in the new cabin and folded her clothes, she finds, discovering her Landmate's favorite mug forgotten on a two-by-four. Helene had sanded the floor, after Jane cleaned it. It's like elves have been in there working while she was away.

For the next few days, she bangs out some more work on it, finishing the roof, installing a heavy lock inside. After her work for the day is done, she paints Willa, as if in a fever dream, late into the night.

Willa dancing in the fire, which spirals up and out, consuming everything.

Willa sitting on the edge of the exam table, swinging her legs, staring us down.

She's never made art like this, without a plan, with whatever is at hand. Not thinking, just feeling. She paints Willa's eyes over and over—one over another, until they're just right. Until her body is spent and she can do nothing but sleep.

Five days after her return, Billie drives into Seattle to see Catalina. After a couple years in mural arts, with Billie as her mentor, Catalina had shifted her focus to psychology. She recently opened her own practice, in a renovated apartment building in Pioneer Square. When the virus hit, she started seeing clients via a video app. Only recently has Cat resumed in-person visits.

The two have an easy familiarity, from working together so closely when Billie was Cat's mentor—but even so, sitting on the couch in Cat's quiet, comfortable space, Billie can't stop her knee from bouncing.

"I've never seen a therapist before," Billie says.

"You don't have to think of me as a therapist," Catalina says. "Think of me as your friend with a very expensive degree."

Billie smiles and nods, blowing her hair out of her eyes. She unlaces her boots and sets them to the side, then pulls her feet up under her on the couch.

I bet I could fall asleep right here, she thinks, suddenly exhausted.

After barely surviving her hurricane of emotions and the long drive home alone, Billie had hermited herself away from her Landmates. She hasn't even wanted to talk to Jane about what she learned in Humboldt. And now she finds she doesn't really want to tell Cat about it either.

"Listen," Cat says. "You kick back right there. I'm going to turn some music on and make us some tea. Then we'll talk about whatever you feel like talking about. No pressure."

Billie nods and leans back into the couch cushions, pulling a blanket over herself. She closes her eyes.

When she opens them again, Catalina is sitting across the room, and a mug of tea is on the table beside her, no longer steaming. Perfume Genius is caterwauling soothingly in the background.

"I fell asleep," Billie says, pushing herself up to sitting. "I'm so sorry...."

"Don't apologize," Cat says. "I'm glad you're comfortable. I don't have any more appointments today."

"I haven't been sleeping well in the new cabin," Billie says. "I installed a lock, but it doesn't really help."

"I see," Cat says. "What were you hoping the lock would help with?"

"Feeling more safe," Billie mumbles.

"Does your old cabin have a lock?" Cat asks. "I can't remember."

"Nah," Billie says. "Never wanted one before."

"I imagine you must feel pretty vulnerable," Cat says. "Out there on your own."

Billie knows that Cat means *on your own in the new cabin,* away from everyone. But Billie also feels on her own in a general sense. First her dad left her, then Randall. Gloria saying at the fire, and on the phone, that she's not alone in this—it helped to hear at the time, but it's hard to actually feel that's true. She *is* alone in it, inside of herself.

"I don't know what to do," Billie says, her voice breaking.

"That must be scary for you," Cat responds. "The project manager extraordinaire, without a plan."

Billie's dark-blue eyes lock on Catalina's brown ones. She crosses her legs, the blanket still over her lap. She reaches for her tea; it's ginger, still warm.

"Sometimes that's good, though," Cat continues. "In times like these. To leave room for whatever needs to come through."

Billie nods. She drinks more tea and it soothes her throat, sore from swallowing back tears. *You're safe,* she tells herself. *She's a professional. And she loves you.*

"So," Billie breathes in, "we figured out who hurt me."

"Okay," Catalina responds, nodding.

"He's this guy Colin Klein." Billie realizes that she's been thinking of Colin Klein as a young guy—the age he was when he hurt her, the age he was in her dream—but of course he's not anymore. He would have been at least twenty then, she figures, to have been an intern in a medical office—which puts him in his late sixties now.

She blinks heavily. "He's a pediatrician in southern Humboldt."

"Oh, no," Catalina says.

"I filed a complaint against him. Saying he hurt me, in a medical office, in 1973."

"Well, that's good," Cat says.

"Yeah," Billie says. "I didn't want to go and see him or anything…I wasn't up to it emotionally, and I didn't want him knowing it was me who filed the complaint. Randall stayed down there, to keep working on it, find out more."

"He told me," Cat says. She and Randall have continued growing a friendship, by text. "He didn't tell me how you figured all of this out though."

"My mom gave us a name—Mars, the doctor in charge of this electroshock study she was part of—and we followed where it led." She chews the inside of her cheek. "But I still don't know what happened. I know who the perpetrator was. I know the when—I was five. Multiple times. I also know where it happened—in this gyno office in Eureka. I know how—I was at this office with my mom, who was part of this study, and sleeping with the doctor. This guy Colin was supposed to be taking care of me."

Cat pulls a legal pad from a drawer and takes down some notes.

Billie continues, "But the what and the why…those I don't know."

"Do you want to know?" Catalina asks.

"I do, yeah. I feel ready to deal with it. I think I need to know what happened in order to move on."

"Okay, well, I have an idea about that," Cat says. "You've heard me talk about Eye Movement Desensitization Reprocessing, or EMDR. I've used it myself, healing my own trauma with my therapist, and it's a powerful tool—the most efficient way I know of to heal trauma. You have enough pieces filled in that, if you want, you can start to do this work. And a lot of the time, in the process, more memories come back."

Billie looks at Cat, her mind slow to absorb the info.

Cat continues, "The main goal of EMDR is to integrate the trauma, so that it's less triggering and you have more control over how you engage with it. You would be holding two pulsing discs, and wearing headphones that also slowly pulse—one hand, then the other; one ear, then the other. We would go back into your memories of happened, and I would guide you through it. But we would have to go into as much detail as possible. It's not easy—you'd have to relive the whole thing."

Billie likes the idea of getting free of the triggers, having more control. The alarms going off inside her helped narrow in on what happened: they were information, clues. But she doesn't need them anymore.

"And like I said," Cat adds, "EMDR often brings up formerly unremembered memories. The pulsing creates an almost-trancelike state, in which you can more easily access your unconscious. It might help you remember more about *what* happened, *how* it happened. And even if it doesn't, it would likely still give you more peace around all of this. I've had a very high success rate, using EMDR. My clients usually come out of the work feeling less victimized, more empowered."

Billie plants her feet on the carpet. "How long are the sessions?"

"One to two hours. We would most likely start, then take a break, then start again. We could stop at any point if it's too much. We would also first establish a safe place for you to go to in your mind, should you get scared during the session. And we would work to replace any negative beliefs you formed about the world—as a result of the attacks—with positive ones. We would likely need several sessions, even as many as ten."

That's how Billie has been thinking of them too: as "attacks." He may have been experimenting on her, too—she has no idea what all went on.

"Okay, let's do it. Can we try the first session on the Land?" Billie asks. "I'm much calmer out there."

"But you don't have electricity, right?" Catalina recalls. "For the machine."

"We could use the portable generator," Billie says. "If we did it in the new cabin, we wouldn't be interrupted."

"Sure, I can come out there," Catalina agrees.

In the new cabin, they'd be safe. And with all the Willa paintings in there…maybe it will feel like she's in the room, too.

They could go digging for the final answers. She knows it will be hard to go back through the trauma. But then it will be integrated into her psyche, like any other memory—and that could change everything.

They'll be rewiring her system—rewriting her story.

Randall is staying in the trailer behind Hank's house in Arcata. Hank is the best man Billie knows; she wishes she could have hooked them up sooner. Hank is fifteen years older than Randall. But, she thinks, true love doesn't make up reasons not to exist—it pushes through them.

Randall pitched an article about Colin Klein to *The North Coast Journal,* Humboldt's alternative weekly, and they're going to publish it. He's still doing research and has scheduled some interviews, including one with a Dr. Jerzy Marszalek, of Manila.

So when Billie tells Randall about the EMDR, and he asks if she wants him to come up for the first session, she says no way. She'll call him afterward, from the bluff—they can process the reprocessing. She misses him but also knows that him being gone is good for her. She had been so focused on him—helping him recover from the overdose, getting to know him again—in the early part of the summer. The distance is good for both of them.

Randall found a photo online of Colin Klein as a young intern, which he sent to Billie. In the picture, he is standing with a group of other young people in white coats. He stares at the camera like he did at Billie in her dream, from the cliff above: dismissive, dangerous. She looks at the photo once and then deletes it from her phone.

Lisa sent a text saying that she had finally gone into Petra's studio to see what shape it was in, and had found several boxes of Joe's stuff in there as well, which she hadn't known about. One of the boxes was full to the brim with photos—a bunch of which were of Billie and her dad. Lisa took pictures of a few and texted them, so now Billie has pics of her dad on her phone, to help her focus on *his* face, and hopefully never forget it.

After breaking her isolation, and talking about the attacks with Cat, Billie becomes almost desperate for comfort and reaches out to her friends, who respond with food, medicine, love. Jane has taken over as the public face of the Land, fielding interest and keeping things running smoothly. Billie has been spending more time with Tulip, has even brought her to the new cabin to spend the night a few times; the dog normally goes to work with Rabbit at the dispensary, but prefers being home on the Land. The softness of her fur and her unconditional love soothe Billie's wounds.

Telling her friends about the case, around the fire at her surprise party, had allowed them to support her through this. Billie needs all the help she can get, and a hug from a friend has the power to put her back together.

At night, Willa hasn't dragged Billie out on any more dream-adventures, but once Billie again discovers that she sleepwalked—the door, which she's sure she locked the night before, is unlocked in the morning. Another time, she wakes to find that she drew something in her black notebook while she was asleep: a square with circles in it, repeated over and over again, some strange dotted grid. It makes her think of the dervishes—from above they, too, had looked like a bunch of circles.

She tries not to obsess about what it means. She tries not to even think about Colin Klein, to give him any more of her energy. It helps that she has the treatment plan with Catalina, which feels productive and positive. In the days before her first EMDR session, she takes care of herself as best she can.

Soon she'll have to go back to her paying work. She dreads the undergrads but misses her grad students. It's always inspiring to see what they come up with, like looking into a prism: little pieces of herself, projected out into the world.

On a Wednesday in late July, Catalina comes out to the Land. Billie meets her at the lodge, and they walk to the new cabin together—Billie carrying the small solar generator and a folding chair, Catalina with the EMDR equipment. As Cat looks up into the trees, Billie notices new lines next to her eyes. She wonders if holding other people's pain takes a toll on her. That's the downside of doing this work with a friend: she worries it will be too much for her. But she knows that she has to focus on her own needs, and trust that Cat knows her limits and will speak up if it becomes too much.

They set up the generator a safe distance from the cabin and plug in the small EMDR machine; it controls the pulsing in the headphones and the small handheld discs, called pulsators. Billie has moved out all of the tools and pushed the Willa canvases and the mattress to the corners. She carried over her grandmother's chair— the one she sat in at the fire party—from the lodge.

Billie locks the cabin door and they sit down across from each other in the center of the tiny room, Billie in Wilhemina's chair and Cat in the comfortable camp chair. Billie is recording the session with her phone. She sees her dad's pipe on the framed window and grabs it, slips it in her pocket.

As they look at each other, Catalina holds tight to her legal pad. She starts by saying, "This is going to be hard, but I know that you are strong enough to handle it. We can stop at any point if you need a break. There were many times in my own EMDR sessions that I needed to stop. That's normal, and it's good to honor your limits."

Billie is nervous, too. But she wants to know what happened to her, and if the EMDR might fill in some gaps, she has to try. She trusts Catalina, and Catalina trusts the tool, so Billie's optimistic. She also feels like she is probably going to throw up at some point and has a bucket nearby just in case.

Crow is on the roof; Wilhemina and Joe guard the front door. The rest of Billie's spirits circle the cabin—to witness, support, and protect.

Billie checks to make sure her phone is silenced, then presses record.

Catalina untangles the cords and gives Billie the two pulsators to place in her palms. Together they adjust the pressure and speed of the pulses, then do the same with the headphones.

Left, right, left, right. Billie is surprised to find the pulsing comforting—steady like a heartbeat.

Catalina takes Billie's hands in hers. The discs pulse at the heart of them. It reminds Billie that Catalina is here with her, and will keep Billie safe.

Catalina turns off the pulses. "Before we start, I'm going to ask you to name a limiting belief that resulted from these attacks. Something that you have felt ever since, even though you may intellectually know it's not actually true."

"'I'm not safe with doctors,'" Billie answers immediately, surprised that she doesn't even need to think about it.

"Okay, good," Catalina replies. "On a scale of one to ten, how true does that statement feel right now? 'I'm not safe with doctors.'"

"Ten," Billie answers.

"Okay. We will work to replace this negative belief with a positive belief that you want to have about the world. Do you have an idea what that might be?"

"'I am safe with doctors.'"

"Good. Okay, if you're ready we can start. Please get comfortable. Remember, I'll be right here, and you can always go to your safe place, any time you need to." On the walk over, they had established Billie's safe place as the redwood forest outside Vinnie's house, where she had been crowned by the golden web of light.

Billie props a pillow in her lap, adjusts the headphones and pulsators, then closes her eyes. Catalina turns on the machine.

Left, right, left, right. The pulses are synchronized, in her hands and ears. *Left, right, left, right.*

"Okay, Billie. I want to take you back to when you were five years old. Your mother has an appointment, and she takes you with her. You drive to a doctor's office in Eureka. When you get there, she goes off with Dr. Mars and leaves you in the care of an intern named Colin. Try to bring to mind the room that Klein took you to."

Not even a minute later, Billie responds, "I'm lying on my back and it's bright. The tiles on the ceiling have holes in them." The square grid from her dream-drawing the other night—she understands it now. Her mind is alert, calm.

"Okay. What else do you see?"

"Cart next to me with stuff on it." She slows down and looks more closely. "Syringe. Glass bottles. Test tubes with black lids. Scalpel."

"Good, Billie. Can you see Klein?"

Billie looks across the room and sees a young man heading toward her. *It's him.* She shivers. "I see him. He's young, like early twenties. Wearing a white coat."

"Good job, Billie. What happens next?"

Billie watches from across the room. Willa is so small on the adult-size exam table—Colin had had to lift her up. In her memories, it had felt like the table was raised up somehow, like on a platform or stage, but Billie sees now that that was just because she'd been so small.

She can feel his hands on her back and butt, as she watches. He pulls her down to the end of the table, near the stirrups.

"The table is cold on my legs. I'm wearing shorts. I want to get up." She starts to shake.

"It's okay, Billie. You're here in your cabin with me. You're safe. If this is as far as you want to go today, that's totally fine."

"No, I want to keep going. He puts a towel underneath me, and it's not as cold. He folds another towel and puts it under my head. He asks if I'm comfortable. I say yes.

"He says I'm special. 'Not many little girls get to do this. You will be helping us doctors a lot. It might hurt a little at first, but it will be worth it.'"

Billie shakes her head.

Left, right, left, right.

The pulses calm her, remind her where she is, who she's with.

"You're doing really great, Billie," Catalina assures her. "We can stop, or take a break if you want to?"

Billie shakes her head again. She was holding this so deep inside, she forgot it. She wants it out of her now.

The little girl on the table is *her*. This happened to *her*.

"He gave me something to drink—very sweet, like fruit punch. I feel calmer. I even start to laugh. This can't be normal. I've never been to the gynecologist, but I don't think it's like this."

"No, it's not," Catalina affirms. "Nothing about this is normal. You are right."

The exam room goes black.

"What do you see, Billie?"

"I can't see anything. Like someone turned off the lights."

"Can you hear anything?"

"I hear a kind of scratching sound. Metal on metal."

"Good, anything else?"

"I think he's talking to himself. I can't understand what he's saying. Everything is dark."

"How is Willa doing?"

"She's not here. I can't see her or feel her anymore."

"Maybe what he gave her to drink knocked her out?" Catalina wonders.

Billie instantly knows she's right. "Yes. That's what happened. She's sleeping."

"Okay, that's good. But Billie, just because Willa is asleep doesn't mean you don't know what happened next."

Billie moves her body, tries to move her arms, but they're restrained. Her legs are restricted, too. She feels dizzy, like she's suspended upside-down.

"Let me *out*!" she yells.

Left, right, left, right.

The pulses bring her back to the cabin. She is crying, her eyes still closed. She squeezes her pillow tightly, her body folding in on itself. Out of habit, she goes to pull her hair forward, to protect her face, but can't with the pulsators in her hand.

Cat is asking her, "Billie, do you want to stop?"

Shaking her head no, she reenters the exam room, feeling herself float to the ceiling, to watch from above. Willa's body takes up only about a third of the exam table, and even then her feet won't reach the stirrups. They are, instead, restrained with tape at the corners of the table.

Billie draws in a ragged breath. "I'm scared," she says.

"Okay, let's stop for a minute," Catalina says. "Okay?"

Billie nods. The pulses stop. She keeps her eyes closed.

Inside herself, she imagines Willa free of the table, the room, the building, and here with her instead. She holds her inner child on her lap, and Willa rests her head on Billie's shoulder. Billie smooths her hair, holding Willa tight. She stays there for a while, crying quietly as she imagines giving Willa the love and care she needed.

Then she opens her eyes, pulling the headphones down around her neck. "Hey."

"Hey," Cat says. "How are you doing?"

Billie says, "I'm okay. That was hard." She doesn't have to throw up, but she does feel a headache menacing.

"You did great, though. And we have another big clue: he knocked you out. Which explains why you don't remember much of the actual attack."

"And how he was able to get away with it."

"Right. Up until you blacked out, you might not have known that he was going to hurt you. It seemed like he was being careful to be nice and polite while you were conscious, maybe hoping you would remember only that."

Cat pauses. "But Billie, just because you were unconscious doesn't mean you can't remember what happened to you. Knowing how sensitive and intuitive you are, you may be able to. When you're ready to—not today—we can go back in and try to remember some of what happened when you were under."

Billie's eardrums start to buzz. She rubs the pipe in her pocket.

"Not today," Catalina repeats. "I just want to plant that seed, that it may be there if we want to look for it. The priority right now, though, is making sure you're okay. Are you okay?"

Billie nods, pulling the headphones down around her neck and resting her head on the back of the chair. *Cat's couch would be nice now,* she thinks. Cat's glasses are a bit foggy, and Billie wonders if she's been crying, too.

Cat says, "That was a huge success, in terms of information. *Huge.* It fills in a lot of the blanks. It's not fun, I know, but it will help you in addressing it."

Billie nods, hugging the pillow into her.

Cat pulls out her phone, looks at the clock, and puts it away. "I can stay as long as we need today, but I don't want to push you to try and do too much, too soon. With trauma, it's a marathon, not a sprint. It's all about not exceeding your threshold, and everyone's threshold is different, so I really need you to check in with yourself as we go. If you sense you're near your limit, we'll stop right away, or go to your safe place. Okay?"

"Yeah," Billie says. "For today, I'm not ready to go into the unconscious stuff, but can we fast-forward to after I woke up?"

"Yes," Cat says. "Good idea. You want to do that now?"

"Yeah." Billie pulls the headphones back on, and grabs the pulsators; Cat ensures that she's holding them in the correct hands, then turns the machine back on.

Left, right, left, right, left, right, left, right, left, right.

Billie imagines that the pulsators are all of her friends, squeezing her hands—first a friend on the left, then one on the right. *Left, right, left, right.* In her ears is the heartbeat of the universe. *Left, right. Left, right.*

She falls into a calm, steady awareness—hyperaware, but detached. Catalina guides her, a gentle GPS in the background, but Billie is in another realm.

She's in the exam room again. It's hazy, out of focus, but Billie can see the outline of a small figure on the exam table. She wades through the fog, pushing it away, but it's physically heavy, like leaning into the wind.

And then she hears the scream. There's a whimper, a sound of movement from the table—Willa pushing against her arm and leg restraints—and then a full-throated scream. It fills the room and adult Billie goes to cover her ears, against it.

Klein quickly puts his hand over Willa's mouth. She tries to bite him. He pulls out a handkerchief and stuffs it in her mouth, to stifle her scream.

Willa is still screaming, though, whether or not anyone hears her. Billie feels it in her, raging through her body, piercing her bones. It was the only way of protecting herself. Her voice.

Something is hurting her from the inside. It gets worse when she tries to move, so she stops. Her stomach is cramped and her head feels murky.

He pulls out the handkerchief and quickly gives her more fruit punch. She tries to spit it out but, lying back on the table, she chokes, and some of his sleeping potion goes down her throat. Soon the room goes black again.

"Billie?" Catalina is asking.

"Huh?" Billie says.

"Are you okay?"

Billie shakes her head. Catalina stops the pulses. Everything is quiet.

The cabin is quiet. Billie can still smell the sickly sweet liquid. She remembers her mom asking what was on the front of her shirt. When Billie told her fruit punch, Petra responded, "You know you aren't allowed to have that."

Billie starts to cry. Cat comes over to her and takes

the discs and headphones, offering Billie a hug. Billie turns her head and rests it in the crook of Cat's shoulder, like Willa's had nestled into hers. Like her head had nestled into her dad's shoulder, when she was little. She can remember seeing the world from that safe place, his powerful arms holding her.

But he hadn't been able to protect her from this.

She knows now that when she screamed, it was because she woke up with the speculum inside her. It was the only time she had been conscious during the attacks, and she had screamed her head off when she came to and found herself strung up and pinned down, with something tearing her open inside. She can remember now how it felt: it felt like that scream sounded.

The sense memories are murky and vague because of the sedative, which also explains why it's been so hard to remember. But the more Billie understands, the sharper the picture gets—the more defined the lines, the more exact the edges.

As Cat continues to hold her, the scream fades a little. Her ears stop ringing.

Billie sits up, feet on the floor. Cat moves back to her chair.

"How could she?" Billie says, her voice quivering.

"Your mom?"

"Yeah. This is on her. How could she not have known? Or was she just enjoying the sex too much to care?" Had Petra been jealous of the attention the handsome young intern had given Willa?

"She may have known only on an unconscious level," Catalina says. "I'm sure she noticed differences in you, but maybe she didn't understand them."

"A parent who was paying attention, who actually

cared about me, would have known."

And that hurts worse than anything that came before—her heart splitting and breaking open inside her.

This is never going to heal.

Tulip

They do a few more EMDR sessions, in Cat's office. Billie is pushing hard to find out what happened when she was unconscious, but she hasn't been able to reach it. With each session, however, the numeric scale for how true the negative belief "I'm not safe with doctors" feels is getting lower, though she's nowhere near believing that the opposite is true.

She knows that it's helping, to have more info about what happened, and to integrate it—but it's also hurting. Going through it again and again, down to the detail, makes her feel like a walking open wound. The other day after a session, her earbuds had fallen out of her pocket and someone had tapped her on the shoulder to give them to her. Billie jumped, and as she turned she flashed to Petra standing right behind her, that night in Petrolia.

Staring at the good Samaritan like he's her deranged mother, on the Seattle streets where people were trying to learn how to come together again after the Covid crisis… They stared at her, and she could see the fear above their masks.

It had been so long since a stranger had touched her. And in the meantime she had learned some godawful things about some truly terrible humans. So many more reasons to fear them, at a time when they all needed less reasons.

She keeps flashing on images of her mom and Ann

having sex in Petra's studio—and others probably, too. That was why the energy in there had creeped her out, and why her mom had protected it so aggressively— it was a space of secrets. Billie and Cat have discussed Petra's relationship with Ann, and they agree that while it does need to be dealt with, along with her mom's care, it doesn't need to be dealt with now. Billie doesn't have the capacity for any more right now.

In fact, she needs to take a break from the sessions. Cat agrees. They can talk by phone anytime, and Cat will be happy to come out to the Land if Billie needs her.

The case has been a rush, in some ways. The thrill of the chase, of getting more pieces of the puzzle. The exhilaration of putting it together. The picture growing, becoming more complete.

But the pieces are starting to feel heavy. They are a lot to hold, and now they are always there. She doesn't get any relief.

Her friends help a lot, but her friends aren't here at the moment. On this night, Billie Knight is alone on the Land. For the first time in a long time, she's cooking herself a nice meal. She's playing the Clash on her phone while the solar battery charges it, and drinking root beer–flavored kombucha that Helene made.

Straight to hell, boy…straight to hell.

In the light of the moon shining through the east window, sustenance sizzling on the stove, Billie moves her body. Chest in, and then out, rolling her body up and out, then drawing in. Like the Aztec dancers she's witnessed at Day of the Dead celebrations, their heavy headdresses adorned with skulls and feathers, their bare feet stamping the earth. Images dart across her mind: Bodies hanging from trees. Smiling and screaming Black people in Gloria's "June Teeth." The chainsaws hanging overhead in the Logger Bar, their blades as long as bodies.

Closing her eyes, hands on her knees, she shakes her head up and down, side to side.

When she opens her eyes, she notices that she's standing where she and Randall had sat across from each other a month ago, when she noticed his gray roots in the sun. *Hank saves me from worrying about Randall, like Lisa freed me from worrying about Dad.*

She needs all of her energy now, every last bit. She's too vulnerable—like her skin's been stripped away. Literally stripped of her defenses.

This is what being brave enough to know the truth looks like. Being willing to get that dark. Trusting you'll find your way back. With no defenses, everything is sensitive, all the time. There's no jacket to put on, no bangs to hide behind. No murals to paint, no plans to make. No sex to have. No other to fall into. No children to spoil, no structures to build, no alcohol to drink, no drugs to take. No protests to organize, no slogans to shout. No students texting, calling, needing. No left, right, left, right to shake things up and shake things out. Just what has been shook.

No TV. In her cabin she has stuff downloaded on her computer, but here in the lodge, no. No Wi-Fi, no cell service—so no therapist to call, no bestie to text with. No online shopping. No Instagram. No art to make— not here in the lodge. In the new cabin there's always a canvas to take it out on.

There's music and there's food. There are herbs: seven shelves of them in alphabetized jars. There's sweet Tulip, who is always up, who never has a bad day.

The darkness weighs you down, it just does. There's no getting around it, on this night when there's no hiding—

when every move she makes can be seen from the outside, in fact, through any of the large windows on all sides of the lodge.

Knowing what happened to her doesn't make her stronger, it makes her more vulnerable.

I have to take care of myself. It's the only way. One foot in front of the next.

Dinner. Tea. Kombucha. Sticky-note happy face on the jug for Helene.

She shakes her body out, all over the kitchen. She stirs the beans, flips the plantains, takes the greens off the heat. She shimmies to the herb shelves, shakes lemon balm and ashwagandha into the teapot, imagines it's her being immersed in hot water.

She remembers her birthday bath in the clawfoot just up the hill. The wish she made echoes down to her. *"Universe. Please help me learn what happened to me. Help me uncover the darkness, so I can get it out of me."*

I asked for this. And now I have it. That's magic.

She makes herself a plate and brings the tea with her to the table. Tulip settles into her bed with a sigh. Billie looks into the darkness outside as she eats, listens to the whistle of the wind. Beyond the deck on the western side of the lodge is a view similar to the one at the bluff: a valley of trees, and then the Salish Sea. Up here, the water is just a little farther away. Though she can't see much in the dark.

Suddenly something scurries across her vision, from the right—near the road that leads to the lodge.

That looked human.

She stands up. Whatever it was, it's faded into the shadows. Her legs feel rubbery.

She moves to the nearby door and locks it, then races

across the room to the other door, turns that lock, too. Though the windows would be easy enough to break, if someone wants in.

And the lantern on the table lights her up, she knows. *So whatever is out there can see* me *perfectly.*

She backs away from the windows and into the kitchen. She grabs her phone, turns off the Clash, puts it in her back pocket.

Tulip goes to the window where Billie saw…whatever that was. The dog's ears go flat against her head as she stares out, body rigid.

Billie turns off her headlamp and blows out the lantern. They look out into the black night.

I can't see shit.

Tulip starts to bark. A loud, sharp, aggressive bark, insistent. Her lip curls.

Billie doesn't see anything. She goes to the big window across the room and looks out, scanning the area past the deck, essentially their driveway. A person would likely come in from that direction. But she can't make out anything but shadows, vague shapes of things. She would see if something moved, though.

Tulip is still barking.

Fuck! There's nowhere to hide in this room. Her heart is going so fast it feels like it will bust out of her.

She grabs the baseball bat by the door and runs to the Captain's room—Randall's old room, past the kitchen and bathroom. As far as she can get from where Tulip is still barking.

"Tulip!" Billie calls her, sharp but quiet. She goes back out into the hallway and calls her again, and this time the yellow dog starts toward her, barking a few more times as she backs away.

"Good girl," Billie says, as she brings the dog into the Captain's room, sliding the flimsy lock across the door. The room is mostly made up of its huge wooden boat bed. There's a desk in the corner and she shoves it against the door.

It's totally dark but for the light of her phone, which she turns to face down. Tulip's ears are flattened back on her head. Billie has never seen her like this. They have never had an intruder.

It has to be a person out there, for her to be this disturbed.

Sitting on the bed, breathing heavy, she says again, "Good girl."

The dog paces the tiny space. Billie is lucky she got her in, because Tulip really wants to be out there. She barks, the noise piercing Billie's ears.

It's like the scream on the exam table. The sound that broke all the windows in Wilhemina's house.

Covering her ears, she tells Tulip to stop. Tulip is just doing her job, but Billie can't take it. She falls on the bed and covers both ears with pillows, breathing heavy.

The flashback enters aggressively, like a strobe lights. She's in a small, dark space. A closet. She sits on the floor, quivering.

Tulip is still barking. It hurts her head. She squeezes the pillows against the images trying to get out, against the sound trying to get in.

The closet was locked from the inside. He knew she was in there, but he couldn't get to her.

Just like now—she's only safe if she stays in here. She's stuck in a box, and he's outside, with the whole world to move around in.

She remembers trying to breathe in that little closet. Locked from the inside, by her. He knew she was in there, but he couldn't get to her.

Just like now. Safe in a tiny box, but only if she stays in here.

Now she remembers: She had been on the table. Her feet and arms weren't strapped down yet and that thing wasn't inside her. He had just given her the drugged fruit punch, and he had his back turned, prepping test tubes by the sink.

She silently let the punch drool out the side of her mouth. The cold sensation on her neck—that's what she had recalled in the café. Sliding off the table, she crept quickly to the closet, closed the door and locked it.

He must have heard the click of the door. He came over and told her to open up, knocking on the door. "Willa! Come out. This is not okay!"

She can hear him, right outside the door. He's breathing heavy. She forces her own breath to quiet, so she can hear.

"It's okay," he says through the cracks in the door, as clear as if he was whispering in her ear. "Don't worry. It's safe. Come on out now."

It's dark in the closet and she's afraid to turn the light on—afraid of what she'll see in there with her. She senses a bucket of bleach behind her. This is where the smell came from. She can feel the chemicals in her head.

She closes her eyes tight—now, then. In the dark.

She can hear him muttering. "Damn it!" She hears him walk over to the exam table, his shoes squeaking. He sees that she spit out the punch, and she hears him make a creepy squeal. He wants to scream, but he can't attract attention.

Then he's back at the door, turning the knob violently, trying to open it with brute force. She feels her five-year-old heart stop. "Willa?" It's awful, hearing her childhood name in his mouth. "Come out and I'll give you a lollipop."

She is still, silent, listening. He's talking to himself, cursing under his breath. He paces back and forth, stops again outside the closet. Then he bangs his head against the door, twice. She's afraid his head will break through.

He stops. She hears him talking to himself again, high-pitched and anxious. Something about the research. Not being able to complete the study.

The study. He *had* been experimenting on her. That's why he's so riled up: he's losing his subject.

He was taking samples from her, to study. That, Billie knows now, is true. He took something from inside her vagina. Multiple times. That's the what.

Tulip has quieted, but is still listening intently, panting. Billie takes the pillows away from her head. Her head is throbbing like the inside of a gong, ringing like a winning slot machine, the literal *dingdingding* that's the sound of her body recognizing the truth.

He was studying her, alright—but he wasn't just doing interviews. That was why he had volunteered to help Mars: he was collecting his own data. Stealing her precious, private cells. Mars had said yes to it, because Klein had made too good an offer.

There must have been more to it—Klein had to have been getting off on his power over her—but the main intention of him being inside her had been science. She knows that now.

Science fantasy.

That was why he was so excited and breathless about it. Why it had been so important to him; why he'd been so persistent, and reckless.

Between the sex her mom and Mars were having, the electroshock therapy, and Mars's own interviews with Petra, Klein had hours of access to Willa. Plenty of time to conduct the interview, drug her, go inside her, and wake her back up. If she was still a little groggy when her mom came to get her—well, Petra was out of it, too, and even on a good day she was never the most perceptive parent.

But then finally, Willa wasn't having any more of it. As soon as he wasn't looking, she spit out the sedative, and then she did what she did best: she ran. She made it to the closet, and locked it; she had been lucky that it locked from inside, and Colin didn't have the key. She is sure he would have hurt her if he'd gotten to her, angry at being denied what meant everything to him.

That was the last time it happened, Billie knows. Because what she did made it stop.

From the closet, she had heard some of what he said, but she had been too young to understand what it meant. So it all just seeped into her, deeper and deeper, till it was unrecoverable without heavy excavation.

But Billie has gotten there. She has her why.

Eventually her mom came, and even then she didn't leave the closet, Billie remembers. Because of course her mom couldn't be trusted either, and neither could the other man calling for her to come out—Mars, she knows now. She can hear Mars asking Klein what he and Willa were doing in the gynecology office, rather than in the intake room with toys that they had set up for the kid interviews.

Mars didn't know what was happening. If he had known, Klein would have gone to get the other doctor's help with Willa much sooner. No, he did everything he could to fix the problem on his own first, to cover his tracks.

There must have been others he hurt; other children of parents in Mars's study. For who knows how long.

Billie holds her head, shaking it side to side, as if to evade this new information.

To calm herself, she remembers sleeping here with Randall. She brushes her bangs out of her eyes and remembers Randall doing the same.

Joe is in here, too, in the wood of the walls. He invested it with his spirit, building this place.

It's time for him to go now. She balls up her fists as she fights the thought. *No! Please don't go away. Don't leave me alone with this.*

She senses the air near her shift, and is surprised to feel a heaviness in her evaporate. It feels like forgiveness. He can go now because everything is cool between them. She hadn't known she was holding on so tightly.

It's okay, she tells herself. *You have your family here. You have everything you need.*

He'll always be here, in the bones of this place, in Billie's bones, too.

Tulip is curled up on the floor next to the bed, as if nothing has happened.

I need to feed her dinner. And my dinner is out there, too.

Billie puts the desk back. She peers out the window, into the dark. The storm seems to have died down. Seeing a tarp bunched strangely on the ground outside, she realizes that what she saw in the shadows could have been the tarp being blown across the deck.

We're never really safe. Out here in the open, or in a castle behind a moat. Safety is only ever an illusion.

Billie has found what she needed to know: She

escaped. By her wits and her senses and her strength and her speed. She should not have had to do what she did, but she did it anyway. She ended it.

She got away.

Elk

$\mathcal{R}$andall and Hank FaceTime Billie from the back-
yard of Hank's house in Arcata. Sharing the screen,
they spend some time showing her around the yard: an
extensive peony garden, baby palms with their sprouts of
triangle leaves, and the vine-covered trailer that Randall's
been staying in.

At the cell vista, Billie shows them the western hem-
lock spread out behind her, and ahead, the Salish Sea.
"Canada is over there," she tells Hank, pointing. "You
have to come visit me."

"I'd like to," Hank says. "You should come visit us, too."

Randall says, "Hank asked me to move into the main
house with him." In the little rectangle, he kisses Hank
on the cheek. "I said yes."

"Oh, wow, congrats!" she says. Her smile is automatic,
and she tries to make it authentic. But her insides somer-
sault, leaving behind an ache in her chest. *I'm alone again.*
She doesn't want them to see her ugly envy.

"Oh, and guess what?" Randall says. "I booked a solo
show down here. At the Outer Space, in the spring."

Her jaw drops open. "I love that place. Seems like
a good place to play—small and dark. All the queers
go there."

"I'm doing my own songs for the first time. I even
recorded something out here." He nods at the trailer.

"Can I hear?"

"I haven't shared it with anyone yet. Not even Hank. But I can sing a little bit right now, if you want."

She nods, putting up her paws and panting like a spaniel. *Let it go, Billie. Just be happy for them.*

"One sec," he says, handing the phone to Hank.

Hank's kind, intelligent eyes look out at her from behind his glasses. "You good?"

She lies back on the ground, holding the phone up above her, pine needles poking through her T-shirt. "I'm good."

She can hear Randall warming up in the background. "The music must be harder without the drugs," she says quietly to Hank.

Hank nods. "Easier, too."

"Okay, ready," Randall says.

Billie sits up. Hank focuses in on Randall. He keeps time with his head to a spirited drumbeat coming from his laptop. Lost in love, Billie watches her friend.

Hank zooms in a little on Randall's beautiful, delicate face. Bare of makeup, suntanned. His hair is growing out gray, the last few inches of strawberry pulled behind his ear.

He starts to sing, and she realizes it's the first time she's heard him sing without someone else's vocals behind him. His voice is high and pristine, but powerful. She sits up again, stares at the screen.

"Small-town life has me down,
All this green and all this brown.
When we walk into town,
Strangers smile and I frown.
The wind blows the sea all around,
$5.99 a pound."

Billie is shocked by how good he is. He breaks, bobbing his head to the peppy interlude, his hair falling in his face. His arms are bare under his T-shirt, and she can see that his scars have faded a bit.

He opens his eyes and smiles at her as the tempo slows.
"Go do another round,
I'll bring you my sound.
Still so tightly wound,
In this tiny little town."
He finishes the song with a flourish and Billie and Hank erupt into applause, whooping and hollering.

Billie is dazed, slightly starstruck. She hadn't realized, until now, how special and unusual Randall's voice was. *Why did he never sing when we were together?* The whole time he'd been sitting on this enormous talent.

But then she remembers, *He did sing—he was always singing. You just didn't hear it.* She feels stupid, fights back tears.

He just sang a new piece for you. Let it be enough. She wonders if she'll ever feel like she's getting enough Randall. All those years he was away from her, there's no way to fill in all the holes. *And now he has Hank....*

She shakes it off. "Randall, that was incredible. Can I come for your show?"

"Sure," he says. "Or Hank will record it and we'll send it to you after."

Billie remembers that her mom's car is sitting unused in Petrolia, thinks of offering it to Randall, so he can get to his shows. But she stops herself, thinking, *I should check with Ann first.* The conversation she needs to have with Ann about Petra's care, and about Ann and Petra's relationship, is daunting. But she knows that if they can get through that stuff, Ann can probably tell Billie more about the electroshock study, about a lot of things.

As Hank takes Randall by the cheeks and kisses him, Billie again feels a sharp twinge in her chest. A love pain. Like the heart-shaped rock, stabbing her with its point.

Randall is flushed as he comes up for air. "Hey, but Bill, the real reason we called—I have something to show you." His head dips off-screen and he comes back holding up a copy of the *North Coast Journal.* "It came out yesterday," he says, his pretty seafoam eyes gauging her readiness.

He opens the paper to the third page, the Local News section, and holds it up close to the screen. As she sees the headline—FORTUNA PEDIATRICIAN ACCUSED OF ABUSING PATIENTS—the alarm bells again ricochet throughout her body like a pinball machine.

Seeing "By Randall Delphine" below the headline makes her feel safe enough to continue reading:

A claim of sexual misconduct was recently filed against Fortuna pediatrician Colin Klein. After the *Journal* reported the claim, several more accusers have come forward. Four women and one man have accused Klein of assaulting them when they were children. The alleged attacks are said to have occurred both in Klein's Fortuna office, and in a Eureka medical building where he formerly practiced.

Dr. Klein, who has headed a pediatric practice in Fortuna for the past three decades, declined to comment. Fortuna police officer Kenneth Jones told the *Journal* that the complaints against Dr. Klein are being investigated, and police have no further comment at this time.

Local lawyer Michelle Tobin, who is exploring whether a class action suit may be filed against Dr. Klein, explained that "California does have a statute of limitations with regard to legally pursuing cases of sexual misconduct, but those restrictions don't apply in the case of felony sex crimes. We are working with the police to determine the nature and extent of the crimes Dr. Klein is being accused of. And of course, more recent accusations may come forward, which could be actionable."

Fortuna residents have been protesting outside the doctor's small office, warning incoming parents about the accusations. "He's not going to get access to another child," Fortuna resident Fern Phillips said, from her lawn chair on the sidewalk in front of Klein's office. "Not ever. Not if we have anything to do with it."

The *Journal*'s reporting on this issue is ongoing. To share any information you may have, please email rdelphine@ northcoastjournal.org. Your safety and privacy will be protected.

If you or someone you know are struggling with thoughts of harming yourself or another, please seek support from a medical professional. The Rape, Abuse, and Incest National Network (RAINN) has a hotline, 800-656-HOPE (4673), providing support of all kinds to survivors of sexual assault.

A shiver passes through Billie, images and sensations haunting her periphery—not just her own now but others', too. The phantoms and detritus of trauma. All the shit it leaves in its wake.

"Billie!" Randall and Hank call her name, bringing her back. She looks at her phone, blinks, then sees them there again.

"Hey guys," she says quietly. "Sorry, I went away for a minute there."

"Are you okay?" Randall asks, tipping his head to try to catch her eye.

She nods, though she is not okay. "Thank you for doing this. All of it. Both of you."

"My longer story about the investigation comes out in a month," Randall says gently. "Depending on how things progress, it may be a cover story."

At the thought of this, Billie's head starts to spin. She

sits back against the log, setting the phone in her lap.

She places her hands on the ground at her side. She imagines her spine extending down through the earth—down, down, down, until she's rooted there.

Billie drives onto the ferry, locks her truck, and walks to the back of the boat. She's headed in to the Seattle Art Institute, to try to convince her dean to let a former student teach her two mural classes this fall. Then she has an appointment with the director of the school's gallery, to see if they want to show the Willa paintings.

The Willas' eyes, Billie knows, are better than any her mom ever painted. Eyes that dare you: *Pay attention!* Adult eyes in a child's body.

Willa, where she should never have been: in a tall tree, on the roof of the new cabin, flying high above on Crow's back. Places where no one was watching. On the side of an exam table, skinny legs swinging. Those eyes peering out from under bangs, staring into your soul, daring you to come in.

Billie knows this is a big ask—and very last-minute. The dean isn't going to be happy. But Billie's limits have shifted, with everything on her plate right now. Recognizing that she may not be up to the task seems preferable to breaking down halfway through the semester. She can still mentor her grad students.

This past week, Billie has started sleeping in the old cabin again. With all the painting happening in the new cabin—and the housing of all the Willas—there's no room to sleep. But also, Billie missed her Landmates, being cozy with them in the evenings, cooking together. Her family. Jane, holding the space. Helene, who makes kombucha and likes to mosh around the living room with Billie. Rabbit, who reads aloud to them, who teaches Billie something new every day, despite being only twenty-five years into this life. Tulip, who is soft, and sweet, as good at kisses and hugs as any human.

They love me no matter what.

It's good to be able to leave her work behind when she's done painting for the day, to come back to the lodge and warm it up with a fire for her friends, coming home soon from their own work. They talk, and play music, and cook delicious food that grew out of their Land. They make each other laugh. She needs to remember that she has a family, and they love her unconditionally, like her dad did.

Alone in the rain at the back of the ferry, slicker hood up, Billie gazes up at the land to the south—her cell phone vista. From here it's hard to see—it looks like a cave on a foothill.

Winter will be coming soon. *Maybe now that I've met my monster, it won't be so hard to face the shortening days.*

I'll finish the Willas, and in spring we could start hosting free artist retreats in the new cabin. At the thought of the tiny space in the forest being used by other artists to find and fight their own demons, her heart swells, inflating till it fills her. *Willa's Cabin.*

Now that Billie knows what happened to her, her healing has started. It will take a lifetime, but it will go by quickly.

Her intuitive powers are back and she's her sensitive self once again. She even made herself a doctor's appointment—pap smear and physical. Cat recommended a female gynecologist, and Gloria offered to go with her.

Healing from trauma is a long game. She knows that

Randall is going to find out more, about what Colin Klein was doing inside her, and who else he harmed. He'd texted that Dr. Mars was going on the record, was even willing to use his name, to try and put things right.

She knows that this thing is much bigger than just her, and that more details are coming—and that she's not ready for them yet. Pacing herself requires knowing herself intimately, listening carefully. Respecting the limitations of this body: this elegant system of inexpressible power.

The scientists, artists, seekers—all in search of what she has found. What she has remembered.

This was the solution to the case, ultimately: knowing that she's inseparable from the rest of the universe. She's not in this alone. This eternal flame, this membership, this undimmable light is alive in her again, powering her up. Ancestors walking at her side. A posse of survivors at her back. Nature and animal spirits above and below.

As the ferry starts to round the corner for Seattle, Billie sees, roughly below the Land, an Olympic elk walk to the water's edge. She's never seen one there before.

His antlers are a massive circuit of soft and sharp: soft like driftwood in the middle, ends sharpened to spears. Billie grew up with herds of elk roaming wild in Humboldt County; she knows that the size and shape of the antlers determine whether the bull lives or dies. Every year around this time, the velvet that covers the antlers and connects them to the head dries up, and soon the antlers will die and fall off. In the spring, a whole new set grows—sharpening, softening.

Looking out at the bull, her head hums with energy. The golden crown spreads to cover her whole scalp, and soon her entire body is tingling with it—as if her cells are made of that bright, sparkling light.

And then they turn the corner, and he's gone. Billie turns to face forward and her eyes fall closed. Below, all of the cars are nestled in tight, like babies in an orphanage. Raindrops drum gently on her hood; the slap of sea against hull is steady and wild.

Hands wrapped around the railing behind her, she leans back, and lets herself be held.

Huge-hearted thanks go to:

Christopher Church

Ocean Mandela Milan

Fancyland and Sacha Marini

all of the activists of the CHAZ/CHOP

my spirit army: teachers, deities, ancestors, nature beings

beloved Humboldt County (and its Native peoples,
flora, and fauna)

the stunning Olympic Peninsula (and its Native
peoples, flora, and fauna)

Laura Costa, Lindsay Kessner, Cara Cordoni

the good folks at Dagmar Miura

September Woods Garland

Elizabeth Hollis Hansen

Emily Joy Schifferling

Mary Anderson

Hisae Matsuda

Britt Sutton

Sue J. Kim

Tara Reinertson

Jimena Flor Mar

tammy lynne stoner

Dahlia Buttercup Howl

Kristine and Thom Adams

the Black Lives Matter movement